Close Disharmony

A DI Ambrose Mystery

P J Quinn

Stairwell Books

Published by Stairwell Books
161 Lowther Street
York, YO31 7LZ

www.stairwellbooks.co.uk
@stairwellbooks

Second Printing

ISBN: 978-1-939269-19-5

Layout design: Alan Gillott
Cover Image: Mike Flippo

Also by P J Quinn
Published by Stairwell Books

DI Ambrose Mystery
Foul Play
Poison Pen
Poetic Justice

By Pauline Kirk
Border 7
The Keepers (eBook)
Waters of Time (eBook)

About the authors

Pauline Kirk is the author of three novels: *Waters of Time*, Century Hutchinson and Ulverscroft, *The Keepers*, Virago (Little, Brown), and *Border 7*, Stairwell Books. Eleven collections of her poetry have been published, including *Walking to Snailbeach: Selected and New Poems*, *Dancing through wood and Time*, in which some of her poems are set to music by the composer, Martin Scheuregger, and the most recent, *Time Traveller*. She is a member of the Pennine Poets group, and editor of Fighting Cock Press. Her poems, short stories and articles have appeared in many anthologies and journals, and been broadcast on radio.

Jo Summers has written numerous articles for the legal press and national newspapers. She co-wrote *Islamic Wills, Trusts and Estates: Planning for this World and the Next* with Mufti Talha Ahmad Azami and Shahzad Siddiqui (Euromoney Books) and wrote *The UK Tax Handbook for Offshore Trustees* (Euromoney Books 2011). Future projects include a children's book aimed at adopted children (having two adopted children of her own).

With thanks to Paul Summers, Nicky Pallis, Peter Kirk; and to our editors Rose and Alan.

For Charlie and Ethan

Prologue

Tuesday 8 December 1959

Creak

The sound seemed to fill the whole bedroom. Pausing mid-step, the intruder moved carefully away from the loose floorboard.

Silence returned, broken only by the sound of gentle snoring. The room's occupant was fast asleep, oblivious to the figure dressed entirely in black standing in the doorway.

The large sagging bed stuck out into the middle of the room. A faint ray of moonlight was struggling through a crack in the curtains. Brass bedposts near the window reflected a pale light. The rest of the room was in total darkness.

Checking the old lady was still asleep, the intruder stopped at the dressing table near the window. The top drawer opened easily. A hand felt inside, between the clothes, and then moved down to the bottom drawer. It jammed, the runners worn and uneven. Very carefully the shadowy figure pushed the drawer back in.

A mahogany wardrobe almost filled the wall opposite the bed. Two empty cases were stacked neatly on top. The intruder turned the wardrobe key gently, and stopping the doors from swinging open, reached a hand through the small gap. Skilful fingers found a jacket pocket. Silently the hand was withdrawn and the doors locked again.

Avoiding the creaky floorboard, the figure crept stealthily out of the room. Once again, everything had been perfect.

Chapter One

Wednesday 9 December 1959

"Oh what a beautiful morning…" DI Paul Ambrose sang softly as he drove.

Actually the day was anything but beautiful. It was cold, with a biting wind, but Ambrose was in a good mood. Solving a crime was always satisfying, especially a nasty one like this. The murder of a shopkeeper had even made the national news. Robbery gone bad? Was no one safe in their own home?

He'd been helping Jenners Park CID with the case. Ambrose knew DI Urwin would have got there in the end: the man was no fool. Unlike the driver of the Ford roaring up behind him, Ambrose decided.

The road was narrow and rose in a long hill. In front a small coach was struggling, puffs of black smoke coming from the exhaust. Shaped like a box on wheels, the vehicle looked distinctly pre-war.

Ambrose knew the road well. There was nowhere to overtake safely for another mile. Even after reaching the top of the hill you had to be careful. The Netherton crossroads were notorious. Anything could come out of those side roads: a tractor, coal lorry or even a muck spreader.

The Ford had caught up. Ambrose could see the driver in his mirror. He looked like a commercial traveller, young and impatient, late for his next appointment. He was driving too close to Ambrose's car, pushing him to go faster. Resolutely, Ambrose resisted.

Still the old coach laboured up the hill. Ambrose glanced in his mirror. The young driver was cleary impatient. "I'm in a hurry too," Ambrose thought. He could have driven straight home instead of going to see Mrs Hemmings, but he'd wanted to tell the widow personally about the arrest. It won't take long, he'd thought. He hadn't bargained on being stuck behind a tractor for over a mile and now this darn coach being so slow.

The Ford pulled out, its driver trying to see around Ambrose's car. Quickly the Ford pulled back into safety, narrowly avoiding a car coming from the other direction. Twice the driver repeated the manoeuvre. Ambrose frowned. There could be ice in the shadows. Leyton Lane was a notorious black spot. Besides, it was never a good idea to 'play chicken' with oncoming traffic.

Anxiously he glanced at the clock on his dashboard. It was nearly one o'clock. He would have to call at Chalk Heath Police Station and file a report before he went home. He wouldn't have long to get ready for the theatre that evening.

A glance in his wing mirror startled Ambrose. The Ford was gathering speed again. It pulled level, overtaking, its engine revving loudly. "Don't be daft!" Ambrose muttered in alarm. Dropping back, he gave the other driver space to pull in behind the coach.

But the Ford didn't pull back. Instead it roared past Ambrose and the coach, up the hill and out of sight.

"Bloody idiot!" Ambrose said aloud. If he'd been in the patrol car, he'd have given chase. Instead he drove on, keeping his distance from the back of the coach and its foul exhaust fumes.

Suddenly, as they reached the brow of the hill, the coach seemed to judder. Grit and dust sprayed from its back wheels: they couldn't hold on the rough surface. A smell of burning rubber filled the air. The driver had slammed on his brakes, without warning. Urgently Ambrose braked too but the old Hillman was heavy. He was hurtling towards the back of the coach.

Gripping the steering wheel hard, Ambrose managed to stop himself from skidding. The coach was swerving from side to side. Somehow the vehicle stayed upright, but it was careering all over the road. The passengers must have been screaming in alarm.

Suddenly the coach skidded to a stop across the road. If he'd been driving any closer, Ambrose would have been sitting in the coach with the passengers by now. With his wheels grinding on loose gravel he managed to stop, three feet from the coach's side.

For a few seconds Ambrose sat still, catching his breath. Then he leapt out of his car and ran towards the coach. The driver was leaning over his driving wheel. Ambrose couldn't tell if the man was injured or just exhausted. Some of the passengers were standing, but several had been thrown from their seats and were now picking themselves up. A lady moved towards the driver, touching him gently on the shoulder. He turned to look at her, so clearly he wasn't badly hurt.

They'd been lucky. At the crossroads fifty yards ahead, a small lorry was facing into the hedge, its side smashed inwards. All around it, broken bottles of pop were scattered across the tarmac, some still rolling where they'd fallen. Just beyond, the Ford lay on its side in a ditch, wheels still spinning, engine roaring.

Ambrose approached the car, looking urgently for any sign of fire. The driver had been thrown forward against the front window and then backwards, almost into the passenger seat. He wasn't moving. Blood trickled from his forehead.

Fortunately the car had tipped onto its passenger side. The driver's door opened as Ambrose tried it. Very carefully he reached in and checked the driver's pulse: he was still alive. Ambrose turned off the ignition. A ghastly silence followed.

Looking around, Ambrose assessed the scene. The lorry had pulled out of Netherton Lane and was crossing the main road when the Ford hit it side-on. The young driver must still have been doing quite a speed, judging by how far the two vehicles had been moved by the impact. Fortunately the lorry had stayed upright, propped up by a hedge. The car must have bounced off it and landed in the ditch.

Ambrose thought quickly. It was a long time since he'd attended a road accident. He needed to call an ambulance. He wished to heaven he had the patrol car. He could have radioed for help. Without it, and in the middle of open country, everything became far more serious.

Quickly Ambrose went to the lorry, picking his way through broken glass. The word 'Corona' was painted on the side of the vehicle. The driver was still in his cab slumped over the wheel. A young lad was lying in the road, where he'd been thrown by the impact, groaning. He was probably riding on the back of the lorry among the crates, ready to leap off to make the next delivery. "Daft but they all do it," Ambrose thought sadly.

Running on the grass verge to avoid the broken glass, he went to his car to fetch his first aid kit. As he passed the coach, a woman appeared at the door. She stared at the carnage for a second, then called inside "Barbara!"

By the time Ambrose was running back from his car, a younger woman had appeared. She half leapt down the coach steps before hurrying towards the boy in the road. Reassuring him, she laid a coat over him to keep him warm. "Looks like his leg'll need a splint," she called to her companion. Then she crossed quickly to the Ford.

The older woman saw Ambrose. "Do you know anything about first aid?" she shouted.

"I'm a policeman!" he shouted back. "Off duty."

"Barbara's a nurse," she called. "She's gone to check the driver."

The older woman seemed to be the leader of the coach party, a capable sort, admirably calm.

"Could one of your passengers run for help?" Ambrose asked her. "The farm up there may have a phone."

"John," the woman called back into the coach. A fair-haired young man, wearing smart shoes and a blazer, appeared.

"You're the fittest of us," she said to him. "Run to the farm and call for an ambulance."

The young man turned to Ambrose. "Do you know the way?" he asked. He was still white and shaken.

Ambrose took John to the side of the road and pointed to the farm on the skyline. "There's a footpath," Ambrose recalled. "Somewhere on the right. You can cut across the fields."

John set off at once. To Ambrose, he looked more like a shop assistant than an athlete, but at least he was willing. Ambrose prayed there would be someone at the farm, and that they had a 'phone.

"What else can we do?" the woman asked. "My name's Evelyn Hulme, by the way."

Quickly Ambrose considered how the coach passengers could help. The situation could have been worse: he could have been on his own. "We need to stop the traffic," he said. "Ask someone to go to the bend and flag drivers down."

To his surprise, instead of calling one of the others, Evelyn picked up a red scarf and set off up the lane herself. "Don't take any risks," Ambrose called after her. "Make sure you can be seen."

Ambrose turned to the boy lying shivering under the coat. He was about fifteen and crying with pain. His left leg was bent oddly beneath him "It's alright, lad," Ambrose said gently. "You'll be at the hospital in no time." He wished he could believe his promise. It would take at least ten minutes for John to get to the farm. Then it would be another twenty or so before an ambulance arrived from Chalk Heath.

Four more passengers had got off the coach, all still rather shaken. At least one of them must have witnessed the accident, Ambrose thought. He should speak to them as soon as he'd dealt with the injured.

"Pass me a couple more coats," he asked. "And something to use as a splint."

An umbrella appeared, a fashionable long Italian type. A pile of coats and scarves followed. As gently as he could, Ambrose straightened the boy's leg. Screaming, the lad passed out.

At least he could no longer feel the pain, Ambrose thought sadly. The boy was about the same age as Joe, Ambrose's son. Joe had wanted to take a job on a milk round, to save up for a new guitar. Ambrose was glad he'd refused permission. Delivery boys were just too vulnerable.

Bending over the lad, Ambrose made a splint for the broken leg, lashing the umbrella with a couple of scarves. As he did so, he could hear the coach passengers talking quietly behind him. "Poor soul!" a woman said several times. Sounding near to tears, she turned to the man next to her. "Oh Wynn, he only looks about fifteen."

"How long do you think we'll be stuck here?" Wynn asked. He spoke with a soft Welsh accent.

"An hour at least, I'd say," the woman answered.

Ambrose looked up. "Make that three," he warned. "The police will need to take photographs and measurements before the road can be cleared. You'll probably be sent back to Leyton Bridge."

"But we must be in Chalk Heath by two!" another man objected.

He spoke with a pronounced foreign accent. "Polish or German," Ambrose thought.

"We'll get the road cleared as soon as we can," Ambrose assured him, forgetting for a moment that he was off duty. "But this is a serious accident."

"Oh Dennis, we'll be late for the rehearsal!" the woman said in alarm.

"If that bloody woman had been on time, we'd have been well ahead of this!" the foreigner almost shouted. "I could ring her bloody neck!"

"So could us all, Anton," Dennis replied more quietly.

Ambrose had almost finished making the splint. Stirring, the boy began to regain consciousness. "You're going to be alright," Ambrose said gently. "That's the worst over." He folded another coat and put it under the boy's head as a pillow.

The lorry driver had climbed out of his cab and was sitting on the grass verge holding a handkerchief to his forehead. He must have got out unaided, as the young nurse was still attending to the commercial traveller. The injured would be safe while Ambrose spoke to the witnesses. He looked towards the group standing beside the coach. "Who's left on board?" he asked.

"Only Angela and Harry," Wynn replied.

"Harry's our driver," the woman explained. "He was badly shaken and Angela's *comforting* him."

To Ambrose's surprise, her tone was spiteful. There was an awkward pause.

"Trust Evelyn to direct the traffic," Dennis remarked, to break the silence. "She'll be in her element, eh, Jackie?"

Ambrose got up from his kneeling position. "Come and hold the lad's hand," he said to Jackie. "He needs comforting as well. I'll have a chat to your driver."

Climbing up the steep steps, Ambrose looked into the coach. Harry was sitting on one of the front seats, sharing a flask of coffee with a strikingly attractive woman. Both turned to Ambrose as he entered.

"Glad you're here," Angela remarked. "You clearly know what you're doing."

"I hope I do," Ambrose replied. He produced his warrant card.

"Ah, a policeman!" Angela said. "That explains it."

"I just wish I could have stopped without skidding," Harry said, probably not for the first time. "There's a lot of loose gravel on the road. My wheels wouldn't hold." He sounded apologetic.

"You did brilliantly," Angela reassured him. "Or we'd all be in the ditch."

To his relief, Ambrose could hear the sound of a distant bell. An ambulance was on its way. Young John had clearly been quick on his feet.

Ambrose turned back to the coach driver. "You ought to go to hospital," he advised.

Harry shook his head. "I have to get this lot to their concert," he insisted.

Angela chewed her lip nervously. "We've sold lots of tickets," she agreed, "And it's a special fund raiser for the theatre. We can't let people down."

Ambrose looked up from his pad where he'd been scribbling. "Is your concert in Chalk Heath?" he asked in surprise.

"How did you know?"

"Because I'm supposed to be going myself."

The woman smiled at the coincidence, her expression softening. For an instant the tiredness and worry lifted from her face. She had perfect features, the sort of classical beauty that lasted.

Ambrose recalled a publicity poster he'd seen at the theatre. The photo on it had probably been taken a couple of years ago, but there was no mistaking the rich, gold hair, or the unusual hazel eyes and clear-cut features. "You must be the soloist, Angela Chapman," he said.

"I am indeed," Angela replied with a smile.

Chapter Two

The last notes of 'In the Bleak Midwinter' echoed round the empty theatre.

"Oh for goodness sake!" Kathy Sutton said, slamming her hands on the piano keys. "What time is it *now*?"

"Five minutes since you last asked," WPC Meadows replied. She stamped her feet slightly. The stage was cold.

Molly Kendrick was working her way along the back stalls, checking for litter missed by the cleaners. She flicked a seat up with a bang. Kathy jumped and turned towards the noise. The dark auditorium made her uneasy, recalling unpleasant memories. She shivered.

"Do you want to try 'White Christmas'?" she asked.

Meadows sighed. "I suppose so," she looked at her watch. "The box office will be opening soon."

"Not at this rate," Kathy pointed out. "They may have to delay."

"Or perhaps they'll cancel?" Meadows looked hopeful. "At least it'll let me off the hook." She laughed nervously. "Save me making a fool of myself."

"Nonsense!" Kathy replied firmly. "You'll be fine. Besides, they'd never cancel the Christmas concert." She twisted back on her stool to face the piano.

Far away, a telephone rang shrilly in the office. They looked at each other in concern.

Molly ran out to the foyer, setting the doors flapping.

"Oh Lor'," Meadows said. "I hope there hasn't been an accident."

Kathy chewed dry skin around a fingernail. She was beginning to feel sick with nerves. If the Calzone Singers didn't arrive soon, there wouldn't even be time for a lighting check before the concert. She wished she hadn't asked Pauline Meadows to help. No substitute could be expected to sing close harmony, unaccompanied, without a rehearsal. The show could be a disaster.

Through the swing doors, Molly's voice could be heard faintly. She sounded worried.

"I can't stand this!" Meadows snapped and half vaulted off the stage.

Kathy followed more carefully. They ran up the aisle, towards the foyer.

Molly met them before they reached the doors. "That was Miss Hulme from the Calzone Singers," she said. "They're on their way. The coach got stuck behind an accident. She tried to call earlier but couldn't find a 'phone box."

"Where are they?" Kathy asked sharply. "If they've still got to get to the hotel…"

Molly interrupted. "They're going to come straight here, Mrs Sutton." She shook her head in concern. "The dressing rooms are locked and I don't have a key. The ladies won't like having to change in the toilets! There'll be ruffled feathers!"

Hurrying back into the foyer, she disappeared.

Kathy smiled ruefully. "She's met choirs before," she remarked.

"My feathers would be ruffled too," Meadows admitted. "First one of them is rushed to hospital, then they get stuck behind an accident."

"You've forgotten the late start," Kathy reminded her. "Still, that's pretty normal. Take any group of musicians on tour and one of them'll go missing." She picked up a programme from the pile near the door. "Do you want to run through any of the songs? You know the carols."

"But I don't know what speed they do them," Meadows replied. "I'm flattered you suggested me, but I do need a rehearsal."

"You'll be fine," Kathy repeated, over brightly. "DI Ambrose was right. You have a lovely voice."

Meadows flushed. "How does he know?"

"He's heard you at chapel."

Thoroughly embarrassed, Meadows looked at her watch. Another five minutes had passed. "OK. Let's have a go at 'Little Drummer Boy'."

They walked back towards the stage.

Suddenly there was loud banging on the theatre doors. Kathy almost yelped in surprise. Even Meadows jumped. A coach was reversing in the car park outside. The banging grew louder.

They reached the foyer just as Molly was unlocking the door. "I'm coming! Just a minute!" she shouted, struggling with the bolts.

As soon as the doors were open people were pushing inside, all talking loudly. They filled the tiny foyer. The ladies had black skirts and white blouses over their arms. The men were carrying dinner jackets and coloured bow ties. Everyone looked cross and hot, though it was bitterly cold outside.

"Why can't we go to the hotel?" Jackie was demanding. "We've been on the road for hours!"

The crowd pushed further into the foyer, almost pinning Molly against the opened doors.

"Ladies! Gentlemen!" a voice called. Immediately everyone paused. Evelyn pushed her way to the front, clapping her hands.

At once, the babble subsided. The choir looked towards their leader.

"Headmistress," Kathy suggested quietly.

"Or ex-army," Meadows whispered back. They kept out of sight, beside the doors to the stalls.

"We're here safe and sound, and that's all that matters," Evelyn announced. "We've still got time to get ready and have a quick rehearsal."

"Can't we even have a cup of tea?" Dennis asked. "There must be a café round here."

Jackie shook her head emphatically. "Tea's not good for the voice," she reminded him. Her manner suggested they were husband and wife. "I told you this tour was fated," she added more quietly. "All we need is Mother to play up again."

"If I don't have something to eat soon, I shall faint," Angela agreed, her beauty distorted by a furious scowl.

"Doesn't look the fainting sort to me," Meadows muttered.

"If you'd turned up at the coach on time, Angela…" Anton started.

Angela didn't give him time to finish. "Are you blaming *me*?" she snapped.

"We'd have been miles ahead of that smash, but for you!"

The leader was losing control. Suddenly she noticed Kathy and Meadows. "Ladies! Gentlemen!" she called reprovingly to the choir. "Our volunteers are here! What *will* they think of us?"

At once, everyone lapsed into shamefaced silence.

Evelyn stepped towards Kathy. "Please excuse us. We're all tired and upset. We've had a perfectly dreadful journey. Now, which of you is which?"

Kathy shook the outstretched hand. "I'm Mrs Sutton," she said. "I'll be playing piano while you're in Chalk Heath. Anne Jacobs, your pianist, and I were at school together."

"She speaks very highly of you," Miss Hulme replied. "The dear lady at Leyton Bridge did her best, but we missed Anne."

Smiling, Kathy turned towards Meadows, carefully avoiding any reference to her job. "And this is my friend, Miss Meadows. Anne asked if I knew a good alto."

"Thank you so much!" Evelyn shook Meadows' hand vigorously. "And these are the Calzone Singers," Evelyn smiled proudly, "one of the best amateur close harmony groups around."

"We're on first name terms amongst ourselves," Evelyn continued. "Since you're going to be part of our Chalk Heath tour, would you permit us to use yours?"

"This is Kathy, and I'm Pauline," Meadows replied awkwardly.

"Excellent. I'll introduce everyone after they've changed," Evelyn promised. "First let's have a look at the music. Then we'll have a quick run-through all together. It's so fortunate Anne sent you the scores in advance. I presume you've heard why she had to cancel at the last minute?"

"She said her children had measles," Kathy replied.

"You can't afford to take risks with measles," Evelyn agreed. "Not with so many people dying this year. But we must get on."

Angela stepped forward to interrupt. "Why isn't someone here from the Friends of the Theatre?" she asked. "Anne promised…"

"The Chairman came earlier," Kathy explained. "I'm afraid he had to leave an hour ago."

It was the wrong thing to say. Furiously the singer glared at her. Turning abruptly, she rejoined the rest of the choir.

Evelyn sighed. "Don't mind Angela," she said quietly. "She can be very difficult, but she has a wonderful voice. Excuse me a moment." She walked over quickly to soothe the soloist.

"Their star. And knows it," Meadows whispered.

Kathy laughed softly. "She might actually be good," she warned.

Evelyn was clapping her hands again. "I suggest we change now," she called to her choir. "If any of the audience arrives early we need to look presentable."

Molly broke the news. "I'm afraid the dressing rooms are locked, Ma'am," she said. "The manager has the key. He won't be here until the box office opens."

"Pardon?"

"Mrs Jacobs said you wouldn't be needing the changing rooms. I'm afraid you'll have to use the toilets."

There was an immediate outcry.

"No changing rooms?" Anton demanded. "That's an insult!"

"Who do you think we are?" Dennis agreed. "Some hick chapel choir?"

"Can't you get the key?" Jackie asked icily.

Molly was not easily intimidated. "I'm afraid not, Ma'am," she insisted. "There's only me here until the box office opens. I'll ring the manager and ask him to come in early, but he's on business the other side of Jenners Park. Maybe if the ladies take it in turns in the toilets, and the gentlemen go to the upstairs bar? We could keep the doors shut until they're ready …"

"I am not changing anywhere except a proper changing room," Angela insisted.

"If that woman complains again, I'll hit her!" John hissed. He sounded like he meant it.

Barbara sighed. "She doesn't mean to put everyone's backs up," she replied. "It's nerves."

"You're very loyal, Barbara," John said. "More than you should be."

Evelyn looked at her watch urgently. "The show must go on," she reminded everyone. "Change as fast as you can, please, then join us on stage. Kathy, could you show the ladies to the toilets? You gents will have to look after yourselves. I'm sure you're very capable of that."

A couple of the men smiled. There was some disgruntled muttering still, but the atmosphere was easing.

"We really will be dropping, Evelyn, if we don't have something to eat," Wynn pointed out. "The hotel might deliver something here."

"What an excellent idea!" Evelyn agreed. "I'm sure this kind lady will phone them."

"Not my job…" Molly began, but seeing the reaction, shrugged her shoulders and turned towards the office. Feeling as if she were back at school, Kathy also obeyed, leading the ladies down the corridor.

Evelyn smiled at Meadows ruefully. "Don't be put off," she pleaded. "We're a friendly group really. What with Gill doubling up at breakfast, Anne having to stay home and then the accident…" She left the sentence unfinished.

"Quite a day," Meadows agreed sympathetically.

Kathy reappeared. "It's a bit of squash in there," she said, "but they'll manage."

"Thank you so much," Evelyn said profusely. "Now let's find the piano. Lead on, my dears."

As they went back into the darkened theatre, Kathy whispered to Meadows. "I'm so sorry. I wish I hadn't involved you. This isn't going to be fun, and you've had to take the day off to do it."

"Don't worry," Meadows assured her. "Everything will be fine now. They can't have any more bad luck, surely?"

Chapter Three

The theatre was packed. Even the seats in the balcony were full. Ambrose looked around with pleasure. The Christmas concert was an important fundraiser for the theatre, as necessary as the Pantomime. With the second half featuring groups from local schools, there were always plenty of proud parents to swell the audience.

This year the Calzone Singers were the real attraction. They were well known. Their secretary being a Chalk Heath girl helped too. Though she'd moved to Uttley on her marriage, Anne Jacobs came back regularly to visit her parents.

"It's such a shame Anne had to stay behind," Mary said, as if reading his thoughts. "I was looking forward to seeing her."

Ambrose nodded. He still couldn't quite believe he'd made it to the theatre on time. He had no idea how the singers would perform after all the drama earlier.

He glanced anxiously towards his son. Usually Joe declared Christmas events 'dead boring', as if moping in his room were far more entertaining. However, he'd surprised Ambrose by joining them at the concert. Ambrose suspected a hidden agenda. He hoped fervently that, whatever it was, it wouldn't cause trouble.

Joe was unusually quiet. He seemed nervous, tapping his fingers on his knee in a constant rhythm. Ambrose realised he had no idea what was going on in his son's head. The knowledge saddened him. He wished he and Joe could start again.

The lights dimmed and a hand tweaked one of the curtains. An expectant hush settled on the audience. With a creak of ropes the curtains drew back on the stage. The backdrop looked like an empty street, with a single snow-covered lamp post. Snatches of 'Have

Yourself a Merry Little Christmas' wafted from the wings, softly at first, then growing louder.

Suddenly, from both sides of the stage, the Calzone Singers entered, blending in harmony. As they strolled about, they tossed handfuls of imitation snow towards each other. Finally the singers stood together near the lamp post, four men and four women, with their leader standing to one side.

"Very effective," Mary remarked. "I told you they were good."

Ambrose smiled in surprise. Half hidden in the wings, Kathy Sutton was sitting at a piano. In a long blue dress and with her hair brushed back, she looked lovely. It was hardly surprising young Sutton had fallen for her, despite her already being married at the time. Ambrose glanced round the theatre and saw PC Sutton with his parents in one of the boxes. "I wonder how Kathy managed to wangle that?" Ambrose thought in amusement. "No wonder the lad wanted the night off!" Then he turned back towards the stage. As he did so, his surprise turned to amazement.

Mary nudged him sharply. "Isn't that Pauline Meadows?" she asked.

"Or her double," Ambrose replied. "What the heck is she doing there?"

"Must be covering for someone, I knew she could sing but…"

The Honourable Marjorie Hodgkiss turned round from the row in front. "Shushh!" she ordered loudly.

Mary stifled a laugh. "Now we've done it," she whispered. "One *must* behave when 'Madge' is around!"

But Meadows had been recognised by others too. "In't that woman a copper?" a man behind Ambrose hissed. "The one on the left?"

"Blimey! That's WPC Meadows," another voice agreed. "Looks a bit different to last week. She brought our Tim back by the scruff of his neck. He deserved it, mind."

The surprise was becoming audible. Quickly the choir leader intervened. After what he'd seen earlier, Ambrose already knew she could command an audience. "Good evening everyone," she said in a clear, confident voice. "Welcome to the Chalk Heath Theatre, and to the Annual Charity Concert. The Calzone Singers are delighted to entertain you at such a happy event. I hear you have some good news too. The Friends group have nearly raised enough for your new theatre. Building work is to begin next year."

At once a cheer went up. The chairman of the Friends Committee stood up in the front row and bowed in appreciation. For a few moments there was a happy babble. Joe was paying little attention however. He seemed to be gesturing to someone in a row behind. Ambrose turned, trying to see who it was. "What's the boy up to now?" he wondered wearily.

Evelyn called everyone to order again. "Let me introduce the members of the Calzone Singers," she continued. She started with the tenors: "Dennis Walters and John Pedderson," she called. One by one the men stepped forward and bowed to the audience. "Now the basses: Anton Gdansk and Wynn Davison."

Then she turned to the sopranos. First she introduced "Our soloist, Angela Chapman," followed by her more ordinary companion, Jacqueline Walters. The altos waited patiently.

"And last, but definitely not least," Evelyn continued, "our altos, Barbara Collier, and your very own Pauline Meadows. Miss Meadows has stepped into a very large breach, taking the place of our regular singer, who is indisposed. We couldn't have performed tonight without her, so please give a very loud round of applause."

Flushing scarlet in embarrassment, Meadows stepped forward and did a slight curtsey.

"Pauline's going to have trouble living this down," Mary smiled.

"What on earth possessed her?" Ambrose thought uneasily. If Meadows performed badly, the whole town would hear. Gossip travelled fast. Being a police officer in a small town had its disadvantages. People noticed everything you did. And everything your family does, he thought ruefully. That was part of the problem with Joe, he admitted. It must be hard for him to live a normal life with his father so well known.

Ambrose sighed. He'd hoped for a quiet, enjoyable evening. It looked like it was going to be anything but.

The choir began to sing, moving smoothly into 'White Christmas' and then on to 'Chestnuts Roasting by an Open Fire'. Meadows seemed to be coping well. There were no obvious pauses or wrong notes. Only a keen-eared musician would have noticed the piano in the wings joining in occasionally, to give the altos their cue. Ambrose knew Meadows well enough, however, to see the strain in her eyes.

People behind were whispering again, but approvingly. "Bloomin' good voice!" one of them said. "Who'd have thought it?" Smiling, Ambrose relaxed a little.

All the same, he sincerely hoped the missing singer would recover quickly. The Calzone Singers had a big concert in Jenners Park and engagements in the town before then, including one of The Shalimar's famous Gala Dinners. He couldn't see how Meadows could continue performing and do her normal duties. She'd have to take the week off, and they had a lot on at the moment, with the recent thefts.

The audience were clearly enjoying the evening. By the time the carols began, many were joining in, or swaying in time. Ambrose glanced at his watch. He was astonished to see nearly an hour had gone by. It was time for the interval.

"It's traditional in our concerts to finish the first half with a solo," Evelyn announced. "It gives me great pleasure to call on Mrs Chapman."

The soprano stepped forward.

"Blimey! What a stunner!" the man behind remarked.

Smiling, Ambrose considered the woman waiting to sing. He'd seen her earlier in the coach, but on stage she looked even more beautiful. He wondered whether the other women in the choir were jealous of her. That sort of beauty often caused trouble, and the others were very ordinary in comparison. Angela's expression when she wasn't singing suggested sadness, however. He suspected she'd been widowed young, in the war perhaps, like so many. Or maybe it was discontent he saw in her face. Whatever it was, she seemed out of place on Chalk Heath's faded stage.

"You always did have an eye for a good-looking woman," Mary whispered, teasing him.

"And I found one," he laughed as he touched her hand. "Sorry. Was I staring? She interests me. There's something not quite right."

"Your famous instinct," Mary teased again.

The choir leader was continuing. "Mrs Chapman will sing one of Handel's loveliest arias," she announced. "'I Know That My Redeemer Liveth', from *The Messiah*. After that there will be an interval of twenty minutes. I'm told that ice creams will be served at the front of the theatre, and tea and mince pies at the back. So, a big hand for Mrs Chapman please."

Joe looked down at his knees. He wasn't partial to Handel or any of 'those old duffers'. "Do I have to?" he pouted.

"Shush," his mother admonished. "It's almost the interval. I'll get you an ice cream."

Placated by the promise of food, Joe lolled back in his chair, his legs sticking out into the aisle. Ambrose considered telling him to sit up, but decided to pretend he hadn't noticed.

The piano struck up in the wings. Several people shuffled. They were not fans of Handel either. One or two near the exit got up, to secure first place at the bar.

Then Angela Chapman began to sing. Slowly the shuffling subsided. The people moving towards the door paused. Ambrose stopped thinking about his son or about anything else.

The woman's voice matched her beauty. The aria seemed to rise and fall without breath, the top notes reached effortlessly, perfectly pitched. She was far too good for an amateur choir, however well known. She should have been starring at a West End Theatre, or gracing a soirée in some great house. Given the right break, she could be a star.

When the last notes died away the applause was tumultuous. Smiling with pleasure, Angela did an elegant bow. She had the bearing of a star.

Then the curtains closed. At once the audience surged towards the refreshments.

"Better than most professionals," The Hon 'Madge' declared. As Life President of the Friends and its chief donor, her opinion was important. "That woman will go far," she predicted. "Her voice is far too big for an amateur group."

"The oracle has spoken!" Ambrose commented softly to his wife. Mary laughed as she darted towards the ice creams.

"Are you enjoying it?" he asked his son afterwards.

"It's ok," Joe said, shrugging. On a scale measured from scowling grunts to "alright", 'ok' was praise indeed.

The interval was the usual chaotic scramble for drinks and toilets. When the bell went for the second half there was no chance of everyone getting back to their seats for another ten minutes. Hopefully the next Christmas concert would take place in a splendid new concrete building with a much bigger bar.

Suddenly, Ambrose noticed his son had disappeared. “Where’s Joe?” he asked Mary in concern.

Chapter Four

"Joe's alright," Mary smiled. "Wait and see."

The choir leader stepped out from the wings and clapped her hands. At once the theatre was hushed. "I could do with her down the Police Station," Ambrose thought dryly.

"Ladies and Gentlemen," Evelyn began. "The Calzone Singers will perform a few more numbers at the end of the evening. First, it is my pleasure to introduce some of the talented youngsters you have in your own town. To open the second half we have The Tramps, from Chalk Heath Grammar School."

As the curtains jerked back, Ambrose had his third and biggest surprise. Joe was standing on stage, guitar at the ready. Either side of him were two of his classmates, Rob and Jimmy. Rob had an old washboard in his hand; Jimmy was about to play what looked like a tea chest. A string was attached to a long pole sticking out of the box.

As soon as the curtains were fully open Joe was pounding away, Jimmy was strumming on the tea chest while Rob rubbed vigorously on the washboard. "It's called Skiffle," Mary whispered.

"I'm not quite such a dinosaur," Ambrose protested. "I've heard it on the radio. I thought Joe was into the more modern stuff."

"He is, but the school wouldn't let them play rock and roll."

The lad on the washboard started to sing. He had a pleasant voice, though the lyrics seemed to consist mainly of the words 'Cumberland Gap' repeated over and over. Joe and Jimmy played vigorously in accompaniment.

"You little …" Ambrose teased, tapping his wife on the nose. "You knew, didn't you?"

"I've been carting him back and forth to rehearsals for weeks," Mary admitted.

Shaking his head at her, Ambrose listened. He was no judge of such things. Skiffle wasn't his sort of music, but he could see that the audience liked it. The younger members were tapping their feet and smiling. Afterwards, there was loud applause. Ambrose was amazed his son and friends could give so much pleasure.

He scarcely noticed the rest of the programme. It seemed only a few minutes until the choir was singing 'Rudolph the Red Nosed Reindeer' and the evening was coming to a close.

The Friends were invited to join the choir for supper at The Shalimar Hotel. "Now come along," The Hon 'Madge' instructed. "I hear the poor choir members missed their tea. They'll be eager to get to their refreshments. I can take three of you in my car and I imagine DI Ambrose can take others."

Ambrose glanced quickly at his wife. "We ought to take Joe home," she pointed out. "It's getting late."

"Surely you'll be coming to the Hotel with us?" The Hon 'Madge' asked. "We ought to see the choir are happy with The Shalimar. They'll be looking forward to meeting you," she added pointedly. "I do think we should have all the committee to welcome them."

Ambrose sighed. He would far rather be going home to congratulate Joe, but he had to keep Marjorie Hodgkiss happy. "Do you mind?" he asked Mary softly. "Take Joe home in the car and I'll make my own way back as soon as I can."

"If you need a lift you can travel with us," a voice beside them invited. Evelyn Hulme was smiling and shaking hands all round. "The coach is waiting outside, and there's room on it for another four. Please do join us. We never did get chance to thank you for all your efforts earlier. I'm sure we'd still be stuck behind that accident now if you hadn't been there."

Ambrose glanced at WPC Meadows. She too was trying to slip away unobserved. "No you don't!" Evelyn said, laughing and catching her by the hand. "You deserve a good supper."

Meadows glanced towards Ambrose, pleading with her eyes. She clearly hadn't told them she was a policewoman. "Could he keep her secret for the rest of the evening?" her expression said. Ambrose nodded slightly.

Obediently they followed the Hon 'Madge' towards the foyer. "Tell Joe he did brilliantly," Ambrose called after his wife.

"Tell him yourself tomorrow," she called back.

After the warmth of the theatre, the air in the car park was painfully cold, frost settling on car windscreens. The choir piled onto their coach, carrying music and bags. They chattered noisily, relieved that the show was over and had gone well. Ambrose found himself sitting beside the young man who'd run for help earlier.

"An excellent evening," Ambrose said. "You're Mr Pedderson aren't you?"

"You've got a good memory," the young man replied approvingly. "Call me John, though. Our esteemed leader insists on first names, being as we're like family."

"I'm impressed you could all sing so well after what happened earlier," Ambrose observed.

"It was a nightmare! We thought we'd never make it on time. The hotel was very good. They sent us a mound of sausage rolls for the interval, but none of us felt much like eating. We'll make up for it now."

"You certainly deserve it," Ambrose smiled.

The man on the other side of the aisle leant forward. "Pleased to meet you properly," he said cheerily, offering his hand. "I'm Wynn Davison. We were all so impressed earlier. Heaven knows how we'd have coped if you hadn't been there. You'll have to bear with us. Nerves get frayed when you're tired." He glanced meaningfully in the direction of the women.

"Is that what it is?" the other bass asked in his broad foreign accent. "Playing prima donna I call it."

"Now then, Anton," Wynn replied in mock reproof. "Don't start stirring it."

Fortunately the women at the front didn't hear, or they chose to ignore him. Ambrose watched them with interest. Meadows was sitting next to her fellow alto. They seemed to be getting on well. At the front of the coach, the lead soprano was sitting with Evelyn Hulme, but the choir leader was turning, chatting to the couple behind her. Despite the babble, Angela Chapman seemed very much alone.

The Shalimar Hotel was just outside town. The road became narrower and the streetlights dwindled. The heath brooded mysteriously in the darkness. Though the coach claimed 'Superior Travel' along its side, it was poorly sprung. The passengers rattled and bumped over the uneven roads. Even with a break at Leyton Bridge, the hundred mile trip from Uttley must have been very uncomfortable.

Unused to the route, the driver had to break sharply at a couple of bends. The rear wheels skidded. "Getting icy," Wynn remarked. "Good job we didn't finish late."

Ambrose was beginning to realise how well Harry had driven earlier, to avoid the accident. The coach turned off the road, through two imposing gateposts, each topped by a stone lion. Beyond, floodlights cast a welcoming glow and a tree twinkled with fairy lights. A painted sign announced 'The Shalimar Hotel' in gold letters.

The coach crunched up the gravel drive.

"Looks ok," John remarked.

"Ooh, how pretty!" Jackie Walters called from the front.

"I hope the beds are comfortable," Dennis replied. "I need a good night's sleep."

A grandiose mock Tudor folly by day, The Shalimar was beautiful at night. The black and white front looked genuinely old, topped by romantic gables and a little tower. Ambrose had been to several of their Gala Dinners in an official capacity, but he'd never seen the building look so attractive.

Several of the Friends group had already arrived. They were being welcomed by Peter and Audrey Tempest, the owners of the hotel, standing almost regally in the porch. It was a big occasion for them. Peter was in his best blazer & smart grey trousers, with his regiment tie of course, very erect and military in his bearing. Audrey was in her customary twin set & pearls, but the skirt and court shoes were especially smart.

As soon as the coach came to a stop, both of them were stepping forward to help with the luggage. "Welcome to The Shalimar," Mrs Tempest said as the choir members clambered down onto the driveway. "Supper is laid out in the dining room. Some of you might want to pop up to your rooms first. We'll do our best to get you all booked in quickly."

Every member of the Shalimar's staff was waiting to help. Jane Fellowes, the waitress, was taking addresses and getting the visitors' book signed. Even Des the chef and Libby the chamber-maid had been called on to carry cases up to the bedrooms. For quarter of an hour, there was controlled pandemonium. "Do go into the dining room and have something to eat while you wait," Mrs Tempest invited. "The Friends group are tucking in."

Several of the choir did go to eat, but the Reception remained crowded and busy. Another group arrived from town, adding to the bustle. Guests came down from their rooms, drawn by the promise of supper. Ambrose recognised two of the hotels' long-term residents, Mr and Mrs Gibbs, occupying the best chairs in the reception area. They were thoroughly enjoying watching.

At last the queue for keys almost disappeared. Most of the choir returned from their rooms and were beginning to move into the dining room. Ambrose lingered by the desk, to have a quiet word with WPC Meadows. "You did very well," he said approvingly.

"Thank you," Meadows replied, smiling with pleasure. "I was all over the place actually. Hopefully no one but the choir noticed." She dropped her voice to a whisper. "Thank you for not recognising me. They mightn't have liked me being in the police."

"Are you going to have to sing with them again?" Ambrose asked.

"I hope not. I managed, but only just. And to be honest…." Meadows paused, trying to find the right words.

Suddenly there was a commotion near them. "It isn't fair!" Jackie Walters was complaining shrilly. "That room simply isn't big enough for two. Just because we're a couple doesn't mean we want to be squashed together."

"I'm so sorry…" Mrs Tempest began, but was cut off.

"Dennis and I were stuffed in a cupboard at the last place, and I'm not having it again! There's hardly room to walk round the bed, never mind open the wardrobe. I demand to be moved."

"Jackie…" her husband pleaded, red faced with embarrassment. "It'll be alright. I can put our cases on top of the wardrobe."

"That won't be necessary," Mrs Tempest assured them, with a practised smile. "We'll see if we can rearrange the rooms so you have one of the bigger ones. Maybe a couple of your colleagues would be willing to share the tower room? That one has two single beds, and it's full of character."

"I'll share," Barbara Collier offered. She turned to Angela. "How about it? Sleeping in a tower sounds fun."

"I never share with anyone," Angela said coldly. "You should know that by now." Turning away, she headed towards the dining room.

"What about Gillian's room?" Evelyn jumped in quickly. "Has her room been re-allocated? You did get the message she isn't joining us?"

"Ah, of course," Mrs Tempest replied with a sigh of relief. "That room is quite a bit bigger. It does mean a bit of a walk to the gentleman's bathroom but I'm sure that won't be a problem."

"Not in the slightest," Dennis replied immediately. He snatched up the key. Then grabbing his wife's arm, he propelled her up the stairs, before she had chance to say anything else.

To Ambrose's surprise, Barbara's eyes were filled with tears. Meadows had noticed too, for she put her hand comfortingly on the other woman's arm. "That was unkind," she said quietly, nodding in Angela's direction.

"It's not just her," Barbara replied, her voice thick with emotion. "It's this whole trip. Everyone's so nice normally. They gave me a lovely birthday last month; lots of cards and presents." She touched her necklace, a pretty silver pendant with a red stone in the centre. "Angela gave me this. 'For being her friend,' she said. Now she's hardly speaking to me. I don't know what's wrong with her, with everyone. Maybe it's not having Anne with us. She keeps us in order." Attempting a smile, Barbara went to find the supper.

"That's what I mean," Meadows said softly to DI Ambrose. "I'll be glad to be out of it. Did that look like a garnet to you, by the way?"

"I'm no expert on gems," Ambrose admitted, "but I'd say that's an expensive necklace." He was about to say more, but the choir leader was clapping her hands.

"I have some wonderful news, Calzone!" she announced standing in the doorway so she could be heard both in the dining room and the reception area. "Gill's husband rang the hotel while we were on our way. It's food poisoning, not appendicitis. Gill should be able to join us for the Gala on Friday."

There was an immediate cheer from the choir. “Isn’t that great?” Evelyn enthused. “Now eat up quickly and then we can give the hotel guests a carol or two.”

“Here we go again,” Meadows said. “I’d better grab a cake while I have the chance.” She headed towards the food.

The reception area was emptying. Quietly Ambrose found his coat and slipped out of the front door. To his surprise, the coach had gone. Clearly Harry was staying elsewhere.

Turning up his collar, Ambrose set off. The walk home would clear his head.

Chapter Five

Thursday 10 December 1959

PC Higgins yawned. He hated doing paperwork. When he joined the Force he'd imagined catching desperate criminals, not completing forms. On such a quiet afternoon, he could hardly say he didn't have time (his usual excuse). There was a lot to enter up too. There'd been a spate of shoplifting during the past week. It wasn't the usual sort either: the odd schoolboy nicking a lipstick to impress his girlfriend.

These thieves were clearly professionals. They took high value goods and disappeared before the shop assistants realised anything had gone. It looked like a gang had moved into Chalk Heath. The Chamber of Commerce had already leant on the superintendant, who'd leant on everyone below. Something must be done. But as usual, quite *what* should be done, 'Top Brass' hadn't said.

The telephone rang, its shrill bell cutting through the silence. Higgins snapped himself awake. "Chalk Heath Police Station," he said efficiently. "Can I help you?"

"I want to report a theft," a woman's voice said.

"Of course, Ma'am. Can you give me your name and address?" Expecting one of the local shopkeepers, Higgins tried to place the voice. The speaker was breathless, probably nervous. She sounded middle aged. Higgins couldn't think who it was.

"Er, yes, my name," the voice replied, flustered. Then she calmed herself. "This is Mrs Harold Budgen of Gateways Farm, Little Steading," she said. "I've been staying at The Shalimar Hotel with my husband." Having got going, words began to tumble out. "We often come to Chalk Heath to do our Christmas shopping. We only have a general store in the village, and it makes a nice break. Mr and Mrs Tempest always make us so welcome and the food's excellent…"

"So I've heard," Higgins agreed, managing to cut short the stream. "What's been stolen?"

"My husband's watch."

"You're certain it was stolen?" Higgins asked. It wouldn't be the first time someone reported a watch had been taken, only to find it in the bathroom.

"Positive!" Mrs Budgen insisted. "I waited till we were home before ringing. I thought we might have packed it, but it's not in either of our cases." The woman's voice became shaky, almost tearful. "It isn't just any watch, officer. It's an antique half-hunter on a gold chain. I told my husband he shouldn't bring it, but we were going to the Christmas concert and he wanted to wear it with his new waistcoat."

Higgins was interested now. He began taking down details.

"It's come down the family," Mrs Budgen continued. "There's a sovereign on the chain with a date on it. I think it's 1837." The woman's voice echoed, as if she was speaking in an empty hall. "We should have got it valued, but you don't think, do you?"

Higgins went through the usual questions. "When did you last see it?" he asked.

"When we went to bed. Harold wore it at the concert. He'd still got it on when we came back to the hotel. He must have taken it off and put it on the bedside cabinet. That's what he usually does."

"But you're not sure?"

Mrs Budgen hesitated. "Not totally," she admitted. "We were both very tired. The choir was in the hotel when we got back, the one from the concert. They were singing carols and there was a special supper. It was all so nice that we didn't get to bed till after midnight. But we don't see how Harold could have lost it before we went to bed. We'd have noticed."

Higgins was trying to establish the facts and finding it difficult. The woman had a way of speaking in sudden bursts that made her sentences hard to follow. "When *did* you notice?" he persisted.

"This morning, but we thought it must already be in one of the cases. Harold's blaming me, of course. I should have checked before we left."

"Could someone have taken it while you were at breakfast?"

There was a pause before Mrs Budgen replied, "My husband started looking for it before we went down, but the gong sounded and we had to go. We can't be sure," she admitted, her voice beginning to shake again, "but it looks like it was stolen while we were asleep. Someone must have come into our room. I hope I'm wrong..."

Higgins could understand the woman's concern. He was alarmed at the idea himself. Could someone really have come into their room at night? They would have to know their way around. Perhaps one of The Shalimar's staff was a thief? Or maybe the gang that was shoplifting in town had got into the hotel? That was an even worse thought.

He said nothing to increase Mrs Budgen's concerns. "Have you told Mr and Mrs Tempest?" he asked instead.

"I've just rung the hotel," Mrs Budgen replied. "Mrs Tempest said she'd ask the chambermaid to check our room. I didn't say it had been stolen. I mean, that's a serious thing to say isn't it? Until you're absolutely sure."

"Why don't you ring again tomorrow and see if it's turned up?" Higgins suggested. "Then let me know. If the watch is still missing, we'll investigate."

"Thank you. You've been very kind. I've never rung a police station before. Harold usually does that sort of thing, but he said I had to, because it was my fault."

"I'm sure it wasn't," PC Higgins assured her. He took an instant dislike to Mr Harold Budgen.

Higgins neatened up his notes, ready to discuss them with DS Winters when he came in. The Shalimar had an excellent reputation. If a theft had been committed by one of their staff, Mr and Mrs Tempest would be down on them like the proverbial ton of bricks.

The next half hour was quiet. Apart from a report that travellers were tethering their horses on the heath, there was nothing new. Higgins continued with his paperwork until WPC Meadows came in. She'd been looking for a stray dog in the park.

"Couldn't see hide nor hair of it," Meadows admitted, taking off her hat. "I got a description though. 'Large fangs and huge burning eyes'..."

Higgins kept a straight face. "Did it have 'Baskerville' on its collar?" he asked.

"Wasn't wearing one," Meadows replied, equally dead-pan. "Anything new?"

"The BBC rang. Wanted to know if they could feature you on *Juke Box Jury*."

For a second Meadows stared at him, red-faced, then she managed to reply flippantly, "Tell them I'm already booked. The London Palladium want me."

Higgins smiled. "Doreen at The Copper Kettle told me," he admitted. "She'd heard it from Gladys, who'd got it from her sister. Word gets round."

"Oh Lor'," Meadows groaned. "I'd better bring sandwiches for the next day or two. I don't fancy Doreen pointing me out to her customers."

She suppressed a yawn. By the time she'd got home last night, it was nearly one. Even so, she'd had to get up for duty this morning as usual. Keeping busy was the best remedy. Going to one of the cupboards, she took out a pack of handmade road signs, and a picture of traffic lights she'd pasted onto a sheet of card. She gave road safety talks at local schools. Tomorrow morning she was speaking at Chalk Heath Junior.

"It sounds like you did alright," Higgins said kindly. "Doreen might even treat you to a stale bun, if you're lucky. How long is your glittering career going to last?"

"Till tomorrow," Meadows replied from inside the cupboard. "The choir's leading a sing-along Messiah tonight. I'll join them later but said I can't make the rehearsal this afternoon. I know it pretty well and there'll be loads of singers to hide my mistakes."

"Isn't there a big concert on Saturday?" Higgins called across. "I saw an advert."

"Yes, at Jenners Park. And they're doing a Gala Dinner at the hotel tomorrow. Luckily, the woman who's been sick should be back for both." Meadows changed the subject. "You've been to the Junior haven't you? What are the children like?"

"Some of the boys can be a handful. The new headmistress may have knocked them into shape by now, though."

Meadows packed the signs and poster into her rucksack. She lifted the bag onto her back to check the weight. It would be awkward as she cycled but not too heavy. She took the bag to the locker room, down the corridor.

Higgins was just thinking about his tea break when a young woman came in. Hesitating at the door, she looked around.

"Can I help you?" Higgins called from the desk, sighing inwardly.

The young woman stepped forward. "I hope so," she said. "I want to report a theft."

"Another?" Higgins almost said aloud. "Certainly Miss. Can you give me the details?" he asked instead. "Your name and address please."

"Miss Barbara Collier, 13, Newdigate Street, Uttley." The woman was in her late twenties, nervous, but used to speaking to strangers. "I'm staying at The Shalimar Hotel with the Calzone Singers," she continued.

Higgins took up his pencil and pad. "And what's been stolen?" he asked.

"A necklace. I've written a description down for you." Taking a note from her handbag, Barbara glanced at it quickly. "A silver pendant on a sterling silver chain," she read. "The chain was about ten inches long and the pendant had a hallmark on it. I remember a lion but not the date. A red stone was set into the pendant." She looked up apologetically. "I don't know whether the stone was a real garnet. Knowing who gave it to me, I'd say it was." Her voice became husky, and she passed Higgins the note to cover her emotion. "It was a gift to me from one of the other choir members," she explained.

Higgins was writing furiously. "When did you notice it was missing?" he asked. He had a sense of déjà vu. Less than half an hour ago he'd been asking exactly the same questions.

"This morning, after breakfast. I overslept and had to dress quickly. We had a late night last night. I didn't have chance to put on my necklace this morning. When I came back up to my room, it had gone. I'd hidden it in a drawer. Someone must have rummaged through my clothes to find it."

In concern, Higgins looked up. "Could that have been while you were at breakfast?" he asked.

"I hope so. Otherwise someone entered my room while I was asleep."

"No, that's not a good thought," Higgins agreed. "DS Winters won't like the sound of this," he added mentally. "Can I confirm you'd put the necklace in a drawer?" he continued aloud.

"The top drawer of my dressing table," Barbara replied. "I've made a sketch of the pendant. It's from memory, but I think it's right." She took another piece of paper from her bag and passed it to PC Higgins.

Higgins placed the description and the drawing in his notepad. "Have you told the Hotel?" he asked.

"Of course. I went to see Mrs Tempest. She was quite upset. She said she'd ask the staff if they knew anything. But she didn't say she'd report it to the police. So I thought I'd better come myself. I suppose she's worried about the hotel's reputation."

Once again, Higgins made no comment, though he scribbled 'not reported by hotel' on his pad. "You've been very clear, Miss Collier," he said. "I'll pass this on to my superiors. One of us will investigate." He paused, thinking what DS Winters might do in such a situation. "I suggest you don't tell anyone at the hotel that you've been here," he advised. "If there is a thief on the staff, we don't want to alert them."

Barbara Collier was just turning to leave when WPC Meadows came in, carrying a cup and saucer. "I thought you'd like a cuppa," she said to Higgins. Then she stopped and stared. "Oh dear," she said, and went bright red.

Barbara stared back. "You didn't say you were a policewoman!" she said accusingly.

"I didn't say I wasn't," Meadows reminded her gently. "Everybody seemed to assume I was a typist. I didn't like to argue."

"Some typist!" Barbara retorted.

Higgins came to his colleague's aid. Evidently Meadows hadn't been entirely Frank with her fellow singers. "She's a lousy typist," he confided to Barbara in an exaggerated whisper. "Makes more mistakes than the rest of us put together."

Meadows gave him a quick glance of thanks, then turned awkwardly to Barbara. "I'm sorry," she apologised. "I didn't mean to deceive you. But you mightn't have liked me being a policewoman. Even my mother doesn't."

Barbara smiled slightly and the atmosphere eased. "You were probably right not to tell us," she admitted. "It was an awful day and everyone was cross. People might have thought you were spying on us. Anton certainly wouldn't have approved. He has some very old-fashioned ideas. I suppose it's with him being Polish.

"I'm afraid things are no better today," Barbara added. "Your colleague will explain. This trip really is fated. My necklace has been stolen: the one Angela gave me."

"That's awful!" Meadows said at once.

"Giving me that necklace was the last nice thing Angela did. She hasn't had a good word for me since, and we used to be such friends." Barbara paused, not sure whether to continue. "What makes it worse," she added, "is that I keep wondering if one of the choir took it."

Higgins looked up. "Why do you say that?" he asked quietly.

Frowning, Barbara paused. "Some money went missing while we were doing our last concert at Leyton Bridge," she explained. "We'd made a collection for the Children's Home and the tin disappeared. But why would anyone take my necklace? It has to be a coincidence." She sounded as if she was trying to convince herself.

"I'm sure it is," Meadows said reassuringly.

Looking at her watch, Barbara made an effort at a smile. "I need to get to the church now," she said. "I think I can remember the way. The coach dropped us off at the shops before the rehearsal. I didn't tell anyone I was coming here or about the necklace. I thought Angela would be furious and it might still turn up."

"I'll see you to the main road," Meadows offered. "You can see the church from there. I'll be along later for the sing-along." She liked the woman and felt bad about unintentionally deceiving her.

At first they walked in silence. It had begun to rain so Barbara put her umbrella up to shelter them both. "Does your mother really not like you being a policewoman?" she asked finally.

"It's not a *nice* job for a woman," Meadows replied, smiling.

"Mine's not sure nursing's very nice either," Barbara admitted. "What with all that blood. I might meet a handsome doctor though, so she puts up with it."

Meadows raised an eyebrow. "I thought you were engaged," she remarked, glancing down at Barbara's left hand.

"The ring's just cover, so I'm not invited to parties at the Nurses' Home. They can be pretty wild."

"But you still wear it for choir?" Meadows asked.

"I forgot and wore it one week. After that I had to keep it on. It's quite useful. Anton can be a bit of wolf and I think John would get ideas if I let him."

"Wynn seems rather sweet," Meadows smiled. "Don't you fancy him?"

Barbara laughed. "All the women do," she said. "But he's married. The best ones always are."

They'd reached the corner. To Meadows' surprise, Barbara gave her a little hug as they parted. "Thank you for being so friendly last night," she said impulsively. Then she turned towards the church.

As soon as Meadows got back to the 'Station, Higgins called to her. "You'd better hold the fort. I'll go and talk to DI Ambrose." He gathered up his pad and the notes. "The choir's here as guests of the committee the DI's on," he added. "He won't like having thefts at The Shalimar either."

Higgins shook his head. "And I don't like thieves going into bedrooms while people are asleep. What if one of the guests wakes up?"

Chapter Six

By early afternoon it was raining hard. "Just my luck!" Sam Winters said as he kissed his wife.

"Ah!" she agreed in disgust. "Orrido!" Sheltering under the porch with little Caitlin in her arms, Francesca Winters looked into the gloom. The weather was so different to her native Italy.

"We will get soak-ed when fetch the others," Fran complained. "I hate your rain."

"It's *soaked*," Winters corrected her gently. They had agreed that his wife must learn better English if she was to help the children at school, but it did not come easily to her. "And it's not my rain," he added, smiling. "I hate it as much as you. Never mind, it'll be Christmas soon and Mama will be coming."

Fran nodded, her expression brightening with excitement. "Four more days!" she agreed. "We meet her at airport? You no go work sudden?"

"Of course not," Winters assured her. "I've booked the leave." He kissed his wife again briefly. A curtain twitched at the window opposite. Looking across, Winters waved cheerily. At once the curtain dropped back.

Fran laughed. "Naughty!" she said and tapped him on the nose. "You take care!" she added more seriously. "We need you. But you not wake us up when you come back."

Winters shook his head ruefully. "Sorry about last night," he apologised again. "I'll avoid the creaky stair."

"If not, how you say? I cut your guts into garters," Fran retorted.

Laughing, Winters pulled his collar up and walked down the path. For an instant he looked back, watching his wife. He saw the brightness of her expression fade, to be replaced by a hint of sadness.

Whenever he saw that expression on her face he felt guilty. She missed her home, missed its sun and laughter, and she missed her family even more. He should not have brought her to this cold country. But he had promised to go back for her when the war was over, and he kept his promises. Besides, he could not stop thinking about her. He had to find her again, though it cost him all his savings. They had had a lot of happy times since then he admitted. He wouldn't have done anything differently given another chance. But it was hard for her, living in a strange land.

Jerking himself back to the present, Winters went out into the street. Yesterday's frost was preferable to this miserable downpour. By the time he'd walked the mile to the shopping parade, he was indeed soaked. Though it was not yet three o'clock, the sky was already dark.

Buchmann's was just round the corner, four shops along. The jewellers shut early on Thursday, but Mr and Mrs Buchmann lived above the shop. He could have sent Higgins or Sutton tomorrow, but Winters preferred to go himself, as soon as possible.

The Buchmanns were the eyes and ears of the shopping parade. Sam Winters gave them individual attention. In return they often passed him information: a description of someone loitering around the pub perhaps, or of children playing truant. Besides, they needed an eye keeping on them. A few of the local hotheads couldn't tell good from bad; not where a German was concerned. Or an Italian come to that, Winters thought grimly.

Even some of his colleagues should know better, he reflected. The jokes in the tea room infuriated him. 'How many gears does an Italian tank have? One: reverse!'. When PC Vernon cracked that old joke yesterday, Winters had almost lost his temper. He'd wanted to retort, "Could you have fought Mussolini and hidden a couple of British soldiers in *your* loft?" But it was no good. The lad wouldn't have understood what Fran and her family had been through.

The jewellers' was in darkness, its window protected by an iron grill, the displays empty. A chink of light shone under an adjoining door. The Buchmanns were home. The bell was taped over so Winters rattled the letterbox.

Footsteps sounded on the stairs. "Who's there?" Mrs Buchmann called.

"DS Winters, I hear you've had a theft."

A key turned and bolts were pulled back. "Come up," Mrs Buchmann invited, hardly opening the door long enough for Winters to enter. The Buchmanns took no chances. Jewellers were always more at risk of a break-in than other shopkeepers, even in Chalk Heath. Fleeing the Nazis must leave you jumpy too, Winters reflected.

The flat upstairs was cosy after the cold outside. Winters hung his wet things in the hall and gratefully accepted the chair beside the fire. "Sorry to trouble you," he began, "But I was passing. We need a few more details: description, value, that sort of thing."

"Yes. We have details," Hans agreed. He poked the fire to a brighter flame. "But first you have tea. Anna has made a new cake. Very good."

It was a ritual for every visitor. Before conversation could begin they must try Anna's latest recipe. Though Winters had eaten he knew better than to refuse. "Delicious!" he announced afterwards, as he always did, and Anna smiled with pleasure, as she always did. "Another piece?" she invited. This time Winters managed to refuse, producing his notebook as an excuse. "You were going to tell me about yesterday's theft," he reminded her.

"Ah, that was a clever one," Anna replied, shaking her head. "All night I think and think, 'Who was it?' Most people yesterday we know. It cannot be one of them. So which of the others took that ring? The couple choosing a wedding ring? They were so much in love. Not them. The old woman who looked at children's bracelets? Surely not."

Her husband took up the list. "Then came a man needing a new watchstrap," he recalled. "And a couple who bought earrings. After them a girl bought a locket for her mother. I cannot think of any other; not between midday and three o'clock."

"So you saw the ring at midday, and missed it at three?" Winters established. "And where was it?"

"In the tray so customers could see, but not help themselves. Except one did."

Winters turned to Mr Buchmann. "Did you see anything suspicious?" he asked.

"I was repairing watches," Hans explained. "I only took over from Anna for an hour. I do not see how anyone could take something, not from under my nose."

"Nor from under mine!" Mrs Buchmann protested. "They were very clever."

"Could you write me a description of each customer?" Winters asked.

"We already write it all down." Getting up, Hans opened the bureau and took out a writing pad. Carefully he tore off the top pages and passed them to Winters.

Thanking them for the tea and cake, Winters got up and headed out into the rain again.

Ambrose was waiting for him at the Police Station. "Higgins asked me to give you these notes," he said. "He's on his break. Two more thefts."

"It's getting to be an epidemic," Winters complained. He'd been investigating the shop thefts for nearly a month now.

"The odd thing is, both were at The Shalimar Hotel," Ambrose added. "A Mrs Budgen rang about a pocket watch. Then one of the Calzone Singers called in about a necklace. Both thefts may have been while the owners were asleep. Higgins thought that would worry you."

"It does," Winters agreed in concern. He didn't mention his biggest worry; that there might be a connection with the Jenner's Park murder, the robbery gone wrong. Quickly he scanned PC Higgins' notes. He knew The Shalimar well: had been to several functions there. Anyone who could afford better than the Conservative Club (and quite a few who couldn't) wanted their wedding reception at The Shalimar. "I'll go down there now," he said. "We need to know whether these are connected with the other robberies."

Ambrose nodded in approval. "The sooner you can sort this the better," he remarked. "The choir leaves on Sunday. They're guests of the town. We don't want them going away with a bad impression."

"Of course not," Winters agreed. He frowned in bewilderment. "What did you say the choir was called?"

"The Calzone Singers."

A smile developed around Winters' mouth. He tried to control it, but his smile broadened. "The Calzone Singers?" he repeated.

"Yes, why?"

Laughter welled up in Winters' throat.

Ambrose stared at him. "I fail to see anything funny," he remarked.

Winters' face was going red. "I'm sorry, sir," he apologised, almost choking. "But I think they've got the wrong word."

Ambrose was mystified. "Explain please," he instructed. "Then I might see the joke."

"They've got their Italian mixed up. 'Calzone' means a trouser leg, but it's also a sort of pizza, folded over. They must have meant 'canzone': a song. Fran will be most amused."

"A folded pizza?" Ambrose repeated, beginning to smile himself.

Winters nodded. "A pizza base folded over, then stuffed, sort of like a Cornish pasty only bigger. Fran's mother makes them. You don't need to eat for a week afterwards."

Ambrose was laughing now too. "So we have the pasty singers here?" he asked.

"Big, stodgy pasties," Winters agreed. "Stuffed with whatever Mama's got left."

Recalling Evelyn Hulme's grand introduction to the choir, Ambrose shook his head. "I don't think we should tell them," he suggested. "They mightn't take it too kindly." He pictured their lead soprano acknowledging the applause,and wondered if she knew. "No. Some of them definitely wouldn't see the joke."

Then he was serious again. "Whatever their name, they don't deserve to have their things stolen," he added. "And we don't want the Chalk Heath Press getting hold of the story, never mind the Uttley papers."

DS Winters took one of the cars, so he wouldn't arrive dripping at the hotel. Before he left, he read through Higgins' notes. He was surprised the hotel's owners hadn't reported either theft. Mr and Mrs Tempest were well respected and their hotel had an excellent reputation. Perhaps that was the point. They didn't want gossip and hoped to trace the thief themselves.

When he arrived at The Shalimar, Mrs Tempest wasn't at the Reception desk. He could hear laughter and chatter coming from the lounge. Winters peered in. Twenty or so elderly people were sitting at tables, urgently shaking dice. Two couples at a table near him were furiously passing the shaker back and forth. "A six!" one shouted in excitement. "I've got a body!"

Amused, Winters paused to watch. It was a mistake. "A man!" a voice shouted. "Come over here! We need you." An elderly woman was standing at a table on the far side, waving urgently. "There's only three of us here."

Mrs Tempest intervened. "That's not just any man. That's Sergeant Winters," she called from a nearby group. "You'll have to excuse me while I see what he wants. Carry on playing."

"That's not fair!" one of the men on her table complained. "We'll be one short."

Everyone else was too cunning to let the interruption affect their chances. Winters laughed. He'd interrupted The Shalimar's weekly beetle drive. He noticed Mr and Mrs Gibbs at a nearby table joining in the fun.

Glancing at Winters in amused apology, Mrs Tempest grabbed the shaker being thrust in her direction.

"Sorry folks," Winters called but very few people looked up. Dice rattled onto tabletops, a few falling on the floor, before being urgently retrieved. Monstrous beetles were being drawn on cards; pencils gripped at the ready. The atmosphere was as tense as in any casino. "A head!" a woman near him shouted. She could have been announcing the relief of an army under siege.

"What's that, Ethel?" her companion demanded.

"I said I'd got a head," Ethel almost bellowed.

"You'd look funny without one," commented a wag at the next table.

One of the men near him grinned. "If you want to get ahead, get a hat'," he sang. For no apparent reason he broke into 'I'm Dreaming of a White Christmas' afterwards.

"Shut up, Reggie!" someone shouted. "I can't concentrate."

"What's new about that?" Reggie called back.

It was all very good-natured. The Tempests were doing their bit for the town's older folk. Winters knew the hotel must make very little out of it financially. The hotels' long-term residents also enjoyed the events. Mr and Mrs Gibbs were shaking their dice vigorously, heads down in concentration. Winters looked round for Colonel Webster and Miss Lacey and was surprised they weren't there.

Mrs Gibbs passed the shaker to the other woman at their table, who dropped it on the floor. Winters walked over to pick up the errant dice. "Nice to see you," he said to Mr Gibbs. "Where's the Colonel? Not unwell I hope?"

Mr Gibbs gave a throaty laugh. "Gone away for Christmas," he said.

Winters wondered why the old man found that funny. He glanced at Mrs Gibbs who shook her head in disapproval. "So has Miss Lacey," she whispered.

Her husband was less discreet. "They've gone away *together*," he said loudly.

"Shush! We don't know that …" The shaker was being thrust at Mrs Gibbs. She had no chance to finish her sentence.

The idea of Colonel Webster and prim Miss Lacey going away together made Winters smile. There must be more to the bluff Colonel than he'd realised; and who knew what passion lurked benath Miss Lacey's lavendar-scented cardigans? Two lonely elderly people living in hotel rooms and watching other people's television. They deserved a bit of happiness. "Good for them!" he said.

"Really officer," Mrs Gibbs reprimanded, but she gave a girlish giggle.

"Beetle!" An urgent cry went up from the back of the room.

Everybody stopped. "That's not fair!" several voices complained. "We were interrupted!"

Getting up, Mrs Tempest smiled. "We'll declare that one null and void," she suggested. "Everyone, stay where you are this time." She turned to one of the younger men. "Mr Kingston, would you take over? I'm just popping out for a few minutes."

Smiling a welcome, Mrs Tempest walked across to Winters. "Good afternoon, officer," she said. "Shall we go into the library and leave these good people to play?"

"My thoughts exactly," Winters replied.

Chapter Seven

"To what do we owe this pleasure?" Mrs Tempest asked, as soon as they were settled by the fire in the library. Though her manner was gracious as ever, Winters thought her expression seemed strained.

"We've had a couple of thefts reported by your guests," Winters began. There was no way of saying it gently. "A watch and a necklace. Could one of your staff be thieving?"

Mrs Tempest was horrified. "Of course not!" she said emphatically. "I can assure you that if anything's been stolen it wasn't by one of our staff. They all have excellent references."

"I'm surprised you didn't give us a call," Winters said carefully. "I gather the thefts were mentioned to you."

Mrs Tempest's mouth tightened slightly. "To be honest, officer, I didn't think it was worth bothering you," she replied. "Guests often lose things and think they're stolen, only to find them the next day. I was sure we would find both items."

"It did look odd," Winters warned her. "As if you were trying to cover things up."

"Goodness, no! I just wanted to be sure before we called you. Libby finds things in the strangest places when she does her big clean."

"So you've never had thefts before?" Winters asked.

"Not actual thefts," Mrs Tempest replied.

It seemed an odd answer but before Winters could press her for an explanation, she carried on.

"Oh, yes, I forgot. We lost some money from my office a few years back," Mrs Tempest continued, "but we've been more careful since. Nothing's been lost recently that hasn't turned up later. Now if you'll excuse me, I must get back to my old dears. They can get quite rowdy if they're left alone." With her usual charming smile, she got up. Clearly, as far as she was concerned the interview was over.

"Do you mind if I have a chat with your staff?" Winters asked.

"Not at all. You have your job to do," Mrs Tempest replied. "I'm afraid Mr Tempest is visiting our daughter, but I doubt if he could tell you any more than I have." She turned towards the door. "Stay to tea if you'd like," she invited. "The choir will be back soon and there'll be food to spare."

"Thank you." Nodding, Winters got up too. "You will ring if anything more goes missing?" he asked. "You wouldn't be bothering us, I assure you."

"Of course."

Winters wasn't sure she meant it.

He decided to speak to the waitress first. Jane Fellowes was as sharp as a knife. If anything was going on, she'd have noticed.

As he'd hoped, Miss Fellowes was in the dining room laying out the cutlery for afternoon tea. With her hair neatly pinned under a white cap, and her spotless frilly apron, she was the epitome of efficiency and old-fashioned service. "Nice to see you Sergeant," she said, greeting him with a wary smile. "Are you here on business or pleasure?"

"It's always a pleasure to come to The Shalimar," Winters replied, closing the door behind him. "But I'm on business today. We've received reports of thefts from guests' rooms. Do you know anything about them? You usually know most things."

Jane Fellowes looked at him in horror, then beckoned him urgently across the room. "Someone might hear through the door," she warned. "What's been stolen?"

"A watch and a necklace."

"Goodness! That's awful!"

"Have you had any thefts before?" Winters asked.

"None have been reported."

To Winters, her reply seemed as evasive as Mrs Tempest's. "Is there anyone on the staff who might be tempted?" he asked.

"Of course not!"

"What about the Chambermaid? They're usually the worst paid."

"Libby?" Jane frowned, considering her answer. "She's not the brightest of girls, but I can't imagine her stealing anything." She thought about the question further. "No. Libby wouldn't risk getting the sack. She's saving up to get married. Silly girl! She's only seventeen."

"How many staff live on the premises?" Winters persisted.

"Only the four of us: Des the chef, Mr and Mrs Tempest and myself. Libby doesn't."

Taking out his notebook, Winters began recording names and details. "What's the chef like?" he asked.

Jane paused, considering her words carefully. "Des doesn't have the energy to steal," she replied. "He just wants a quiet life until he can retire."

"I gather you don't think much of him," Winters remarked.

"He's worked at some of the best hotels," Jane replied, "but no waitress thinks much of her chef. It's usually mutual."

Winters smiled. He liked Jane Fellowes. "Whose room is nearest to the guests?" he asked.

"Mine," Jane admitted. "I'm right at the back, where the smaller bedrooms are. The choir are in those at the moment but they're often empty. Although tonight, only the choir is staying. A group left this morning and no one else is due until tomorrow."

"So the choir has the poorer rooms," Winters thought in surprise. "I bet they don't like that, but then if they're not paying, what do they expect?"

"Before you ask, I didn't steal anything," Jane said firmly, "And I'm quite sure Mr and Mrs Tempest wouldn't. It would ruin them. If something's been stolen it has to have been by one of the guests, or an outsider. There's a back door into the garden. From there you can cut into town or onto the heath. Your thief might be an intruder."

"Aren't the doors locked at night?" Winters asked in concern.

"Of course. Mr Tempest locks up at ten thirty prompt, unless a guest has made special arrangements." Jane paused, an anxious expression settling about her eyes. "But however many times you ask guests to use the front door and hand in their keys, some don't. They find they can go out the back and use the short cut. They take their keys with them, and then lose them!" Jane clearly didn't have a high opinion of the average guest.

"Aren't the locks changed afterwards?" Winters asked, his concern growing.

"It's too expensive to do it every time."

So perhaps an outsider found one of those keys, Winters thought. Or maybe a former guest had just kept one. He didn't like the implications. "Thank you for being so helpful," he said, getting up. "I'd better let you get on with the tables. I'll see myself out."

Instead of going back to the reception area, however, DS Winters went down the corridor, following the smell of food. A door opened onto a huge kitchen, a relic of days when The Shalimar was a private house with half a dozen servants seeing to one family. At first, Winters thought the room was empty. Then he saw a broad figure slumped in a chair beside the range. Trays of sandwiches and cakes lay waiting on the table. Pots were bubbling and a kettle was whistling but the chef seemed to be asleep. Winters stepped inside.

At once the chef woke. "Who are you?" he barked, leaping up. He was a big man, with muscular arms and large belly encased in checked trousers and white jacket.

"DS Winters from Chalk Heath Police Station," Winters replied, feeling like a schoolboy caught trespassing. He produced his ID. "Sorry if I startled you."

"What do you want?" Des demanded. "This is my kitchen." His tone was almost menacing.

Winters decided to keep the interview short. "I'm investigating reports of thefts from guests," he replied. "I wondered if you'd heard about them."

"Why should I?" Des retorted. "I'm stuck in here all day. Not even a bloody kitchen maid to peel the spuds. I do the friggin' lot."

"I just wondered if you could help," Winters replied in a conciliatory tone. "I imagine you know all the staff well."

"If anyone's nicking things it'll be that silly Libby Nunn," Des retorted. "Always going on about her wedding. If she had any sense she'd save up for a house first." Grunting, he returned to his pans. "The lad's only a carpenter," he added over his shoulder. "You'd think he was Prince Charming. Now clear off. I've got to get on. Her ladyship'll be ringing the gong for tea soon."

Winters decided he'd get no further with the chef for now. Leaving the kitchen, he stood in the corridor listening. Judging by the chatter from the lounge, the beetle drive hadn't finished yet. There would be no chance to speak to Mrs Tempest again. He was about to look for the chambermaid when Libby herself appeared. She was lugging an old-fashioned vacuum cleaner down the back stairs and almost dropped it when she saw him. "Oooh, I'm ever so sorry," she apologised. "Was I in your way? I'm ever so sorry, sir."

Since it seemed she would go on apologising until he said something, Winters cut in: "Not at all," he assured her. "Here. Let me carry that. It looks heavy."

"I couldn't let a guest carry it."

"I'm not a guest. I'm a policeman," Winters said.

At once Libby flushed deeply. "Have I done something wrong?" she asked. "I didn't mean to, honest, whatever it was."

"It depends whether you've taken any of the guests' things," Winters replied, picking up the vacuum cleaner.

"Me sir? No, sir. I'd lose me job."

"You would indeed. And you'd go to prison," Winters warned.

The girl looked so frightened he regretted it afterwards. "But I haven't done anything!" she insisted. "You won't lock me up, will you?"

"No," Winters assured her, putting the cleaner down in the corridor. "Not if you're honest with me. You get here early in the morning, I imagine?"

"Six thirty, sir."

"When you arrived yesterday, was the back door locked?"

Libby screwed up her eyes, trying to remember. "I can't say, sir," she replied. "It wasn't when I shook my duster outside. Maybe someone went out for a smoke before breakfast. Mrs Tempest won't let anyone smoke inside, sir."

"Maybe," Winters agreed. But the girl's reply worried him.

There was the sound of an engine and voices in the distance. People were getting off a coach in the car park, chattering to each other. The choir must be returning. Winters thanked the chambermaid and made his way back towards Reception. As he did so, the front doors opened and the Calzone Singers burst in.

They were in a good mood. They'd enjoyed rehearsing with the local church choirs. Now the singers were looking forward to a good tea at the hotel, before their coach took them back for the evening performance. Still chattering noisily, they stood at the desk waiting for their keys. Mrs Tempest dealt with everyone with her usual efficiency.

For five minutes the reception area was full of bustle and noise. Pretending to read a newspaper, Winters watched, trying to assess whether any of the choir members looked likely to steal. It was impossible to tell. No one had 'thief' written across their forehead. He frowned. Something wasn't right. He couldn't say what it was, but something definitely wasn't right.

Chapter Eight

It was a tight turnaround. No sooner had the Calzone Singers gone to their rooms than the Beetle Drive ended. The reception area filled with elderly people waiting for lifts or taxis. Others set off to walk back to town, despite Mrs Tempest's invitation to stay until the rain eased. "A drop of English water never did any harm," one resolute gentleman declared.

"It shrinks you though," Reggie quipped. "I was six foot seven this morning."

For ten minutes there was good-humoured chaos. People hunted for missing umbrellas and unfolded plastic rain hats as they said goodbye. In the dining room, cups and plates clinked as the choir's tea was laid out. A notice on the door stated firmly, 'Calzone Singers Only.' Mr Gibbs seemed inclined to ignore it but his wife intervened. "We'll have our dinner later," she promised, leading him away from the door.

Winters decided to accept Mrs Tempest's invitation to join the choir for tea. It would give him chance to ask discreet questions, and hopefully speak to Mr Tempest when he returned. Winters joined Mr and Mrs Gibbs as he waited for the choir to reappear.

"She does everyone proud, doesn't she?" Mr Gibbs nodded in Mrs Tempest's direction.

"Looks after us like family," Mrs Gibbs agreed.

"Are you still thinking of moving?" Winters asked. Since the Gibbs were always talking about leaving, it was a safe opening gambit.

"We'll stay a while longer," Mrs Gibbs replied. "We had a weekend at the coast. It wasn't as comfortable. Not a patch on The Shalimar."

Winters smiled. "Wouldn't you like to join your daughter 'down under'?" he asked.

Mr Gibbs shook his head vigorously. “Went once,” he replied. “Too bloomin’ hot.”

The grandfather clock near them whirred and made a hiccuping sound. Intrigued, Winters looked towards the dial. It was exactly six o’clock. Yet the clock hadn’t struck the hour. A casement clock on the wall opposite gave a similar hiccup five minutes later. “Something wrong with the clocks?” Winters asked.

“She’s turned them off,” Mr Gibbs explained. “Guests complained they couldn’t sleep.”

Winters assumed ‘she’ was Mrs Tempest again. “At six o’clock in the evening?” he asked.

“You’d be surprised what time people sleep,” Mr Gibbs remarked darkly.

“Don’t be silly,” his wife chided. “It’d take ages turning the chimes on and off.” She turned to DS Winters in explanation. “Mr Tempest used to collect clocks. There are two more upstairs. It wasn’t half a racket when they all chimed.”

Four of the choir members were coming downstairs, dressed ready for the evening’s performance. Mrs Tempest returned to the reception desk. “Tea’s almost ready,” she assured her guests. “How did the rehearsal go?” She was the perfect hostess, taking an interest in everyone.

“Great fun!” one of the men declared. “Massed ranks of sopranos in funny hats.”

“Exaggerating as usual, Anton,” the woman beside him laughed. “They took their hats off before they sang.”

Winters seized the opportunity. “I must go and meet the choir,” he apologised. Getting up before the Gibbs could protest, he crossed to the reception desk and introduced himself. “DI Ambrose asked me to check you’re all ok,” he explained.

“Pleased to meet you, officer. I’m Jackie Walters,” the woman replied, offering her hand. “And this is my husband Dennis. Please thank Mr Ambrose for his concern. He’s been ever so good to us, ever since the accident.” She glanced towards the reception desk, clearly meaning to be overheard. “The rooms are a bit pokey, but the food’s very good.”

As she spoke another of the singers ran down the stairs. “Something strange is going on,” she announced, as soon as she was near enough to be heard. Everyone looked in her direction.

“What is it Barbara?” Wynn asked. His soft Welsh voice was probably very appealing to the ladies, Winters observed.

“I’ve found this beside my bed.” Opening her hand, Barbara displayed a necklace. A pendant swung on a silver chain, flashing red in the firelight.

“Beside your bed?” Mrs Tempest repeated. “There! I told you it would turn up.”

“But I didn’t leave it there.”

Mrs Tempest smiled. “Perhaps you forgot,” she suggested.

“I did not!” Barbara snapped. “I left it in my top drawer, not beside my bed.”

Winters went towards her. “Is that the one you reported stolen?” he asked. Taking the pendant, he examined it carefully. It fitted Higgins’ description, even to the lion on the hallmark. If the original had been swapped for an inferior piece, the copy was excellent.

The other choir members were looking on in bewilderment. “Stolen?” Jackie repeated. “You didn’t say…”

“Don’t look at me like that!” Barbara snapped. “Someone has been in my room.”

“I’ll ask the chambermaid,” Mrs Tempest promised in a conciliatory tone. “I imagine she found it on the floor and put it safe for you. All’s well that end’s well.”

“I’ll cancel your report when I get back to the ‘Station,” Winters offered.

“Somebody is trying to make me look like an idiot!” Barbara retorted furiously. “Yes. Cancel my report.” Her face red with humiliation, she turned back up the stairs. Wynn started to follow her, but she didn’t look back. Shaking his head, he let her go.

“Oh dear,” Jackie said afterwards. “I’ve never seen Barbara so angry.” She turned to Winters. “She’s normally very patient.” She lowered her voice. “She’s the only one of us who can cope with …” She broke off, reconsidering. “I hadn’t better say any more,” she ended lamely.

Anton guffawed. “You mean she puts up with our Prima Donna?” he asked.

"Shush," Dennis warned. Angela was coming down the stairs, chatting to Evelyn.

"What on earth's wrong with Barbara?" Evelyn asked as soon as she joined the group.

"She thinks someone's been in her room and moved a necklace," Jackie explained. "She'd reported it as stolen."

"Poor Barbara!" Angela remarked, shaking her head. "Always so sensitive. I'll go and have a word."

"Would you dear?" Evelyn asked, with obvious relief.

With an elegant sweep of her skirt, Angela turned, and followed Barbara upstairs.

"I can never make that woman out," Jackie admitted. "Sometimes she can be so nice."

While they were talking, John Pedderson appeared. "I'm the new boy," he joked, as he introduced himself. To Winters' practised eye, the young man wasn't completely at ease.

"Come along," Evelyn instructed her charges. "We have to be back at the church in an hour. The other two will join us when they're ready."

Balancing a cup and saucer in one hand and a plate of sandwiches in the other wasn't easy. Winters was glad to accept an invitation to join the Walters at one of the tables. Jackie seemed a chatty type, likely to tell him about her fellow choir members. "Have you been with the choir long?" he began, as they put down their plates.

"Six years," Dennis replied.

"Seven," his wife corrected him.

"And you still enjoy singing?" Winters asked, genuinely curious.

"It's our chief interest," Jackie admitted. "Dennis' job is pretty boring. He's an estimator at Uttley Boxes. I used to be a secretary there, but my mother was ill and I had to give up. I'm finding looking after her pretty dull too." Smiling ruefully, she chattered on, clearly glad to have someone to talk to. "We've had to put Mother into a home so we could come away. We both feel bad about it, but what could we do?" She sighed. "We're hoping to bring her to live with us, you see, but our house isn't big enough, and we can't get planning permission for an extension. It's nice to get away for a bit."

"Some of the neighbours have objected," Dennis explained.

"It's all very awkward," Jackie continued. "We live next door to Angela, and she was one of those who objected. Thankfully she's changed her mind, or I don't think we could have come away with her."

"Do the others also work at Uttley Boxes?" Winters asked.

"Goodness, no! Angela used to, but she's in the Education Department now. Anton works in a restaurant; came over with the Polish Air Force and never returned. He's ever so interesting. Evelyn teaches singing, and Wynn's an architect."

"You've missed John," her husband reminded her.

Jackie giggled, dropping her voice. "John's a buyer for the ladies' underwear department at one of our big stores," she explained. "Poor man. He's got a degree in something useless like Classics. He'd be ever so cross if he knew I'd told you."

As she spoke the other two women returned, Barbara looking red-eyed but calmer, Angela talking quietly to her. "Looks like they're friends again," Evelyn whispered, leaning across from the neighbouring table. Her obvious relief interested Winters. Clearly there were tensions in the choir. They might explain the disappearance of Miss Collier's necklace. He decided to try to talk to Evelyn more privately.

His opportunity came later, as they queued together at the serving table. "You must feel like a mother bringing a large family away," he remarked, smiling.

Evelyn laughed. "They need as much looking after," she admitted.

"I gather there have been complaints about the rooms."

"The rooms are fine," Evelyn replied firmly. "We're very grateful for the town's hospitality. The trouble is, our tours are the only holidays some of our members have. They forget we're singing for our supper."

Winters helped himself to a piece of lemon meringue pie. He wouldn't need to go to The Copper Kettle that night. "Singing must mean a lot to them," he remarked.

"Oh it does!" Evelyn agreed, taking a second slice of cake. "Though I say it myself, we've reached a very high standard, and you don't do that without lots of rehearsals. We all have to devote most of our spare time."

Mr Tempest had returned, full of apologies for being late. "I got stuck at the level crossing," he explained. "It was ages before the gates opened." He began walking round the room, chatting, making sure the guests were enjoying their tea. He greeted Winters cheerily. "Evening officer," he called across. "Nice to see you." It was impossible for Winters to speak to him privately.

There was the sound of coach wheels on the drive. Harry was returning from his digs on St George's Crescent. Winters wondered whether Harry had even been invited for tea at The Shalimar. Perhaps the Tempests' generosity didn't extend to the choir's driver.

Evelyn looked at her watch. "We'd better be going," she announced, clapping her hands. "Ten minutes to pop up to your rooms, then meet in Reception." At once the singers began gathering their things.

"Cheer up!" Anton said to Barbara as she rose from her seat. "You're supposed to be enjoying yourself."

"Would you enjoy yourself," Barbara retorted, "with someone coming into your room? Frankly, I wish we could go home. At least I'd be safe there."

Chapter Nine

The dining room was very quiet after the choir had gone. "Phew!" Jane said as she cleared the serving table. "I didn't know eight people could make so much noise." She handed a stack of plates to Mrs Tempest.

Together the two women walked towards the kitchen, carrying trays loaded so high they could hardly see over them. Mr Tempest was cleaning cake crumbs from the tablecloth. Winters seized the chance of a quick word with him.

"We've had reports of items being stolen from rooms," he said. "I thought you'd want to know." Mr Tempest looked at him aghast. "One's turned up though," Winters added quickly. "A necklace. It was in the guest's room after all but there's still a watch missing. Have you had any thefts before?"

"Certainly not," Mr Tempest declared emphatically. "We've had guests lose things, but they've always turned up. I'm sure the watch will. You'll have to excuse me. We have several bookings for dinner." He moved hurriedly away, carrying another tray down the corridor.

Peter Tempest was a charming host, with his military bearing and old-fashioned manners. Yet his reply seemed so curt as to be rude. For a few moments Winters waited, expecting the man to return, but the lounge remained empty. Frowning, Winters knew there wasn't much more he could do now. He might as well return to the 'Station.

Instead of going out the front door, however, he decided to explore the back entrance described by Jane Fellowes. First, Winters went down the corridor and turned left into the Garden Room. Pulling back the curtains he looked through. As he recalled, a pair of French doors opened onto a terrace, filled with pot plants, tables and chairs. In summer, guests could sit and enjoy the sun, but on a wet

December night the only light came from a strip of bulbs attached to a fir tree nearby. There were bolts on the inside of the doors and no keyhole or handle on the outside. An intruder could only enter at night if an accomplice left the doors unbolted and slightly ajar.

Winters was just drawing the curtains when he sensed someone else was in the room. "What do you think you're doing?" a voice demanded.

Turning round quickly, he found the chef standing behind him. For so heavy a man, Des could move surprisingly softly. With his big arms folded and a belligerent scowl on his face, he looked thoroughly intimidating.

"I'm checking security," Winters replied.

"What for?" the chef demanded. "We didn't ask you to."

Winters wasn't going to be bullied. "Now why would you want to stop me?" he said firmly. "Surely you want to know the hotel is safe? Unless, of course, you've got something to hide."

The chef didn't want trouble. With a lopsided smile of apology he replied, "Don't mind me. I don't get to meet people much. You don't need to check those doors though. No one goes out there this time of year." Unfolding his arms, he took a packet of cigarettes from his trouser pocket and tapped one on the back of his hand. He'd presumably come there for a quiet smoke before serving dinner.

"And no one enters either?" Winters persisted.

"Not if the doors are properly locked."

"Jane mentioned a shorter way to town," Winters continued. "Could you show me it?"

"If you want." Shrugging his shoulders, Des lead the way out of the Garden Room, back into the corridor and turned left towards a door marked 'Gardens'. They passed the back stairs where Winters had earlier spoken to Libby. On the wall, a sign pointed up the stairs to 'Guest Rooms 8-16'.

Recalling the singers' complaints about pokey rooms, Winters asked the chef, "Is that where the choir's been put?"

"Yeah. Well they're not payin' are they? And they're perfectly good rooms. Just a bit smaller. The view's good: over the gardens."

"Can you get to these stairs from the other rooms?" Winters asked.

"Of course. From the landing."

Winters tried to visualise the hotel layout. He'd never been up to the bedrooms, but he'd stood on the stairs for a wedding photo and seen the ornate landing from there. "So you can walk along the landing and down the main staircase to the front door," he remarked, thinking aloud, "or cut down these stairs and out the back." He tried the door. It was unlocked.

"That's about the size of it," Des agreed. "Dunno why the door's unlocked. Mrs Tempest usually checks it after dusk. One of the guests must have come in this way and left it open."

"They'd need a torch," Winters commented. All he could see was the outline of bushes, and an overweight cherub guarding a fountain, surrounded by crazy paving. A path led off into rain and darkness. "Presumably there's access onto the lane?" he asked.

"There's a wooden gate in the wall," Des explained. "Guests have two keys: one for the front door and the other for this one and the gate. They like to use the short cut to town during the day. We ask them to lock up after them, but they forget." Lighting his cigarette, he stood at the door smoking as he talked. Now he was more relaxed, his manner was far less threatening.

It couldn't be easy being the only chef in a small hotel, Winters reflected; with no home of your own and little leisure or privacy. Judging by the man's sallow skin and lank hair, he rarely had chance for more fresh air than he could snatch at this back door.

"Aren't you worried about an outsider coming in?" DS Winters asked.

"I always keep my room locked."

They stood together in the shelter of the doorway, looking out on the rain. The scent of the chef's cigarette made Winters feel edgy. He'd given up smoking a month ago, after working out the money he saved would pay for his eldest daughter's school uniform. Over a whole year, it would help pay for their annual visit to Fran's family in Italy. But he was finding it difficult to quit and standing next to someone smoking set him craving for a cigarette.

Turning away, Winters concentrated on the darkness ahead. He could just make out the beginning of the wall around the gardens. He tried to picture the hotel as he'd seen it last time, by daylight. On the approach, the road was bordered by a stone wall. There was a sharp bend up to the gates of the hotel. Then, the drive swung in a broad curve round to the left before reaching the front entrance. The Victorian businessman who'd built the house had set it at the end of a winding drive, so the front entrance faced towards the heath, not the town. The gardens backed onto the lane.

Winters began to understand the guests' desire for a short cut. To leave by the main entrance, you had to walk along the landing, down an impressive flight of stairs, through Reception and out onto the drive. Then you had to follow the drive to the gates and up the lane round a lengthy bend. Go out the other way and you could dart down the back stairs, take the garden path and be straight onto the lane, saving five, perhaps ten minutes.

"Where can you get to from that gate?" Winters asked, pointing into the darkness. "Other than onto the lane?"

"There's another footpath almost opposite," Des replied. "That'll take you to the old church. From St George's you can walk through the new estate to the bottom of the High Street. It saves you about two miles, so long as you don't get lost."

Winters smiled. He'd been on the new estate recently, investigating a 'domestic', and got thoroughly lost himself. Every street was called 'St George' something or other: Crescent, Court, Grove, Garth and so on. The planners had no imagination. "Do you go that way much?" he asked.

Des took a long, thoughtful drag on his cigarette. "Nah," he replied. "Too many dogs and kids. If we've got a thief coming in, they're probably from down there."

It was an interesting idea. Thanking the chef, Winter left him to enjoy his cigarette.

As soon as he got back to the 'Station, he went to see DI Ambrose. "Can you spare a moment?" he asked, peering round the door. "I'm back from The Shalimar."

"How did you get on?" Ambrose asked, putting down his pen. "Any leads?"

"Plenty," Winters replied, shaking his head. "I'm sure the Tempests were holding out on me. They knew about the thefts, but not that they'd been reported. Presumably they're worried about their reputation."

"Odd," Ambrose agreed. "I'd have said Audrey and Peter are as honest as anyone in this town. Possibly more so."

“I reckon the thieving’s been going on a while, so it must be one of the staff,” Winters added. “What do you know about them? The chambermaid seems the most likely.”

Ambrose sighed. “She is,” he admitted sadly. “The Tempests gave her a job when no one else would. She’s one of the Davey kids; changed her name to her foster parents’ a few years back.”

Winters let out his breath in surprise. The Davey family was one of the roughest, and largest, in Chalk Heath. If a bike was missing or a fight started, the first thing you did was see if there was a Davey around. Old man Davey was a nasty piece of work; even his family feared him. His wife was a poor weak woman who thought her boys could do no wrong. In return her boys adored her and did exactly as they pleased. “I’d forgotten there were a couple of sisters,” Winters admitted.

“The old man had it in for them and they were put in care,” Ambrose recalled. “Libby’s the brightest of the lot; been in a bit of trouble herself but she wants to work and get on. She’s engaged to Stan Harding; he’s the best thing that ever happened to her.”

Smiling, Winters nodded. He admired the way DI Ambrose could recall backgrounds and people. The DI made it his business to know what was going on in the town and he had an excellent memory. They’d solved several cases by following Ambrose’s suggestion as to who might be involved.

“If Libby’s stealing, it’ll be because her father’s making her,” Ambrose continued. “And perhaps the Tempests think they can sort it out without us.” Leaning back on his chair, he paused, turning his fountain pen over reflectively. “Libby Nunn couldn’t steal from a shop under an assistant’s nose though,” he admitted. “Certainly not from the Buchmanns. It’d be way out of her league.”

“You reckon we’ve got two different thieves on the go, then?” Winters asked.

“Probably. Though I wouldn’t put it past old man Davey to be involved in both. He’d fence stuff for an outsider, even if he couldn’t steal it himself.”

They both had the same thought at the same time. Ambrose voiced it. “If Libby leaves a door unlocked at night for her Dad, or she just tells him the guests sometimes do … and he tells his new mates …”

Winters finished the sentence. "We could have a problem," he agreed.

There was a knock on the door. PC Higgins was peering through the glass panel. Ambrose beckoned him in.

"What is it?" he asked.

"Something for the DS. Peter Tempest's just rung. They've found the pocket watch. He was most concerned you knew it hadn't been stolen."

"Now that's interesting." Winters frowned. "Where did they find it?"

Higgins pulled a face. "Well it's the weirdest thing," he replied. "Apparently the chambermaid found it in rather an odd location."

"Did she now," Winters glanced meaningfully at Ambrose. "Where *exactly* did she find it then?"

"In a drawer of a bedside cabinet."

"What's odd about that?" Winters asked.

"It was in the tower room. No one's slept there for over three months."

Chapter Ten

Feeling unexpectedly nervous, Pauline Meadows looked around. She'd never been in St Wilfred's hall before. The Church of England and Chalk Heath Methodists didn't have much to do with each other, though they were on opposite sides of the main road. The hall was empty apart from a small group waiting near the door to the adjacent church.

An organ was playing in the church, punctuated by some shaky top notes. The rehearsal was running late. Meadows sighed. Like the other latecomers, she'd hoped to join the choirs at tea time. An ample supply of refreshments waited, guarded by two equally ample ladies.

"No! No!" a voice shouted beyond the closed door. The organ stopped.

"Oh dear," one of the ladies said. "Mr Yarm isn't happy."

Beyond the door, the organ started up again, accompanied by a blast of 'hallelujahs'.

"We won't be able to keep the tea urns warm for ever," her companion warned.

There was the sound of a conductor's baton being rapped. The 'hallelujahs' skidded to a halt.

Suddenly the door opened. "Come in," the Vicar whispered. "We could be a while yet."

Sheepishly, Meadows and the other latecomers trooped into the church.

Mr Yarm rapped his baton again. "Reinforcements!" he said with evident relief. "Do take your places."

Meadows looked for the Calzone Singers. To her embarrassment they were sitting on the front row of the choir stalls, in prime position. An empty space waited for her, between Evelyn and Barbara. Evelyn smiled and beckoned. Like truants from class, the other latecomers were pushing along the rows to their seats. Feeling very conspicuous Meadows walked to the front.

"Glad to have you back," Evelyn said softly.

She didn't need to whisper. Pleased to have a break, everyone else had begun to chatter, clear throats or fumble in handbags. Every choir in Chalk Heath was there, plus others from surrounding villages. The choir stalls and front thirty rows of pews were packed.

"Anything I need to know?" Meadows asked, opening her music.

"It's going at a canter," Evelyn advised. "The organist was too slow at the beginning. I made the mistake of asking him to take it faster and the dear man got huffy. We've barely kept up since."

"At least we'll finish early," Anton joked, swivelling round towards them. He was sitting on one of the soloists' chairs at the front. Beside him a very tall young man was waiting nervously. Meadows recognised him as the lead tenor from a local village choir. Angela was on the far side of the podium, staring ahead. Beside her was a contralto in a strikingly blue dress, with hair to match. Meadows sighed. Mrs Gifford used to have a splendid voice. Lately it had developed a wobble. She could sing a scale in a single note.

Once again the baton rapped. "Ladies and gentlemen! Please!" Mr Yarm pleaded. "We must get on! Part 2."

Barbara stabbed at the place in the music, then they were off. It was a gallop rather than a canter. There was barely time to breathe.

At last the conductor looked at his watch. "That will have to do," he announced. "Or there won't be time for tea. It'll sound better when there's a congregation. Please be at the Town Hall by six thirty."

The Vicar stood up in his seat. "You're all doing brilliantly," he said more encouragingly. "You deserve your tea, but I suggest you keep an eye on your valuables while you eat. We've had a spate of thefts recently."

There was a mutter of concern. "I don't know what's happening to the world," an elderly gentleman complained.

Leaning across Meadows, Evelyn spoke to Barbara. "We owe you an apology," she said. "Perhaps someone did take your necklace, and then put it back."

"Thank you," Barbara replied simply. "I wasn't going nuts."

Evelyn shook her head emphatically. "Of course not! The lady next to me had a fur cape stolen."

She nodded towards the woman on her right, who smiled ruefully.

"I shall have to tell everyone to be very careful at the hotel," Evelyn said. "It's not nice to think thieves may have got in there too. I'd better give the police a ring, unless the hotel has already."

Getting up together, they made their way towards the church hall. There was a crush at the door. Seeing some of her usual choir, Meadows went to speak to them. "Promotion eh?" one of the basses teased.

By the time Meadows got away most people in the hall were already eating. 'Tea and Biscuits' was actually plates of egg sandwiches and buns. "Do have something," one of the church ladies pleaded. Meadows had eaten at her 'digs' after coming off duty, but she accepted a very pink fairy cake.

The Calzone Singers were gathered around a special table with its own tea urn. Crossing through the crowd, Meadows joined them. Since they'd eaten at the hotel, most of the group were refusing further refreshment, "But you must try one of my specials," a lady pleaded, offering a plate of scones like small cottage loaves.

Nobly, Dennis agreed. "You'll never get the top notes after all that food," his wife warned.

"Glad you managed to come, Pauline," John said in greeting.

"We're all pretty well 'hallelujahed' out," Wynn admitted. "And there's quite a high screech factor. It should tone down when the hall's filled."

Meadows laughed. "Anything I should mark up?" she asked. "I've sung with Mr Yarm before. He likes his crescendos."

"I'll go through the score with you," Anton offered. "Let's find a quiet corner." With a gallant gesture, he led Meadows to the far side of the room and pulled a chair out. Then he sat beside her.

Together they went through the score, Anton making remarks in an exaggerated manner that made Meadows smile. "Lots of welly here," or "as gentle as a breeze" he would say, flourishing a pencil. He was good company and with his powerful frame and dark good looks, rather handsome. His manner was probably an act, Meadows decided. Underneath, the man seemed insecure. His accent intrigued her. It sounded Polish but was slightly different to the Polish family that ran a stall in the market.

Finally they put down their scores. "Where do you come from?" Meadows asked

"Uttley, my dear. We're all from Uttley."

"I mean originally."

Sighing, Anton looked into the crowd. "My homeland is Poland, or it was," he said. "I cannot go back. The Ruskies have taken it over. Maybe one day, when they have been sent packing, then I will go home."

"Did you come over in the war?" Meadows asked.

"Just before. I flew here, how you say? Literally. When we knew the Germans were coming, we took our planes and brought them here. Then we flew and flew against them. It was our revenge for what they did to our poor country."

"You were with the RAF then?" Meadows replied, impressed.

"Yes. I was a fighter with the 242 Squadron. I long to go back, but it is not possible…" With an expressive gesture, Anton shook his head. "So I work in a restaurant. One day I shall own my own place. Maybe I shall serve Polish food." He laughed. "But you English are too timid. You like your meat and two veg, not cabbage stew."

"We do indeed," Meadows agreed. She was warming to the man. For a while they sat together, talking of Anton's childhood in Poznań and his holidays in the beautiful countryside that surrounded the city. "My grandparents had a summer house you know," he added proudly. "Not your poky little shed in the garden, but a big house in the woods …"

Meadows was so interested, she didn't notice someone standing beside them. "I've come to rescue you," a voice said.

Looking up at Angela, Meadows smiled, "I'm quite enjoying myself," she said honestly.

Turning back to Anton she saw an expression of annoyance, even anger, cross his face, but he laughed good-naturedly. "I must not monopolise our pretty alto," he agreed.

Taking her hand, Angela guided Meadows back to the rest of the choir. "Our Anton can be a bit of a wolf," she warned softly. "Come and chat to Dennis. He was only in the Home Guard. Much safer than the Polish Airforce."

Glancing back at Anton, Meadows saw his expression. "Now that *is* interesting," she thought in surprise. "If looks could kill…" She said nothing however, merely smiling an apology. In embarrassment, she saw Anton wink at her in return.

It was time to start going over to the Town Hall.

Evelyn caught them up. "The Vicar's wife has had a word with the organist," she whispered. "She took him a nice cup of tea and smoothed his feathers. Hopefully it'll be a more sensible pace this time."

"What would we do without Vicars' wives?" Wynn asked, smiling.

The Town Hall had been built to seat five hundred. Nowadays the gilding was fading, but the room was still impressive. The organ pipes took pride of place behind the raised choir stalls. Above, the splendid balcony was filling rapidly. People pushed past each other along the rows, chattering like starlings. By seven fifteen the Town Hall was packed, and still the stewards were trying to find more seats. With the old boiler turned up and so many people crammed in, it was getting hot. Programmes wafted back and forth, fanning expectant faces. Many of the ladies were wearing large, florid hats; hardly likely to be popular with the row behind. Fur mittens and woolly scarves were being shed. Some of the congregation had brought their own scores.

"Goodness! They're not going to follow us are they?" Barbara whispered as they sat in the front of the choir stalls.

"Half of them will have sung it themselves," Meadows warned.

She looked around her with a mixture of affection and amusement, recognising many of her chapel friends. DI Ambrose was sitting in the balcony. "Good of him to support us two evenings running," she thought.

Then she realised she'd thought in terms of 'us' rather than 'them'. She was beginning to feel like part of the Calzone Singers. They were pleasant people really, even if they couldn't get on with each other.

The Reverend Timms was mounting the steps to the podium in front of the choir stalls. The chattering died back.

"Thank you everyone, for coming," he began. "All of you: singers, congregation, our special guests …" He was about to begin one of his speeches.

Suddenly the organ burst into an elaborate introduction, drowning him. Mr Yarm grabbed his baton and rapped for attention. Urgently the singers opened their scores. The tall young tenor leapt up, his first words coming out in a hurried gasp: "Comfortyecomfortyemypeople..."

Mercifully the organist slowed down afterwards and the choirs could gather their musical wits. Even so, for ten minutes Meadows barely noticed anyone else's part except her own. When Anton began his first solo she was able at last to look up. His full rich bass filled the whole hall. "Thus saith the Lord, the Lord of hosts," he sang as if he really meant the words. Everyone around her stopped shuffling their music and listened. When Angela followed, there were soft murmurs of appreciation from the audience. "I'd heard they were good," a woman behind Meadows whispered. "But those two are more than good."

Chalk Heath had rarely enjoyed such an exhilirating evening. The 'hallelujahs' echoed around the balconies; the organ had not been played at such volume since the Coronation. As the last chorus ended, both singers and audience were exhausted but happy. For a few seconds there was silence, then a storm of applause.

As it died away the Reverend Timms leapt onto the podium. "Well done everyone!" he said enthusiastically to the assembled choirs. "Do stay for refreshments. We have lots of cakes left. I hope the Calzone Singers will be joining us."

To Meadows' relief, Evelyn shook her head. "Thank you, but I'm afraid not," she apologised. "We're having supper at The Shalimar."

"It'll be most enjoyable I'm sure," the Reverend agreed. "Then let's give our visitors a special round of applause. They've lifted us to heights we never knew we could reach." He looked towards the sopranos who laughed in agreement.

Initially Meadows stayed in her seat as Calzone stood up and bowed, but Barbara whispered, "You too." So, thoroughly embarassed, she stood with them. Then the evening was over. Chattering and wrapping scarves around them, the audience began to head towards the doors. Anton and Angela left their places at the front to join the rest of their group.

"Well done!" Evelyn said. "Well done every one of you!" Relief made her face ten years younger. "Now for our little party."

"We always have a party half way through a tour," she explained as she led Meadows into the school room. "You'll join us, won't you?"

Meadows hesitated. She was on 'earlies' that week, which meant getting up about five in the morning. It would be more sensible for her to have an early night. But that would take some explaining …

"Yes, do come," Angela invited. "We always have a good time."

"Everyone comes armed with something light to sing or play," Evelyn added. She dropped her voice. "You'll be amazed how much talent there is in the group."

"But I haven't prepared anything," Meadows protested. "And I'm no good at solos."

"You can sing with me," Anton suggested. "I have a book of duets. All easy."

"If you'd rather, you could read a poem," Wynn said. "I saw a couple of poetry books in the library."

It was impossible to refuse. So against Meadows' own good judgement she went back to the Shalimar.

The short coach journey was a babble of jokes and conversation. All the previous tensions within the choir seemed to be forgotten in a happy commentary on the evening's performance. "I nearly missed that entry…" "Pity about the contralto…" "You did brilliantly Anton," "And you Angela…" For the first time, Meadows could see why the choir meant so much to its members.

As soon as the coach pulled up outside the hotel, Audrey and Peter Tempest met them with tiny gold-rimmed glasses of sherry. The fairy lights had been lit on the Christmas tree and the reception area was beautifully warm. "Supper is laid out in the garden lounge," Audrey announced. "I've put a notice on the door so no one will interrupt you." She turned to Evelyn. "The piano's ready, just as you asked."

Feeling very out of place, Meadows waited while the choir darted up to their rooms to change. She was wondering how to smarten her choir outfit when Barbara returned with a skirt over her arm. "You're about the same size as me," she suggested. "Pop into the Ladies and put this on. I'll find one of those poetry books Wynn saw."

It would have been churlish not to accept Barbara's kindness.

Meadows need not have worried. It was one of the best Christmas parties she had been to since she was a girl. As Evelyn had promised, there was a surprising amount of talent within such a small group.

Each of them had prepared 'a party piece' announced by Evelyn as if she were introducing The Royal Variety Show.

"A big hand to welcome three little maids from school," she began. Three men stepped forward, producing tiny fans from their pockets and holding them provocatively across their faces.

Jackie was already giggling. ""They were rehearsing at our place last week," she confided to Meadows. "I nearly died!"

They were all in danger of choking with laughter as Wynn and John transformed into delicate young girls, and Anton sang Peep-Bo in an improbable falsetto. After that, Angela set feet tapping with Scott Joplin's Maple Leaf Rag played on the hotel's piano, and Wynn fetched an old violin and followed her with a couple of dance tunes. Then Evelyn announced, "Our very own Anne Zeigler and Webster Booth."

"I'd like to earn half their money," Dennis commented drily as he got up, but when he and Jackie sang 'We'll gather lilacs in the spring again' both their faces were softened by the beauty of the words. "Like old times," Jackie said afterwards, looking at Dennis wistfully.

So the evening went on, Barbara singing a Doris Day number and Evelyn producing a recorder from a carrier bag. Angela followed, singing a lullaby so exquisitely she brought tears to everyone's eyes.

Thoroughly enjoying herself, Meadows glanced towards the door, her attention caught by a slight movement. Two faces were peering in through the glass.

Angela had seen them first however. "Stop a minute," she asked. "The old couple who live here are outside. Can't we invite them in? They're rather sweet, and very lonely."

So Mr and Mrs Gibbs were invited in and given a sherry each, on condition they did not interrupt or tell any one else afterwards. Settling in a couple of armchairs the old couple smiled as if Christmas were here already.

Meadows began to worry about her own contribution, but her reading of 'The Listeners' went down well. "Creepy," Anton said, applauding loudly. "You sing with me now. You know 'Mary's Boy Child'?"

She did indeed know it. To her surprise, she and Anton sang well together.

"If ever you come to Uttley, we'll have you two on the programme," Evelyn pronounced afterwards. "Now Angela, let's have a few numbers on your old squeeze box."

Fetching a battered black box from a chair, Angela took out an old accordion and began to play a couple of tunes that sounded exotic and French. The expression on her face as she played intrigued Meadows. It was even more wistful than Jackie's had been.

As Angela finished Meadows looked at her watch. It was nearly midnight. "I shall have to go," she apologised, getting up quickly. "It'll take me nearly an hour to walk home."

"Nonsense!" Anton objected. "You cannot walk alone this time of night."

Meadows wondered what he would say if he knew she would be walking her beat alone all next week. "I'll be fine," she replied.

But the choir would not hear of it. "You shall have a taxi," Evelyn insisted, "and the choir funds will pay for it."

Chapter Eleven

Friday 11 December 1959

Greg Sutton took the call. The woman's voice was tight with emotion. "I need to speak to DI Ambrose," she said. "At once."

"Who's speaking?" Sutton asked. He recognised the voice but couldn't place it.

"Mrs Tempest."

PC Sutton grabbed his pad and pencil. He wondered if Audrey Tempest was ringing to report another theft. "What's it about, please?" he asked.

"One of our guests…" Mrs Tempest stopped, controlling herself. "One of our guests has died. I'm afraid it looks like… It can't have been an accident …" She couldn't bring herself to speak the word.

At once Sutton was totally alert. His heart raced, despite his training. Murders didn't happen often in Chalk Heath. He looked up, hoping to see someone who could call the DI. The corridor was empty. Urgently he went through his mental checklist. "Who's died?" he asked. "Do you know the name?" As he spoke, he wrote 'Friday 11th December, 1959,' on his pad. 'Time of call: 12.20pm.'

"One of the choir. I must tell Inspector Ambrose."

"Of course," PC Sutton agreed. Again he looked down the corridor. "Tell me who's died."

"Angela Chapman."

Sutton wrote the name down quickly. "How?" he asked.

The reply was little more than a whisper. "I think she's been stabbed."

Higgins appeared at the end of the corridor with a file in his hand. Sutton beckoned him urgently. "Fetch the boss," he whispered.

"I've just called DI Ambrose," he said to Mrs Tempest, trying to sound reassuring. "He'll be here shortly." He could hear quiet sobbing in the background.

Ambrose appeared from his office and looked towards the desk with a quizzical expression. Sutton put his hand over the mouthpiece, gesturing frantically.

Ambrose hurried over. In relief, Sutton pushed the pad across to him. "The DI's here now," he said into the telephone. "I'll pass you over to him."

It took Ambrose a few seconds to read the scribbled notes. "*No*!" he almost shouted. He felt a deep sadness. The woman was probably difficult, but it was awful to think of such beauty and talent being cut off so young. He also had an awful feeling of having known something like this would happen, but not being able to stop it.

"Tell Higgins to call the Forensics boys," he whispered to PC Sutton. "Make sure they bring the camera, you know the routine. Get Tom Vernon to take over here. I need you with me."

"Mrs Tempest," he said as he took the phone. "I'll be with you straight away. Where are you?"

"In the office."

"Where are the other guests?" he asked.

"In the dining room having luncheon. They don't know yet."

The sobbing grew louder and then choked into silence.

"Don't let anyone leave the hotel until we get there," Ambrose instructed.

Looking at his watch, Ambrose thought quickly. He could hear people talking in the distance and, further away, the sound of a vacuum cleaner. Life was still going on normally at the hotel. The murder must only have just been discovered. It was rare to see witnesses' initial reactions, before they had time to forget details or to influence each other's stories. If he acted quickly he might gain a lot of useful information. "Don't say anything to anyone," he instructed. "Keep your guests eating their lunch. Who's in the room with you?"

"Miss Collier. She found Angela. Miss Hulme's here too. We've called an ambulance."

"It'll only take me five minutes," Ambrose assured her. "I'll probably arrive about the same time as the medics."

He frowned. DS Winters wasn't due at the station for another couple of hours. He would come in earlier if Ambrose called him, but that would cause trouble with Fran, and there was no need to incur her wrath. Sutton would do for now. When Winters' shift began, he could take over.

"Can I tell Libby to shut that awful vacuum cleaner off?" Mrs Tempest asked. "It seems so… irreverent."

"Just say it's noisy and it's disturbing the guests," Ambrose replied. On the pad he wrote, "Chambermaid upstairs, still vacuuming. May have seen something."

"It's the Gala Concert tonight!" Mrs Tempest remembered. Her voice rose in panic. "The choir are singing."

"It'll have to be cancelled," Ambrose said gently.

"What am I going to say?"

"Leave that to Miss Hulme," Ambrose advised.

"I'll have to tell the choir Angela's not well, and the others are looking after her," Mrs Tempest insisted. "They won't carry on with lunch otherwise."

PC Sutton appeared. "All done," he mouthed.

"We're on our way," Ambrose said and put down the phone.

At the door, he paused and turned to Greg Sutton in alarm. An awful thought struck him. "Is your wife at The Shalimar?" he asked.

"No, thank God," Sutton replied. "She's booked for tonight, but she had a couple of pupils this morning."

"Tell her to keep well away," Ambrose instructed. "We'll need to check with her pupils, but she should be in the clear. I'll need to talk to her though." He paused. "And where's Meadows?" he added sharply.

"Out on a job, sir. Something to do with the thefts."

"Where was she this morning?"

Once again Sutton could answer with relief: "Here, cleaning a cell after Old Tom."

Ambrose nodded. Old Tom's scent was notorious. Any cell he slept in needed fumigating. "Was she singing tonight?" he asked. "Do you know?"

"I don't think so. She said the woman she replaced was coming. Shall I leave a message?"

"Tell her I'll want to talk to her. She may have overheard something."

Every junction was against them. The shift was changing at Carpenters' Sugar Factory; buses and bicycles clogged the main street. Swathes of workers in overalls crossed the road, heading towards the factory gates. Another crowd was leaving and rushing in the opposite direction. "I would catch this lot!" Ambrose thought in annoyance. Turning on the bell would alarm everyone. It would probably lead to even greater chaos. He would get through just as quickly if he picked his way between the crowds. Once he reached Chalk Heath Lane he could speed up.

Sleet was falling in a fine, chilling mist as the police car turned off the lane and through the gates to The Shalimar. Fairy lights twinkled on the fir trees near the door. The hotel still looked warm and welcoming, but an ambulance was parked to one side of the drive, tactfully out of sight of the restaurant windows. There was no one beside it. Ambrose tucked the police car near it, also out of sight. Then he and Sutton walked quickly towards the front porch.

A wreath of berried holly hung from the doorknocker. Beyond the open door, they could see a large Christmas tree in the reception area, decorated with red bows. Paper chains hung in loops across the ceiling and around the banisters. It was all so festive and cheerful, and now so utterly out of place.

Ambrose put his finger to his mouth, indicating they shouldn't speak. For a moment he paused in the foyer, listening. There was no one at the Reception Desk. The emptiness was eerie. Mrs Tempest usually appeared at the first sign of a visitor. Voices came from the restaurant, however. Knives and forks chinked on plates. People were chatting as normal, still oblivious to what had happened.

The office was on the left of the entrance, its door facing the Reception desk. Gently Ambrose knocked, PC Sutton waiting beside him.

Mrs Tempest let them in, closing the door quickly behind them. She was pale, her face drained. Barbara Collier was sitting in a chair beside the desk. Clearly she'd been crying. Evelyn Hulme stood beside her, shivering and holding a screwed up handkerchief to her mouth. All three women looked towards Ambrose in appeal, as if somehow he could make the whole nightmare go away.

Ideally, a WPC should be present when he interviewed the women, but Ambrose didn't have time to wait. Sutton got out his notebook, ready to record everything they said.

"Tell me what's happened," Ambrose began. "Who found Mrs Chapman?"

"I did," Barbara said. Her voice shook. "She was late for lunch. We were meant to start at noon, so we could rehearse at the church this afternoon. She'd told me she was going to wrap some presents for her nieces. So I went up to see if she'd forgotten the time. She always buys something for them, everywhere we go. That's why we were late setting off the other day…" Realising she was rambling, Barbara stopped.

Softly Sutton moved to a corner and leaning against the wall, began to write.

"What time did you decide to look for her?" Ambrose prompted. He needed to establish the exact timeline.

"Probably just before quarter past twelve."

"Go on," Ambrose invited. He felt his sadness deepening and had to push it aside.

"I knocked, but got no answer," Barbara went on. "So I thought Angie might be ill and pushed the door. It wasn't locked. She was slumped over her bed, as if she'd fainted. But then I saw the blood. There was blood everwhere; on the counterpane, the pillow, the wall…."

Evelyn gave a great gulp and blew her nose. "Poor, poor Angela!" she said. "It's awful! A nightmare! How will we manage without her?"

Ambrose turned back to Barbara. "Carry on," he said gently.

"I didn't see the scissors at first," she replied. "I was too upset by the blood. But when I stepped forward to feel the pulse on her wrist, I saw them in her hand. And that's how I got blood on my sleeve." Barbara lifted her arm to show the stain on her blouse. "There was no pulse. I think I may have screamed, but only quietly, more a gasp than a scream. Then I ran out into the corridor. Evelyn was coming up the stairs so I called to her. She ran down here for an ambulance."

"And you?" Ambrose asked, turning to Mrs Tempest.

"I was in here," she replied. "Miss Hulme came rushing in. She said we needed an ambulance, that Mrs Chapman was hurt."

With an obvious effort, Evelyn took up the story. "I didn't know she was dead," she said. "I thought she'd fallen or fainted."

"So you're the only one here who's seen Mrs Chapman?" Ambrose asked, turning again to Barbara.

"I hope so. I shut the door in case someone passed."

"You seem to have acted very sensibly," Ambrose commented. He was puzzled by Barbara's reaction. She seemed unnaturally calm. "Mrs Chapman was your friend, I believe?" he asked.

"Yes, but you're really asking why I'm not having hysterics or swooning, aren't you?" Barbara replied perceptively. "I've worked in Emergency wards. I know what death looks like."

There was a long, difficult silence. Ambrose waited.

"The ambulance men are upstairs," Mrs Tempest said at last. "I took them up, but I didn't go in with them. I thought it best to keep out of the way."

There was a noise on the landing above. Mrs Tempest leant forward to look through a small window near the door. It gave a clear view of the reception area and the stairs. "So that's how she knows a guest's waiting," Ambrose thought. He too looked through and up the stairs. One of the ambulance men had left Angela's room and was coming down. "Stay here," Ambrose instructed as Mrs Tempest got up. He wanted to be the first to hear what the ambulance men said. "Sutton, come with me please."

Jack Malton recognised Ambrose straightaway. "Afternoon, Inspector," he nodded a quiet greeting. "You'd better come upstairs." He led the way back up to the landing and along the corridor, towards the guest rooms overlooking the gardens at the back. "Stabbed in the neck with a pair of scissors I'd say," Jack continued matter-of-factly. "The wound's not large, but it's deep. The blade must have nicked the artery. That's why there's so much blood. The odd thing is, the scissors are in her hand."

His colleague was waiting beside the open door, writing on a clipboard. "Afternoon," he said, equally businesslike. "The Coroner's Officer is going to have to deal with this. Nothing we can do. We'd best go. That ok with you? We're short staffed today."

Nodding, Ambrose turned to PC Sutton. "Come in with me. I need you as witness." It would be hard on the lad, but it was part of the job. Not that you ever got used to it, Ambrose admitted. No matter how often he did it, he had to steel himself before he went in to see a victim, and he'd known this woman slightly. He was glad to have someone else with him.

Sutton nodded. He'd gone rather pale, but he followed Ambrose into the room silently, notebook in hand.

They stood near the door. The dead woman was slumped forwards over the bed, as if she'd fallen to her knees before collapsing. Her head was turned towards the window, eyes wide open. Her right arm was stretched out, the fingers clutching a small pair of scissors. They didn't look big enough to kill someone. The other arm was bent forward, under her. Ambrose could just see something in the victim's left hand, almost completely covered by her body. He wondered what it was.

Angela's beautiful auburn hair was tumbled forward over the counterpane, beginning to soak up the blood. Beside her a blouse was laid out, as if she was about to change for lunch, and a toilet bag had been placed on the pillow. The wound was on the right hand side, as was all the blood.

Ambrose looked round the room, trying to work out where victim and attacker had been standing. "Do a quick sketch for me," he asked Sutton. It would keep the lad from thinking too much and could be useful later. Photos rarely caught the whole room in one shot.

The bedroom was quite cramped. It had the look of a larger room that had been divided. The ceiling coving didn't match the walls. A dressing table and chair stood under the window. The wall to the right was almost filled by a wardrobe and the bed took up most of the wall opposite. There was a small chest of drawers near the foot of the bed. Angela Chapman was slumped over the bed with her back to the door. Her prone figure reflected in the mirror on the dressing table.

Ambrose frowned. It was hard to tell from the victim's position whether she'd just entered, or was already in the room. Perhaps her attacker had been there first and was surprised by her entrance. But how would the attacker then strike from behind? If Angela had already been in the room, wouldn't she have called out or tried to defend herself when a stranger entered? And even if it wasn't a stranger, surely she'd have turned if someone had come in behind her?

Crossing carefully he glanced out of the window. There was a good view of the gardens, but the back door was hidden behind bushes. Even if Angela had been looking out she wouldn't have seen an intruder entering the hotel. She might have heard them on the back stairs but thought it was just one of the other guests or a member of staff. He must check whether the back door was locked.

As Ambrose looked at the dressing table, his throat tightened at the pathos of the gifts laid out. Angela had pushed the mirror back so she had room to wrap her nieces' presents. A small cardboard box was half filled with doll's house furniture, another tiny chair and a peg doll lying beside it. String and a sheet of wrapping paper covered the rest of the dressing table, ready to cut to size. Scissors were the only items missing from the table. Presumably they were the ones in Angela's right hand.

With a last quick glance around, Ambrose checked he'd missed nothing. The other guests must be wondering why there were so many people coming and going. One of them would surely pop out of the dining room soon to see what was happening. It was time he went downstairs. He needed to watch Evelyn Hulme give the awful news.

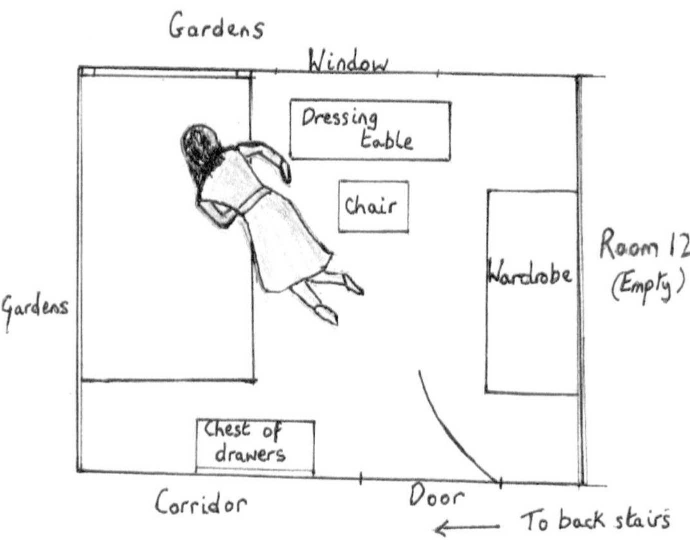

PC Sutton's sketch of the victim's room

Chapter Twelve

The chatter greeted them through the dining room door. With so small a group, the tables had been drawn closer so the diners could talk to each other, and to be nearer the fire. The remains of an ample buffet were spread along the sideboard near the wall. Lunch was almost over. Jane was wheeling a trolley from table to table, serving tea from a huge metal pot. The whole scene was one of relaxation and friendliness. It was about to be disturbed forever.

Ambrose felt a spasm of anger. Someone had stolen the life of a beautiful, talented woman and affected everyone connected with her. Whenever he had to investigate a murder he felt a similar anger. It gave him a steely determination to find that person. Whatever their excuse, as far as he was concerned, a killer acted out of selfishness; a total lack of consideration for others.

He glanced at the three women beside him. Evelyn's face was white and strained but she was no longer weeping. With the choir needing her direction, she walked firmly, staring ahead of her. "She's had to give bad news before," Ambrose guessed. "Probably seen active service."

Mrs Tempest stood stiffly, her expression equally controlled. As she turned towards Ambrose, though, he saw the distress in her eyes. She was looking at ruin for the hotel: cancelled dinner bookings, an empty Christmas week, gossip in the town. The Shalimar's reputation and income would never recover. Yet she hadn't cried. "Taught not to," Ambrose thought with sympathy. The great British stiff upper lip at work.

Barbara, too, was calm. All three women were made of strong stuff. He was glad they weren't the hysterical sort. That would have made the next few hours even more difficult.

Mrs Tempest and Evelyn had entered first. "Just serving the tea Ma'am," Jane said cheerfully. Then she saw DI Ambrose. Still pushing the trolley, she came towards Mrs Tempest. The wheels squeaked on the polished floor. "Hope there isn't a problem," she said softly.

"I'm afraid there is," Mrs Tempest whispered back. She looked for her husband. "Have you seen Mr Tempest?" she asked.

"Just taken a tray of pots to the kitchen," Jane replied. Her cheerful smile faltered. She looked from Mrs Tempest to the others.

"We'd better wait," Mrs Tempest said to Evelyn. One by one, the diners stopped talking and looked in their direction. "Is Angela alright?" Wynn asked from the nearest table. "Not poorly I hope?"

Evelyn didn't reply. A bewildered whisper began to spread around the room. Ambrose watched every face, trying to judge whether they knew of Angela's death. All seemed equally mystified.

"What on earth is the matter?" Anton called to Evelyn. "You look like there's been a death in the house." He began to laugh, but stopped when Evelyn remained silent.

Mr Tempest reappeared, carrying an empty tray. His wife crossed to him and whispered something that made him look at her in alarm. Together, they waited beside the serving table.

"For goodness sake, Evelyn, what is it?" Wynn demanded.

With an obvious effort, the choir leader began her announcement. "I'm afraid I have some very bad news," she said in a small, tight voice.

"What did she say?" Mr Gibbs asked his wife. They were at the far side of the room, apart from the choir.

Taking a deep breath, Evelyn continued, "There's no easy way of saying this. Mrs Chapman has died."

There was a gasp of alarm and disbelief.

"What?" Dennis asked. "If this is your idea of a joke…"

"She isn't joking," Barbara said. Shivering, she sat in an empty seat beside John. "I found her in her room."

"*Angie?*" Wynn repeated. "There must be some mistake. She was fine when I last saw her."

"We were shopping together," Jackie agreed, the colour draining from her face. "She was buying presents." She turned to Mr and Mrs

Gibbs in explanation. "For her nieces, she always likes to buy something for them …" Her words tailed off in confusion.

"Angela is dead," Evelyn insisted quietly.

There was a horrified babble, and then stricken silence.

Ambrose looked round the room. For once his instinct seemed to have deserted him. Shock, bewilderment, disbelief; all the expressions seemed genuine. Either no one in the room had any warning of what had happened, or someone was an extremely good actor. "It *can't* be true!" Jackie said, putting her hands to her eyes. She pulled them away sharply, as if hoping she'd been dreaming. When she saw Evelyn still standing there, her eyes filled with tears. "Poor Angie!" she said. "What was it? A heart attack? Some awful illness?" Fumbling in her bag, she looked for a handkerchief. Her husband passed her his own and she blew her nose noisily.

Barbara started at the sound and put her head in her hands. As she did so, her cardigan pulled back, showing the blood on her sleeve. Urgently she covered it over, too late to stop John from seeing. He caught his breath but made no comment. Almost imperceptibly, he touched Barbara's hand in a gesture of comfort. Looking up, she gave him a wan smile of thanks.

Ambrose watched Mr Tempest. The hotel owner was standing with the empty tray sliding slowly through his fingers. Just before it dropped to the floor, his wife whispered to him. Mechanically he put the tray onto the table. Standing straighter, he tried to look his usual dignified self.

"What happened?" Dennis asked. "Please tell us."

"She was found stabbed," Evelyn said. "Whether in some awful accident or …" She had to pause to steady her voice. "Or deliberately, isn't clear."

At once the babble broke out again, more loudly and in greater distress. "*No*!" several voices pleaded. Mr and Mrs Gibbs looked at each other in horror and began to gather up their things.

"You mean she was murdered?" John asked.

"Good Lord!" Mr Tempest said, shaking his head. "Who could have done such a dreadful thing?" He didn't add, "here, in our hotel?" but his meaning was clear. Like his wife, he could see the implications.

"That's what we intend to find out," Ambrose replied. He was aware of using a cliché but it was true. "If any of you know something, please tell me now."

"But none of us would hurt Angie!" Anton protested. "We're her friends."

Several people murmured agreement. "Of course we wouldn't!" John said. "We wouldn't hurt one of our own, even if we were the sort to harm anyone. And we're not," he added lamely.

Footsteps echoed in the tiled hallway. Ambrose sighed inwardly with relief. The Forensics Team had arrived. PC Sutton would let them in and take them upstairs. They seemed to have taken a long time coming, but when he looked at his watch it was only half an hour since he'd arrived at the hotel himself.

The sound of heavy footsteps convinced everyone that what was happening was real, not just some dreadful joke or nightmare. "Is that more Police?" Mrs Tempest asked.

Ambrose nodded. "The pathologist," he replied. "We should get some answers from him."

Mr and Mrs Gibbs got up from their table and started walking towards the door. "Can we go?" Mr Gibbs asked, like a child wanting to leave the classroom.

Mrs Gibbs appealed to DI Ambrose. "We're very sorry about what's happened," she said, "but we don't even know the lady, and Mr Gibbs isn't feeling well."

"Would you like a drink of water?" Mrs Tempest asked, at once concerned.

"He'll be alright once we're in the fresh air," Mrs Gibbs insisted. "Thank you all the same. This is all so unpleasant. Please let us go."

She looked pleadingly at DI Ambrose. He was about to refuse. Though elderly, the Gibbs were suspects like everyone else, and a pair of scissors weren't heavy to lift. But it was hard on them, keeping them in a hot dining room with strangers and in such an unpleasant situation. "You can go if you stay in your room," he replied. "One of us will talk to you later." He knew they didn't have a car, so they were hardly a flight risk.

Without the Gibbs, the choir could speak more freely among themselves. Ambrose let them talk. After all, they were grieving for a friend and colleague. He listened to their conversations, hoping one of them might reveal something.

Jane had been standing in silence beside the trolley, as if afraid to speak out of turn. She took the opportunity now to turn to Mr Tempest. "What do we do about the Gala Dinner?" she asked.

"Oh, yes, the dinner," Mr Tempest recalled. He turned to DI Ambrose in concern.

"It will have to be cancelled," Ambrose answered.

"Couldn't we go ahead while you do your business in another room, the library perhaps?"

"Sorry, but we can't have dozens of people trampling all over the place."

Mrs Tempest let out her breath in a long sigh. "There will be an awful lot of wasted food," she said sadly. "I'll have to ring round all the guests and stop them coming. I think most of them are on the 'phone." Her manner was brisk but her expression showed how difficult those calls were going to be.

"Chef's already preparing the main course," Jane pointed out. "Oughtn't I to tell him to stop?"

Ambrose couldn't let her speak to the chef in private. "I'll ask PC Sutton to go," he replied. "He'll be back down in a minute."

Evelyn sat down beside Barbara and John. "The concert on Saturday will have to be cancelled as well," she said, sighing. "I'll have to make some phone calls too. And we need to stop Gill's husband bringing her this afternoon." She began chewing some skin on her bottom lip. "This is awful!" she said. "A nightmare!"

"It must have been someone from outside," Jackie said suddenly, so loudly everyone turned towards her. "It can't have been one of us," she insisted.

"Didn't you think someone had been in your room, Barbara?" Evelyn asked.

"I know they were!" Barbara retorted. "Someone took my necklace and then put it back in the wrong place." She turned to face her colleagues. "If any of you were playing a silly joke, please say so. I don't mind any more."

Ambrose nodded. "It would clarify things," he agreed.

No one answered.

"There you are!" Anton said with relief. "It *was* a thief. Angie must have surprised him."

Jackie nodded. "She always liked to wear her jewellery when we came away," she agreed. "I told her it wasn't safe."

Several heads nodded in agreement.

"Poor Angie!" Wynn said.

The shocked chatter began again. "Shall I pour everyone a cup of tea?" Jane asked. "The pot's still warm. I think we could all do with a cuppa."

It was a sensible suggestion and Ambrose nodded. In relief, everyone took the cup of lukewarm tea and sat waiting to be told what to do. The smell from the buffet was making Ambrose feel slightly queasy. It was Mary's WRVS day. He was proud of Mary taking on voluntary work, but it did mean he and Joe went without a proper cooked breakfast. He'd had no lunch either. He wished Mrs Tempest would cover the food over.

Mr Tempest was returning to his usual efficient self. "What do you want us to do, Inspector?" he asked. "I suppose you'll need to question us all." He looked towards his wife for support. She nodded, her mouth set in a grim, determined line.

"I'm afraid so," Ambrose agreed. "No one can leave the hotel until they've given an account of their movements this morning."

"But that's preposterous!" Anton objected. "We haven't done anything! What right have you to keep us here? This is like the Gestapo!"

Ambrose ignored him. "I'll be interviewing each of you in turn," he continued, "including the staff. DS Winters should be here soon. Until he can set up an interview room I'd like you to wait here together."

"I thought you did things differently in England!" Anton almost shouted, getting up from the table. "You should be out there looking for the thief, not keeping us imprisoned here."

"Oh do be quiet, Anton!" Evelyn said sharply. "The sooner we co-operate with the police, the sooner we'll all be allowed to go."

With a growl of protest, Anton flopped back in his chair. He seemed to have shrunk, his barrel chest becoming flab rather than muscle.

Wynn rubbed his eyes. "Inspector, this has hit us badly," he said. "Angie might have been difficult, but she was one of us. I can assure you none of us would have harmed her. We needed her. Calzone will be nothing without her."

Evelyn sighed. "We won't ever replace her," she admitted.

"Even if we look all over Uttley," Barbara agreed. "Angie was special. If things had turned out well she'd have been on a London stage not stuck in a job she hated, longing for her big break. She always had such rotten luck…"

Unable to continue, Barbara lapsed into silence

"Tell me about Mrs Chapman," Ambrose invited, turning to the group. "I'd like to know. In what way did she have bad luck?"

"Well, losing her husband so young…" Wynn broke off, unable to explain.

Jackie helped him out. "She was only nineteen when Jim was killed," she said. "He was in the Merchant Navy. His ship was one of the last to be hit by a u-boat, off the Isle of Man. Most of the crew survived, but Jim didn't. And before that, she caught Scarlet Fever, just as she was hoping to study music."

Jackie was the sort who knew about people. Ambrose encouraged her. "That was rotten luck," he agreed.

"Angie had it ever so badly," Jackie continued, "all her books and music had to be burnt afterwards, so she couldn't catch up at school or get into music college. But she's tried ever so hard since. She's well known in Uttley, appears in ever such a lot of shows, as well as singing with us. Someone's bound to notice her soon …" With a stifled sob Jackie broke off, realising that she was talking as if Angela were still alive. "Only she won't ever have the chance now," she added.

PC Sutton knocked on the door. "Can you come upstairs, sir?" he asked as Ambrose answered. "The pathologist would like to speak to you."

"Take over from me here," Ambrose instructed quietly. "Don't let any of them leave. Let them talk and listen for anything of interest. They're not under caution yet." He wished DS Winters would come soon.

"I found the chambermaid on her own upstairs," Sutton continued. "She was still cleaning in one of the bedrooms. Do you want me to bring her in?"

Ambrose looked into the hallway behind Sutton. Libby was standing near the telephone table, shivering as if with cold, a feather duster still in her hand. "Nobody told me," she said immediately she saw him. "I'd have stopped if I'd known. Honest. I didn't know anything about it, honest..." Her face was deadly white. She looked absolutely terrified.

"Go in and sit down," Ambrose told her. He guided the girl gently to the door to the dining room.

The front desk bell rang, startling them all. DS Winters had arrived.

Chapter Thirteen

DS Winters was waiting beside the Reception desk.

Ambrose greeted him "Thanks for coming so quickly," he said. "I thought you might help as you were here only yesterday. Doc Halstead's upstairs with Forensics. Sutton said he wants to speak to me. I'd like you to come up too. You might spot something I miss."

"I doubt it," Winters replied. "But I'll try."

Ambrose led him upstairs. "There's a lot of blood," he warned. "I hope you haven't just had your lunch."

They walked along the ornate landing and down the corridor leading to the back bedrooms. Winters glanced at the grandfather clock as they passed. "You never know what's coming, do you?" he asked reflectively. "It's barely twenty four hours since I was here and everything was fine then: Beetle Drive and a special tea. I saw the victim come in. She struck me as a bit of a beauty." He sighed. "What a waste!"

Ambrose sighed too. "It's a bad business all round," he agreed. "It'll probably finish this place."

"How are the Tempests taking it?"

"Stiff upper lip, as you'd expect, but they've realised how much harm it'll do."

"Do they have to be interviewed?" Winters asked. "This place means the world to them. They wouldn't shoot themselves in the foot by harming a guest."

"We have to treat them as suspects," Ambrose reminded him. "Mr T could have known the victim way back. Mrs T might have found out and been jealous. There are all sorts of possibilities."

Winters nodded. "True," he agreed. "Keep an open mind and all that. OK. Are there any obvious suspects?"

"None." Ambrose frowned. "I'm a bit stumped so far. It might even be a random killing; someone from outside who's scarpered since. We don't stand much of a chance if that's the case."

The door of Angela Chapman's bedroom was tightly shut but there was the sound of movement inside. Ambrose knocked.

The pathologist greeted them. "Afternoon, Gents," he said, as if they had merely met in the street. His tone clashed with the chaos of the room.

Winters caught his breath slightly. "What a mess!" he remarked, but he was utterly professional as he looked round. The Forensics team were still at work: taking photographs, dusting for prints, measuring angles. The tiny bedroom was full of people, all busy doing their job.

Ambrose had already seen the room, but he felt a sense of shock again. It was indeed a mess. "What have you got for me?" he asked Doc Halstead. "Time of death?"

"Very recent. There's no rigor yet but pallor mortis is present. Look at how pale her face is."

"Can't you be more accurate?" Ambrose frowned.

"I'll confirm when I do the post mortem, but given her temperature I'd say around noon, give or take half an hour each way."

"That fits," Ambrose said reflectively. "Her friend found her when she didn't appear for lunch. That was just around twelve fifteen apparently. The choir returned from shopping at elevenish and she was alive then. So we have only a small window of opportunity. Cause of death?" he added.

"Looks like a pair of standard nail scissors, the sort you'd find in a manicure set or first aid kit." The pathologist nodded towards a pair of scissors lying in an evidence tray. "We'll need the PM to confirm, but the blade's the right shape. Nicked an artery. On the way out I think, rather than in. If they'd been left in her neck and the wound bound tight, she'd probably have survived. I've seen hospitals treat worse."

Winters shook his head. "That's one of the basic things they teach in first aid," he sighed. "Leave the knife in. Don't pull it out." He looked back at the door, and then towards the window, and the dressing table beneath it. A puzzled expression settled around his eyes. "Why's she over here?" he asked.

Doc Halstead shook his head. "That's not the only oddity," he agreed. "The scissors were in her right hand, and the wound's on the same side too." Lifting Angela's hair, he showed them. "You've got an obvious question straight away: 'Did she pull the scissors out herself? Or did her attacker do so, and then put them in her hand?' If it was the assailant, they'd have got blood on them. It would have spurted from the artery, onto their hand, probably onto their body. So, the first thing you need to look for is a pile of bloodstained clothes. Or better still, someone seen with blood on them."

"The lady who found her has blood on her sleeve," Ambrose noted.

"There should be a sight more blood than that on the attacker, I'd say," the pathologist replied, "given how much there is on the bed and wall. There's no obvious void in the blood either, which you'd expect if someone was standing there. The angle suggests she was bending over when she was hit," he continued. "It's quite a shallow blow, almost sideways. It's just possible she stabbed herself in the first place. It seems an odd thing to do, but I've known stranger suicides."

Ambrose looked at the doll's house furniture on the dressing table. "When she was packing presents for her nieces?" he asked. "It doesn't seem likely."

Barry Brooks stood up and prepared to examine the wardrobe. Ambrose turned towards him. "Any useful fingerprints?" he asked.

"Not so far," Brooks admitted. "There are lots of smudges, as you'd expect in a hotel bedroom. Nothing's clear."

"And on the scissors?"

"Too early to tell. With all the blood, we'll need to take a closer look in the lab." Brooks shook his head. "In any case," he warned, "if she was using the scissors, her fingerprints will be all over them."

Like Winters, Ambrose couldn't make sense of the position of the body. "There was something underneath her when I came earlier," he remarked. "Have you found it?"

With gloved hands Charles Murdoch passed him a small bloodstained bag. "I think you call it a jewel wrap," he explained.

"The sort of thing a woman might take on holiday. It's lighter than a jewellery case."

"Is there anything in it?"

Murdoch took out two necklaces and a ring.

"May I see?" Winters asked. Putting on a pair of gloves himself, he examined the items. "These look expensive," he remarked, holding up the necklaces. "But I'd say the ring's sentimental value only." His expression softening, he considered it more carefully. "This reminds me of the engagement ring I bought Fran," he admitted. "Cheap paste, bought on a serviceman's pay."

"That would make sense," Ambrose agreed.

Winters passed the jewellery back. "You say the bag was under her?" he asked.

"She was lying across the bag," Doc Halstead agreed. "She could have been protecting it. Or she might just have fallen on it."

Ambrose looked around the room, wondering if there were any possible hiding places. Apart from the wardrobe or under the dressing table, he could see none. "Could she have been attacked by an intruder?" he asked. "Supposing she came into the room and surprised them?"

Winters paced out the distance from the door to the bed, and then to the dressing table, almost bumping into Barry Brooks as he did so. "She's facing the right way for having just come into the room," he said thoughtfully, crossing to the wardrobe. "But you'd have thought she'd have seen if there was a thief in here. Logically, she'd have either run straight back out, or confronted them. Unless they were hiding in here." He opened the wardrobe door. It swung outwards softly on well oiled hinges. Inside, the space was dark and roomy.

Ambrose joined Winters. Behind the few clothes hanging from the bar, there was ample space for someone to crouch unseen. "You'd better fingerprint in here too," he said to Brooks. Trying to form an image of the dead woman, he glanced at the clothes hanging in the wardrobe: a long black skirt and white blouse he recognised as the choir's uniform, a smart jacket and dress, three blouses, two skirts and several silk scarves. Though he would be the first to say he knew little about fashion, Angela Chapman's clothes suggested a woman who liked to be stylish, and bought a few good items rather than a lot of cheap ones. "Have a glance in her pockets while you're at it," he added. "There might just be a love letter or blackmail note. I've known it happen."

Turning back to Doc Halstead, Ambrose frowned. "If someone was hiding in here, they could have surprised her after she'd been in the room a few minutes," he admitted. "But I can't see why they'd attack her if she was bending over the bed. Why not just run out of the door before she had time to sound an alarm?"

"Unless there was a fight and she tried to grab the jewel wrap?" Winters suggested, though he didn't sound convinced. "That doesn't fit, though. Presumably she was using the scissors to cut the wrapping paper. There aren't any others. So why would she have them over here? Unless she was defending herself with them?"

"Precisely," Ambrose agreed. It was always good to have DS Winters working with him.

"There are no signs of a struggle so far," Doc Halstead warned. "Not on her hands any way." He indicated the dead woman's left hand. The nails were still beautifully manicured, the fashionable red varnish unchipped.

"She definitely died as you see her," Doc Halstead added, "given the way the blood's pooling in her legs."

Ambrose nodded, then turned back to DS Winters. "Ask Sutton to list who was in the hotel this morning. And anyone who called in."

He turned to go. There was nothing more he and Winters could do here and the room was too small for so many people. "Let me know when you've finished," he asked the team. "We'll have to ship the body to the mortuary afterwards."

"What a wretched business!" Winters said as they walked back down the stairs. "Seeing that ring got to me I'll admit." Then he was business-like again. "Do you want to start interviewing straight away?"

"Yes. The sooner the better. The library should be private enough."

They set the interview table between shelves of beautifully bound books. The day's newspapers were laid out on a reading desk, carefully ironed into a leather holder. Everything in the library was discrete and quiet, the chairs upholstered in a tasteful burgundy, the central table polished mahogany. It was all totally out of keeping with a murder enquiry.

"Who do you reckon for prime suspect?" Ambrose asked as soon as he and Winters were alone.

Winters barely paused to think. "Barbara Collier," he replied. "She could have pretended to be fetching Mrs Chapman, stabbed her, then acted like she'd only just found the body."

"My thoughts exactly, "Ambrose replied. "She was altogether too calm when I first interviewed her. The timing's a problem, though. Could she have gone up to the room, committed the murder, cleaned herself up and then called for help?"

"She did have blood on her sleeve, you said," Winters noted.

"Which makes it more unlikely, not less. Did she really kill Angela, change her clothes and then go back in to the body to get blood on her sleeve? It seems rather unlikely and she was only upstairs a short time."

Pursing his lips, Winters frowned. "It's possible but it doesn't sound right," he admitted. "It's more likely there was some bad feeling between whoever came into the room and the victim said something that was the last straw. That'd mean the murder wasn't premeditated."

"It'd also explain why there was no sign of a struggle or forced entry. Mrs Chapman opened the door."

Sitting at the desk, Ambrose looked in the drawers until he found a pencil and a writing pad. "Right," he said in an efficient tone. "Let's see." Quickly he jotted down the names of all the suspects. "Quite a long list," he remarked, shaking his head afterwards. "Usual approach. We talk to everyone informally first, then bring the most interesting into the 'Station under caution. Feel free to ask any questions that occur to you as we go along."

Winters nodded, getting his pad and pencil ready to take notes. It was a formula that had worked well in the past. "Who do you want to start with?" he asked.

"The hotel staff. They seem the least likely. Let Miss Collier stew for a while. It might make her nervous."

There was a tap on the door. Winters went to see who was there.

"Sorry to disturb you," PC Sutton apologised. "But the chef's causing bother. He insists he has to go back to the kitchen. He says he must see to the food that's left out. Apparently the butter and eggs need to be put on the cold slab soon."

Ambrose could understand the chef being upset about the cancelled dinner. "We'll see him first," he agreed.

"Dunno what it's got to do with me," Des protested, sitting heavily in the chair indicated to him. "I'm sorry if one of the guests has died, but I didn't even know it till your young copper fetched me. I've been stuck in the kitchen since six this morning. First there was the breakfast to cook, then the lunch to prepare, and then I'd got the dinner to see to and no bloody help from anyone. Didn't even get a sit down to eat my own meals. Had 'em standing up as usual." He rubbed his back. "It doesn't half get you," he grumbled. "And now they tell me the Gala Dinner's bloody well off. What am I supposed to do with all the food? I got three plump fowl special. Nothing but the best for Her Ladyship."

He paused for breath, and Winters nodded sympathetically. Then the tirade began again. "I've plucked and dressed 'em already. The giblets'll go off if they're not cooked soon …"

They hardly needed to question the chef; just let him grumble on, in his own time.

"Can anyone confirm you were in the kitchen?" Ambrose asked when the flow finally slowed.

"Course not," Des retorted. "Like I said, nobody comes near me. I told him that yesterday." Frowning, he turned towards DS Winters.

"What about Jane?" Winters reminded him. "Didn't she come in?"

"Of course. Brought the breakfast orders and collected the plates." Des sighed. "Then she dumped the dirty ones back. I didn't even have Libby to help wash up this morning. Too busy cleaning she said."

"And at lunchtime?" Winters persisted. "Didn't people come in then?"

"You taking the mick?" The chef scowled in irritation.

Winters shook his head. "I'm trying to help you, Des," he insisted. "I'm trying to establish whether you really were on your own and whether you had long enough to disappear upstairs."

Puzzled, Des paused. Then he began to understand. "Well, no, not when you put it that way," he admitted. "There was someone in or out all morning, from seven thirty. First Jane doing the breakfast orders, then Mr and Mrs T collecting cutlery and plates for lunch, and Jane laying out the buffet. It's just that no one ever helps with the cooking."

"Did you stay in the kitchen the whole morning?" Ambrose persisted.

"I went to the lavatory a couple of times, but there was no time to go anywhere else."

"Just to be sure," Ambrose repeated. "Where were you between eleven and twelve thirty today?"

"In the bloody kitchen!" Des almost shouted in exasperation.

"That's all we wanted to know," Winters assured him with a smile. He showed the chef to the door.

Jane was easier to interview: impeccably polite and ready to answer their questions. She was very discreet however. Ambrose had the feeling that she would only give information if asked directly, and then in a manner that sounded good but said little. It was rather like interviewing a politician. "You were serving breakfast and then getting lunch, you say?" he repeated. "What time did you start?"

"Getting breakfast or lunch?" Jane asked.

Ambrose sighed. "Both," he replied. "Take us through your morning," he invited.

"If it will be of interest," Jane replied. "I got up at my usual time, six o'clock, and then came down for six thirty, to start laying the breakfast tables. If I can, I do it the night before, but there wasn't time last night. The first guests came down for seven thirty, so I took their orders, and served them. Everyone had finished by nine. I gather the choir had a shopping trip and had to get their coach. Mr and Mrs Gibbs always have their breakfast in their room."

"And then?" Ambrose prompted.

"I had breakfast with Libby, and had a short rest in my room afterwards. Then I started setting out the cold meats and cheeses for the buffet."

"What time would that be?" Winters asked.

"About ten thirty. I worked through till Mrs Tempest and the Inspector came into the dining room."

"So you were in and out of the kitchen most of the morning?" Ambrose persisted.

"Of course."

Winters recalled the figure slumped in the chair when he peered into the kitchen yesterday. He tried a more direct approach. "So you keep an eye on Des most of the time?" he asked. "Our Des is a bit 'work shy', isn't he?"

"Goodness, no!" Jane replied in a shocked tone. "I like to keep him company. And so does Mrs Tempest. He can get very lonely in that big kitchen."

Ambrose smiled inwardly, acknowledging the woman's tact. "It's a long day for you," he commented. "Do you ever get chance to have time off? To pop home perhaps?"

Jane shook her head. "This is my home, officer," she replied. "I get a day off once a week, but if I go out it's usually to town shopping, or perhaps for a walk on the heath."

"You have no family, then?" Ambrose asked.

For the first time he saw a flicker of emotion behind the polite smile. "I have a sister," she replied, "but I haven't seen her for years. I never married. The Luftwaffe saw to that." Looking down at her skirt, Jane smoothed a crease away. "Inspector, hotels like this are full of people on their own. Des has no family either. Nor do our resident guests. Libby does, but she'd be far better off without them, well her real family that is. We make a good life for ourselves here. I can assure you, not one of the staff would do anything to harm the reputation of The Shalimar. It would be harming ourselves." A note of conviction, almost of defiance, had entered her voice.

"We're not casting any aspersions," Winters assured her, more gently. "We just need you to confirm that Des couldn't have left the kitchen without you noticing. Can you honestly say that?"

"I did have to leave occasionally to set out the buffet, but he wouldn't have had time to go upstairs and kill a guest if that's what you mean. Perish the thought! Des may be difficult at times, but he would never do that!"

Ambrose nodded, accepting her assurance. "And you?" he asked. "You were in the dining room or the kitchen the whole time from eleven o'clock to Miss Hulme telling you what had happened?"

"Yes." Frowning, Jane paused and reconsidered. "Mrs Tempest asked me to go upstairs to tell Libby to stop vacuuming," she recalled. "That would have been around twelve thirty, when we were waiting for a couple of the ladies to arrive for lunch." Pausing again, she shuddered. "Poor Audrey must have know about the murder then," she realised. "No wonder she didn't like the noise."

"And where was Libby when you went up?" Winters asked.

"Right at the front of the house. Now if you will excuse me, I need to help Des salvage tonight's dinner. We'll have to feed everyone, whatever's happened."

Getting up, Jane gave a little nod of farewell that reminded Winters of a curtsey, and turned towards the door. Ambrose was about to tell her she shouldn't leave the hotel, then decided she had nowhere else to go anyway.

He let out his breath slowly, considering the interviews. "Well, we've established a few things," he said thoughtfully. "Neither the waitress nor the chef had much chance to reach the victim's room, and by the time Jane went upstairs to speak to the chambermaid, Libby was as far as she could be from it. Any other thoughts?"

"Jane's holding out about something," Winters replied. "Just as she was yesterday and the Tempests were too. Something's going on. Whether it's to do with the murder, I just don't know."

Chapter Fourteen

"Get Meadows down here," DI Ambrose said, frowning. "We need to talk to her. She might have noticed something useful. What shift is she on?"

"Earlies." Winters looked at his watch. "She should be back at her digs by now."

"Get her here for a few hours. She'll probably appreciate the overtime."

"I'll ask the 'Station to call her." DS Winters picked up the telephone. "Who do you want to interview next?" he asked afterwards.

Ambrose paused. "We'll leave the chambermaid stewing," he decided. "If this attack is to do with the thieving, she's our most likely suspect."

"Libby wouldn't kill anyone," Winters said emphatically.

"No, but her Dad or his friends might. If she knows anything, she'll try to contact them. We'll keep an eye on her. Let's eliminate Peter Tempest. He probably knows least."

Getting up, Winters stopped. "Did you have anything to eat?" he asked.

Ruefully, Ambrose shook his head.

"I'll mention it," Winters replied. "It's a shame to let that buffet go to waste."

Before Ambrose could protest, Winters had left the room.

Peter Tempest entered and sat stiffly in the chair. "Forgive me if I seem uncooperative," he began. "But I really can't help you." He pushed his fingers through his hair, still thick and wavy, with only a tinge of grey. "I've been very busy today. I have no idea what happened to poor Mrs Chapman."

"What about just before lunch? Did you see anybody go upstairs?"

"I had a long telephone call with a supplier. I'm afraid I didn't see who was where. I can't tell you anything much about the choir either. They only arrived a few days ago. They seemed nice enough: very professional. It's all quite dreadful!" Shaking his head, Peter began to rise from his chair. "Can I go now?" he asked. "There's an awful lot I need to do. Cancelling tonight's Gala Dinner is going to be very difficult."

He spoke too evenly, as if it were a prepared speech. Ambrose couldn't let him go so quickly. "We'd be grateful if you'd answer a few more questions," he said.

Sighing, Peter sat down again.

"Can anyone confirm you were on the telephone?" Winters asked.

"The telephone operator and the people I spoke to. I was on the phone for ages. We've been having problems with the meat supply. The chef isn't happy with the quality. Fosters' fobbed me off and I had to ask for the manager."

"We'll check," Ambrose agreed. "You definitely didn't see anyone go upstairs just before lunch? You can see the stairs from the office can't you?"

"I phoned from our flat, on the top floor. Audrey was busy in the office and I didn't want to disturb her."

"So you have two telephone lines?" Winters asked in surpise.

"Actually we have three," Peter replied proudly. "We have a private line in our apartment, the business line in the office and a public phone in Reception.'

"Could one of your staff have had a grudge against Mrs Chapman?" Ambrose asked.

"Of course not!"

"So it has to have been an outsider?"

Straightening a cuff link, Peter Tempest replied, "I can't see any other explanation."

"What about the choir?"

Peter raised an eyebrow. "They all seemed very dedicated. Attacking one of their number would be madness. It would make no more sense than Audrey or I harming The Shalimar."

Ambrose smiled to himself. "Nicely put," he thought.

Winters tried a different approach. "What were you concealing from me yesterday?" he asked abruptly.

As he'd hoped, that startled the hotelier. Sitting even more uprightly, Peter paused before replying. "I can't think what you mean," he said finally.

"I came to investigate two reports of theft," Winters reminded him. "I had a strong impression you knew about them, but pretended you didn't."

"I don't see what this has to do with Mrs Chapman's death," Peter replied.

"It may have a great deal to do with it," Ambrose said firmly. "It's possible Mrs Chapman surprised a thief in her room. How long have items been going missing? And why didn't you report it?"

"Because it would have wasted your time and ours. Guests are always losing things." Peter's tone suggested that as an officer and a gentleman, he didn't expect his judgement to be questioned.

Winters began to feel irritated. He disliked anyone 'pulling rank', especially when he knew they'd spent most of the war in the payroll department. He glanced at DI Ambrose, hoping he'd pursue the question.

Ambrose shook his head slightly. He felt some sympathy for Peter Tempest. The man had worked very hard to make The Shalimar a success before the war. His wife had worked equally hard keeping it going while he was away. They'd both gained the respect of the town. None of which was relevant, Ambrose reminded himself. Like Winters, he felt Peter was withholding something, but the hotelier would probably give honest answers later, after the enormity of what had happened really hit him.

"Thank you for your time," Ambrose said instead. "Please ask your wife to come in next. She may be able to assist us."

Audrey Tempest was indeed more helpful. Immaculate as ever, she was at first controlled and precise in her answers.

"Could you tell us where you were just before lunch?" Winters began. "We're trying to eliminate people."

"In the kitchen talking to Jane and the chef about the dinner." Mrs Tempest sighed. "And now we have to cancel it. What a terrible business!"

"Did you see a stranger go up to Mrs Chapman's room this morning? You can see the whole Reception lobby from your office can't you?"

Audrey Tempest nodded. "I've racked my brains," she admitted, "but I didn't. I saw the choir come in from their shopping trip around eleven. They went straight up to their rooms. They came back down in dribs and drabs. I didn't notice Mrs Chapman was missing until I went into the dining room just before mid-day. I was there when Miss Collier went to find her. After the choir started serving themselves, I went to my office to read a couple of letters."

"And then?" Ambrose asked.

"Miss Hulme came running down looking very distressed. I opened the door and beckoned her in quickly."

"What did she say?"

"That Mrs Chapman was hurt and needed an ambulance. I called immediately."

"When did Miss Collier come down?"

"A few moments later. She was white as a sheet. I could tell something awful had happened and didn't want others to see her. So I took her into my office too."

Audrey's voice was snagging with grief and horror. She had to pause before she could continue.

"To be honest, I don't remember the next half hour very well, not after Miss Collier told us what had happened. The two ladies were in tears and I was, well, shocked I suppose. None of us could believe it. I remember ringing the police station and being very glad to hear you were coming. I think I felt you could make it all go away." Sadly, Audrey looked at them both. "Which you can't, of course," she admitted.

"Did either of the ladies suggest who might have attacked Mrs Chapman?" Ambrose asked.

"No. They were far too upset."

"Can you?"

"I know none of my staff would have done it," Audrey replied firmly. "Otherwise I don't have the least idea."

"What did you think of Mrs Chapman?" Winters asked.

"She seemed nice enough," Audrey replied, "a bit demanding perhaps, but I can't see why anyone would want to kill her. It's like a bad dream."

"Was she a nuisance?" Winters asked, picking up the questions.

"Of course not," Audrey assured him. "We're used to catering for guests' tastes. Mrs Chapman liked to have her eggs poached rather than fried, that sort of thing. Nothing we couldn't accommodate."

Ambrose nodded. "But her fellow choir members might have found her irritating?" he persisted.

"Perhaps. I did overhear some arguments."

"Might one of the choir have attacked her?" Winters asked.

Staring down at her hands, Audrey thought carefully before she answered. "I suppose it's possible," she replied. "Though it seems a very silly thing to do, especially with a big event this evening. It'd be like cutting your nose off to spite your face." She twisted the rings on her hands. "Quite frankly I wish we'd never agreed to have the choir here. They have been rather trying. And now this …"

"You've been having quite a few problems, lately, haven't you?" Ambrose said gently. "With thefts from guests' rooms too. Why didn't you tell DS Winters about them yesterday?"

"Because I wasn't sure whether they were thefts or not," Audrey said, less certainly. "Guests often lose things."

Winters frowned. "I felt you weren't being entirely honest with me," he replied. "Not like you at all."

Flushing slightly, Audrey looked up at him. "I hoped the things would just turn up," she admitted, "as they did in the end. And I wondered…" Pausing, she considered how much to say.

"You wondered what?" Ambrose prompted.

"Whether one of the choir might be the culprit. I knew none of our staff would be. I hoped the problem would go away once the choir left."

"I see," Ambrose replied, thoughtfully. "Is that why your husband also pretended to know nothing?"

Looking even more uncomfortable, Audrey stared ahead. "Peter cares more about this hotel than anything else," she replied carefully, "except his family of course. He was simply trying to protect our reputation. And the choir's too. If the local papers had reported thefts, both our reputations would have been ruined. There was no deceit intended."

Ambrose wasn't sure she was telling the whole truth even now, but he dropped the topic. "Thank you, Mrs Tempest," he said. "You've been very helpful." They would have to check she was in the kitchen at the time she said, but that should be easy enough.

Winters got up to open the door for her. Audrey was about to leave, then she paused uncertainly.

"What is it?" Ambrose asked.

"It's just occurred to me: I've been assuming the thief was staying here, but supposing he, or she, was an outsider, someone from the council estate perhaps? The back door is left unlocked sometimes, however hard we try to keep it secure." She shuddered. "Perhaps Mrs Chapman disturbed someone in her room? Oh, the poor lady!"

Soon after Mrs Tempest had left, Meadows cycled up the drive to the front door. Only the dark rings under her eyes suggested how little sleep she'd had over the past few days.

"I gather you need me," Meadows said, as Winters walked with her from the reception area. She'd only just got home after her shift when the call had come through.

"We need you to confirm where you were this morning," Winters replied. "You're a bit too close to this case for comfort."

Meadows looked at him in bewilderment. "You mean the thefts?" she asked.

Winters paused, realising she hadn't been told of the murder. "No," he replied, wishing he didn't have to break the news. They hadn't always got on in the past, but he respected her commitment to whatever she took on. She'd probably become quite close to the choir. "One of the Calzone Singers has been killed," he said.

"What?" In surprise, Meadows stared at him. "How?" she asked.

There was no way of saying it gently. "With a pair of nail scissors," Winters replied. "It's a nasty business."

Standing beside the reception desk, Meadows tried to stop herself feeling sick. "Who was it?" she asked in a tight voice. She had a dreadful feeling she knew the answer.

"Mrs Chapman." Winters watched her reaction. "You're not surprised, are you?" he asked.

"I'm surprised anyone would do something so dreadful," Meadows said, trying to stop her voice shaking. "But Angela's the victim sort …" She corrected herself. "Was."

"Come and tell the DI why," Winters instructed.

For a second Meadows still held onto the desk, steadying herself. Then she followed DS Winters into the library.

"Sit down," Ambrose invited. "You look as though you need to."

"Thank you," Meadows replied, sitting in the chair. "I am a bit puffed after cycling over here."

Ambrose left it at that. The girl was never going to admit weakness. "Mrs Chapman was killed sometime between eleven this morning and twelve fifteen this afternoon," he said. "As a member of the choir, even if temporary, you're a suspect. Do you realise that? You need to account for your movements this morning."

Chapter Fifteen

Meadows caught her breath. "Of course," she said. Her voice sounded odd in her ears, but she was determined to reply calmly.

"I was on duty this morning, Sir, at the 'Station from six onwards," she recalled. "Around eleven thirty, I was seeing to a prisoner being discharged, and then cleaning the cell out afterwards. PCs Higgins and Sutton can confirm that. Several others saw me too. I can give you their names.

"I left at two and called on an old lady from chapel on my way back: Mrs Perkins. I had lunch there. She likes to make sure I eat properly." Meadows half-managed a wry smile.

Nodding, Ambrose waited while Winters noted her reply. "You'll need to make a formal statement," he said. "It's fortunate you have such a clear alibi. You could have found yourself under suspicion."

Meadows flushed deeply and looked away.

"Let this be a bit of a warning," Ambrose continued. "You need to consider very carefully what you take on in your free time. A police officer can't have the same social life as someone outside the force. Not in a small town like ours, any way."

"I'm sorry, sir," Meadows said, looking down at her feet. "I was asked to help out in an emergency. I didn't think things through. Is this a formal reprimand?"

Smiling slightly, Ambrose shook his head. "Just friendly advice," he replied. "Don't let your laudable desire to help others get you into trouble. Not that you could have predicted what would happen," he admitted.

"I'll be more careful in future," Meadows promised huskily.

"As it happens, your being in the choir may prove very useful," Ambrose continued. "Tell us anything that might help us, any arguments you overheard."

Straightening up, Meadows nodded. "There were tensions," she agreed. "I think their pianist normally held them together. She was their secretary too, so she organised things a lot. They'd had a horrible accident on the way, and they were all tired and edgy when they arrived. They blamed Angela, Mrs Chapman I mean, for making them late in the first place. They would have been ahead of the smash if the coach had left on time."

Ambrose nodded his agreement.

"Anything more?" Winters asked. "None of that seems sufficient reason to kill someone. You told me Angela seemed the victim sort. What did you mean?"

"She seemed to have had a lot of bad luck yet she was good looking, talented, and a widow. The men were probably around her a lot. She could also be…" Pausing, Meadows considered her words. "A 'prima donna' one of the men called her. I don't think she meant to be difficult. She could be kind. But she was their star and she knew it."

"Interesting," Ambrose commented. "But none of that sounds sufficient motive. Did you hear anyone threaten her?"

"Several times, but I wouldn't think they meant it. We all say things like 'I could strangle her' when we're really exasperated, but we don't actually do it. If one of the choir did kill her, I'd say it was because of something I didn't see or hear, something back in Uttley perhaps."

"Go on," Winters prompted, smiling slightly. Having Meadows as an 'insider' was indeed useful.

Meadows thought carefully. "They knew each other well before they came," she replied, "not just through the choir. I think the Walters and Angela were neighbours and there was some bad blood about a planning application. Jackie Walters told me it was sorted out but it mightn't have been. And I wouldn't be surprised if Angela had had an affair with Anton. The atmosphere between them was strained. Maybe she'd ditched him for another man back in Uttley or maybe even Dennis or Wynn in the choir. She wasn't happy and when you're not happy you often look around for love."

"Indeed," Ambrose said, resisting a smile. "Thank you. Go upstairs now and have a word with Mr and Mrs Gibbs. They're residents here. You'll find them in their room. We need to know their whereabouts this morning. After that, find a quiet corner and write down anything you can recall that might be relevant. You should be able to sit in the lounge. You'd better keep clear of the choir as much as you can. They may not appreciate seeing you in uniform. Sutton's minding them until we've had chance to talk to everyone."

"Yes sir," Meadows said, getting up. She paused uncertainly. "I shall have to explain myself sometime," she admitted. "That's not going to be easy." She shut the door quietly behind her.

For a moment Meadows stood in the hallway. In different circumstances she would have admired the hotel with its grand stairs but now all she could think about was getting through the rest of the day. The sleepiness had gone but her head ached. "Pull yourself together!" she muttered firmly.

As she went upstairs, Meadows suddenly realised she didn't know which room the Gibbs were in. She wondered if DI Ambrose knew himself. She decided she'd just have to work it out.

A corridor opened off the landing. On the wall a sign pointed one way to 'Guest Rooms 1-7' and the other to 'Guest Rooms 8-16'. Permanent residents would want a large room, Meadows reasoned, and larger rooms were likely to be at the front. Walking down the corridor towards the far end, she tried tapping on doors.

Almost immediately, an elderly woman stuck her head out of a room. "Have you come to talk to us?" she hissed. "About time too!"

"Mrs Gibbs?" Meadows asked.

"We've been waiting for ages," the old woman whispered, as if afraid of disturbing other guests. "Mr Gibbs is very upset." She almost bundled Meadows into the room. "They can't keep us here," she said more loudly. "We haven't done anything. We hardly knew Mrs Chapman. I told your inspector but he wouldn't listen. It's upset Mr Gibbs terribly."

Since Mr Gibbs was sitting calmly in a chair, reading a newspaper, Meadows didn't think he looked particularly upset.

"About time too," he repeated putting the paper down.

"I'm sorry to disturb you," Meadows began, taking out her notebook, "but you might be able to help us."

The Gibbs' room was large and furnished like a bed-sit. One end of the room contained a bed with a wrought-iron frame, a wardrobe and a chest of drawers. The other end, nearer the door, contained a settee, two chairs and a small table. Natural light flooded through two tall and gracious windows.

Indicating the settee with a grand gesture, Mr Gibbs invited Meadows to sit down. "About time too!" he said again.

"What do you need to know?" his wife asked quickly.

"Where were you between eleven and twelve fifteen this morning?"

"Eating lunch," Mr Gibbs replied.

"Not all that time!" Mrs Gibbs added with a nervous laugh. "We came down ready for lunch, but we didn't start until the gong went at noon. It isn't usually until twelve thirty but the choir asked for it to be brought forward."

"What time did you go down?" Meadows asked as she scribbled her notes quickly.

"About a quarter to eleven, I think." Mrs Gibbs said with a slight shrug.

"What did you do while you waited?" Meadows continued, turning towards her.

"Miss Fellowes brought us our usual pot of coffee in the lounge. We watched the choir return in their coach. Then we went for our constitutional."

"You went for a walk?" Meadows interpreted.

"Always do, my dear," Mr Gibbs agreed. "In the gardens or on the heath. One or the other," he nodded vigorously. "One or the other," he repeated.

Meadows nodded. "So where did you go today?" she asked.

"On the heath," Mrs Gibbs replied. "Around the gardens first and then onto the heath. There's a stile you know. It's a bit tricky but we help each other over. Sometimes we go further up the lane to the gate. That's easier."

"And which did you do today?" Meadows persisted.

Mr and Mrs Gibbs looked at each other. "Every day's much the same," Mrs Gibbs admitted. "I think we went over the stile today. Yes. We went over the stile."

"Did you see anyone?"

Mrs Gibbs thought carefully. "The choir," she said with an air of triumph. "We saw Mr and Mrs Walters, and then Miss Hulme."

"Where?" Meadows asked.

"In the gardens."

Meadows sighed inwardly. She didn't seem to be getting very far. "What time did you see them?" she continued.

"Before lunch," Mr Gibbs said. "I was getting hungry."

Meadows wondered whether the couple's vagueness was genuine. Their room was neat, a few ornaments and photographs displayed above the gas fire and on the table. A pack of playing cards sat ready on the window ledge. The Gibbs seemed to be making a good life for themselves at The Shalimar. "Far better than in an old people's home," Meadows thought, recalling visits to her grandmother. The Gibbs had money to afford such accommodation. It would be interesting to know their background.

"So you went down for your coffee at a quarter to eleven?" Meadows directed her question to Mrs Gibbs, as she seemed the most reliable.

"Absolutely. We always come down then, so Libby can do our room. We know when to be out. She's a good girl."

Meadows tried one last question. "What did you think of Mrs Chapman?"

"She was very pleasant," Mrs Gibbs replied, "not snooty like some of the others." Looking up sharply, she stared hard at Meadows. "You're very young," she commented, "and it isn't natural for a woman to be in the police. But I hope you catch whoever hurt that nice lady."

Thanking the elderly couple, Meadows went downstairs. She could hear voices coming from the dining room, muted and hesitant, as if people were afraid to speak; like a dentist's waiting room, she thought.

Quietly she explored the hallway and found the door to the lounge. A long window seat filled the bay. The windows were ill-fitting, letting in a cold draught, but the light was better there. Sitting down, she read through her notes of what Mr and Mrs Gibbs had said. She still felt there was something odd about their replies, not so much what they said but how they'd said it.

She considered Ambrose's request to write down anything she thought relevant. For a while she couldn't think how to begin. Her memories were a jumble of voices and music. If only she'd known what agreeing to Kathy's request would lead to.

Writing down the name of each choir member, Meadows started to list her impressions, exactly as they came to her:

Anton – thinks a lot of himself, handsome, bit of a ladies' man. Very good bass voice. Angry with Angela about something. Looked daggers when she interrupted us. In the Polish airforce and proud of it, but accent funny.

Dennis and Jackie – Jackie bosses him about, but she's pretty dithery otherwise. Always talking about her mother. Doubt if Dennis so keen on Mum coming to live with them. Been some issue with Angela over the planning application. Dennis in the Home Guard, so either had health problem or in reserved occupation. What? Could be a dark horse...

The door opened, startling her.

Audrey Tempest came in. Not noticing Meadows, Audrey flopped into one of the armchairs and put her head in her hands. Trying not to disturb her, Meadows wrote on, softly.

Taking out her handkerchief, Audrey blew her nose and sat up straighter. Then she saw Meadows in the bay window and started visibly. "Oh! I'm so sorry, officer," she apologised. "I didn't mean to interrupt you. I wanted to be quiet for a few moments. The inspector said I could go about my business again."

"You're not interrupting me," Meadows assured her.

Pausing, Audrey considered her face. "Don't I know you?" she asked.

Sighing, Meadows nodded.

"You sang with the choir, didn't you? You were the one Miss Hulme made a fuss of because you'd stepped in when someone was sick. I didn't realise you were a policewoman."

"No," Meadows agreed. She tried to look back down at her notes, but Mrs Tempest was persistent.

"Do the choir know you're a policewoman?" she asked.

"One of them does but I'm not sure about the others."

"Oh dear. I doubt if they'll take kindly to it," Audrey warned. "Especially now. They'll think you were spying on them."

"I just wanted to help," Meadows replied. She wasn't sure why she felt the need to justify herself.

To her relief, Audrey nodded. "It must be hard always being on duty," she agreed. "Like running a hotel." Sighing, she shook her head. "I don't suppose we'll be doing that much longer," she added. "This is going to ruin us."

Getting up restlessly, she wandered around the room, straightening pictures and puffing up cushions. A film of dust on the new television cabinet caught her eye. Running her finger over it, she tutted. "I shall have to speak to Libby," she said.

Despite her control, the woman seemed to be in a state of shock, not really concentrating on what she was saying or doing. "Having a death must be a nightmare," Meadows said sympathetically. "Especially like this."

Audrey turned towards her. "It is," she admitted. She seemed to have aged, her normal bearing slipping for an instant. "We have eight bookings for the weekend," she said. "And another twelve next week. If we cancel them, we'll have to refund the deposits, and Christmas is one of our busiest times. It'll just about wipe us out…" Pulling herself erect again, Mrs Tempest stopped. "I'm sorry," she apologised. "It's no concern of yours."

"If you spoke to the inspector, he might advise you what to do," Meadows suggested. "He's a reasonable man."

Nodding, Mrs Tempest turned away. With a last tweak of one of the cushions, she left the room.

Looking back at her notes, Meadows began to write again. She couldn't see what earthly use her impressions would be. Still, the DI had asked for them, and she respected his judgement.

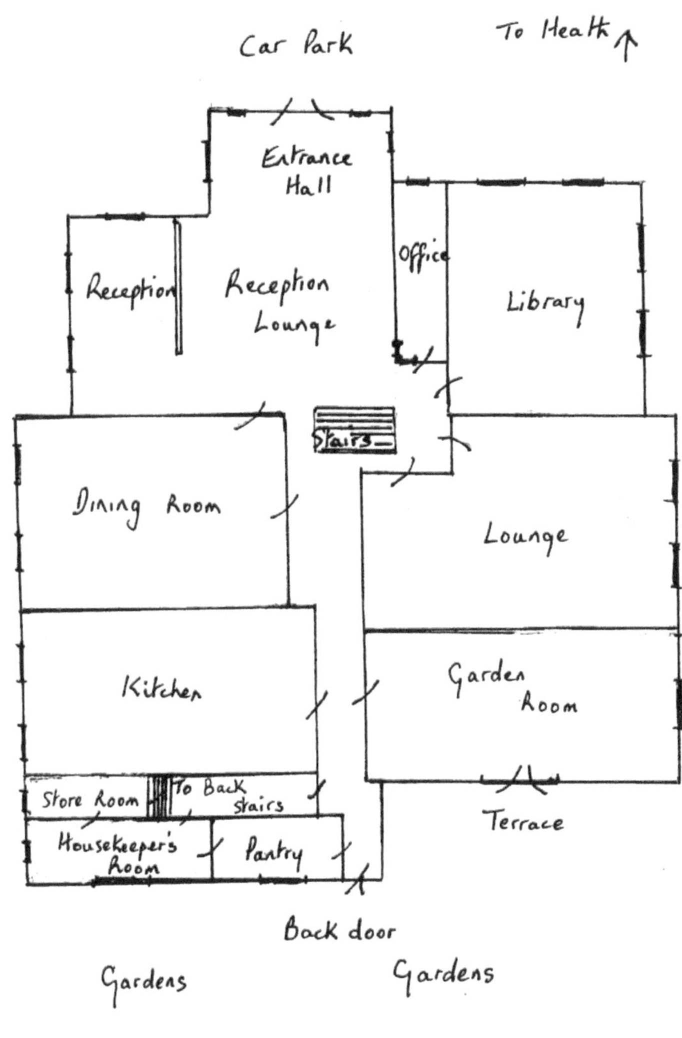

Sutton's plan of the ground floor

Chapter Sixteen

Winters took the call. "Kathy Sutton," he whispered, his hand over the mouthpiece. "Do you want to speak to her?"

Ambrose took the phone. "Thank you for ringing," he said. "I'm afraid I have some bad news." Before she had time to worry about her husband, he added, "Mrs Chapman has been found dead."

"Angela?"

It was several seconds before Kathy spoke again. Ambrose waited. "That's awful!" she said at last. "What was it? Meningitis? She seemed fine last night."

Ambrose liked Kathy Sutton. He wished there was an easier way of breaking the news to her. "Mrs Chapman was killed around lunchtime," he said simply. "Possibly murdered."

"No!" Again there was a long silence at the other end of the line.

"I'm afraid we need you to tell us where you were," Ambrose continued. "We have to eliminate you and Meadows. You're both possible suspects. Everyone who had anything to do with the choir is."

"Of course," Kathy replied in a tight, small voice. "I was at home, teaching two of my young ladies."

"Their names?" Ambrose asked, gently.

"Frieda Lawson and Josephine Cordell. Frieda came at ten thirty, for an hour. Josephine arrived a bit early, before Frieda left. She finished at one, then we chatted for ten minutes until her bus was due."

"So she didn't leave until about ten past one?" Ambrose confirmed.

"That's right."

Ambrose glanced towards Winters and mouthed "She's in the clear."

"We'll have to check with your pupils," he said to Kathy, "but it sounds like you've nothing to worry about. Can you drop their addresses off at the 'Station?"

"Of course." Kathy's voice was becoming husky with emotion. "Poor, poor Angela! Don't tell me how she died. I don't want to think of her like that. I want to remember her as she was at the Town Hall last night, so beautiful and with that wonderful voice."

"Can you think why anyone would harm her?" Ambrose asked.

"I'm sure none of the singers would. Losing Angela will ruin them."

"Did you overhear any arguments?" Ambrose asked.

"Several, but they were just little flare-ups about her being late or wanting her own way. I think they were all a bit jealous of her." Pausing, Kathy tried to remember what she'd heard. "There was one spat that sounded odd, during the interval at the Christmas Concert. I heard John asking Angela to keep quiet about something. He was almost pleading with her. I've no idea what it was about."

"Now that *is* interesting," Ambrose agreed. "If you remember anything else, give us a ring."

"Sounds like John Pedderson might have something to hide," Ambrose remarked as he put down the phone.

There was a knock on the door, followed almost immediately by Higgins peering round. "Sorry to interrupt you," he said quickly. "But it's quite urgent."

Ambrose and Winters turned towards him. "Yes?" Winters asked impatiently.

"Mrs Harpur, the singer who was sick, should be arriving in a few hours. Her husband is picking her up at the hospital in Leyton Bridge. Miss Hulme asked if we could send them back to Uttley instead. There should be time to get a message to them before they leave."

"We don't want yet more people around," Ambrose agreed. "Ring the hospital and speak to the matron," he instructed. "You won't get any joy otherwise. Use the telephone in the office. While you're at it, check whether Mrs Harpur really has been in hospital till now. It wouldn't be impossible to drive over from Leyton Bridge, kill Mrs Chapman, and then get back before the hue and cry started."

"Now that's a thought," Winters agreed.

"Oh and while you're at it, call the Uttley planning office and find out what happened with Mr and Mrs Walters' application for an extension."

Nodding, Higgins left, holding the door open for Libby to come in next. She sat watching Ambrose like a frightened rabbit. She tried to answer his questions, but was having difficulty speaking.

Ambrose reassured her. "You're not in trouble, Libby," he said gently. "We don't think for one minute you murdered Mrs Chapman. We just need you to tell us what you did this morning. You might have noticed something that will help us find the killer. What time did you arrive here?"

"Quarter to seven, sir. I was a bit late. I've apologised to Miss Fellowes."

"Why were you late?"

"My foster mother is sick and I had to take her some breakfast before I left."

"Of course," Ambrose agreed. "And you did your usual jobs once you got here?"

"Yes sir. I cleaned the dining tables and helped lay the cutlery for breakfast. Then I started on the lounge and reception. I had to rush them a bit."

"When did you go up to the bedrooms?"

"When the guests were at breakfast. I started on Mr & Mrs Tempests' private rooms. I hadn't done them this week, we've been so busy, what with the choir and all. Then I started on the back bedrooms."

"Did you clean number 11, Mrs Chapman's room?"

"Yes sir."

"Was she there?"

"No sir. The choir were out on their trip. I was a bit glad about that."

"Why?"

"Mrs Chapman likes to chat, asking about when I'm getting married, that sort of thing. She's always ever so nice but I don't really have time to talk." In horror, the girl paused. "She won't be able to ask me any more, will she?"

"No, Libby, I'm afraid not," Ambrose said. He found the girl's simplicity rather touching and had to remind himself she might be a thief. "Where did you go from there?" he asked.

"I finished the other rooms that end of the corridor. Then I went along to do the front rooms. We have more guests staying soon, you see."

"What time did you move to the front?"

"I'm not sure, sir."

"So where were you when lunch was being served?"

"Vacuuming the long carpet near the big staircase. I didn't know anything had happened. The vacuum's ever so noisy. You can't hear yourself speak when it's on. They ought to get a nice modern one. That'd be a lot lighter too."

"So you were still cleaning when Jane Fellowes came upstairs?"

"Yes. She asked me to stop. She didn't say anyone had been hurt. Just that it was too noisy with lunch being served."

The girl spoke quickly and breathlessly. Winters was writing furiously. Ambrose gave him a moment to catch up. The next question was too important to rush. "Did you see anyone come to their bedroom?" he asked.

"Oh yes sir. They all came up after the coach arrived. The choir I mean. Then they went back down for lunch."

"Did you see anyone use the back stairs?"

"Miss Hulme, sir."

"What time was that? "

"It was about quarter past twelve sir. I saw the time on the grandfather clock in the corridor."

"Can you be a bit more precise?" Ambrose asked. "It might be important."

"No sir. It's one of those fancy ones. There aren't any proper numbers, just stars. But the finger looked like it was at the quarter-past."

"It's a star and moon clock," Winters explained to Ambrose quietly. "Peter Tempest used to collect rare clocks."

"And what happened after you turned the vacuum off?" Ambrose asked, turning back to the girl.

"I carried on cleaning without the vacuum for a bit, then the policeman fetched me. I've been in the dining room since. I couldn't half do with going to the lavatory. Can I go now, sir? "

"One last question, Libby. Have you ever taken anything from the guests' rooms?"

Libby's eyes opened in horror. "No I haven't, not now nor never. The sergeant asked me that yesterday. I told him then. I'd lose me job if I took things and I wouldn't get another."

"I hope you're telling the truth Libby," Ambrose said with a note of warning.

"I am! Cross my heart and hope to die! I haven't ever taken anything since I took that bike and got into all that trouble."

"I believe you," Ambrose replied, honestly. He didn't think Libby was a good enough actress to feign such conviction. "Sergeant Winters will take you along to the lounge. There's a policewoman there. She'll escort you to the Ladies' Room and then back to the others." He turned to Winters. "We'd better speed things up," he said. "Bring Miss Hulme back with you. And tell Miss Collier to be ready." Lowering his voice he added, "She should be getting nervous enough by now."

The room was going dark. As soon as Winters left, Ambrose got up to switch on the light. Crossing to the window afterwards, he looked out. Rain spattered against the window.

Ambrose shuddered. It wasn't just the cold that made him uneasy. Try as he would, he couldn't see any clues in what he'd heard so far. Some vital fact was missing, he felt. He couldn't keep the choir confined much longer without charge, and once they were free, they could destroy any evidence he hadn't yet seen. With their concerts cancelled and a horrible death, everyone would want to go home as soon as possible. He had no grounds to prevent them. He could hand the case over, of course, but Uttley CID would be working even more blindly than he was. He had to make progress before everyone left, otherwise this case could remain unsolved, perhaps for ever.

Ambrose was still standing at the window thinking when DS Winters returned with Evelyn.

The choir leader was pale, but she was calm. She took the chair and sat in silence.

"I'm truly sorry to intrude on your grief, but we need to ask everyone a few quick questions," Ambrose explained.

"Of course." Sighing, Evelyn looked ahead, steadying herself. "It's a terrible nightmare. I keep thinking I'll wake up and it will all have gone away."

"Sadly, it won't," Ambrose replied. "The sooner we find out what happened, the easier it will be for everyone."

"Life will never be the same though," Evelyn said, her voice catching. "We'll never replace Angela."

"No, I imagine you won't," Ambrose agreed. "Let's get this over as quickly as we can. Where were you this morning? We're asking everyone the same question."

"I had breakfast with the others, then we all got on the coach for the shopping trip in Chalk Heath. We left here just before nine. We got back at about eleven. I took my bags up to my room. After that I went for a walk."

"Where?" Winters asked, looking up from his notes.

"I decided to explore a bit. I found the back gate from the gardens and went up the lane. There's a stile onto the heath, so I went up the path for a bit. It was cold but I had a headache and the fresh air did me good."

"What time did you get back?"

"About twelve fifteen, maybe a few minutes before. The walk took me longer than I'd intended and I was late for lunch. I'd given everyone a bit of a talking to about being on time, so it was a bit embarrassing being late myself. I had to dash up the back stairs to my room to change, after my walk. My shoes were far too muddy to wear to lunch."

She shuddered. "That was when I saw Barbara. She was coming out of Angela's room, white as a sheet. She said Angela had been hurt and needed an ambulance."

"Can you think of anyone who'd want to kill Angela?" Ambrose asked sharply, making her uneasy, as he'd intended.

"Absolutely not," Evelyn replied hotly. "None of the choir would ever have deliberately harmed Angela. She was our star. Our success depended on her. We've known each other for years. We're all in total shock since we heard she was dead."

"Can anyone confirm you were out on the heath?" Winters asked.

"I saw a man out walking his dog. We stopped to chat. He had a Labrador just like the one we had when I was younger. I think he was local but I don't know his name. The dog was called Brutus."

"We can ask around," Ambrose agreed.

"Oh, and before that I saw the old couple who live here. They were in the garden. I think Jackie and Dennis might have been there too but I didn't see them clearly."

As Evelyn left, WPC Meadows entered with her notes.

Urgently Ambrose glanced down them. "Some useful observations here," he remarked. "But they still leave the field wide open. As far as I can see, just about everyone had a motive to be annoyed with the victim, but not to commit murder."

"Maybe something happened while the choir were at their last place?" Winters suggested.

"Leyton Bridge? That's an idea."

Higgins knocked on the door.

"Mrs Harpur has been sent home, and she's definitely been in the hospital since early Wednesday morning," he reported. "Matron confirmed. I've also called Uttley town planning."

"And?" Ambrose prompted.

"There's no doubt the Walters' application was turned down," Higgins replied, "but the planning officer was a bit vague as to why. She kept saying we should see the paperwork. Something about objections, but that's all I could get out of her."

Ambrose sighed. He hated these 'jobsworth' types, who pretended to be helpful but gave the minimum information possible. Standing, he stretched his back and made a decision.

"What time is it now?" he asked no one in particular. Then without waiting for a reply, he carried on. "Higgins, take the patrol car to Uttley. If you leave now you should get to the planning office before it closes. I'll square it with the bean counters back at the 'Station. I want to know exactly why the Walters' application was refused. And if someone did object, I need to know who it was. Better still, get a photostat of the letter. Whatever you think looks relevant."

Higgins looked at his own watch. He'd be pushing it to do the hundred or so miles before the council closed. He'd better call the planning officer again and see if he could sweet talk her into staying until he got there. Better still, he'd get Sutton to do the call. Higgins guessed the planning officer was a 'lady of a certain age', so she might respond better to a younger man's charm.

"And whilst you're at it," Ambrose carried on. "Find out whether the Walters knew they'd been unsuccesful again."

Nodding, Higgins added, "Miss Collier's waiting. Do you want me to bring her in?"

"Yes please. Then sort out your route while we see her."

Barbara was very quiet as she sat down. As soon as the usual formalities were over, Winters glanced at Ambrose, who nodded his agreement.

"We think you might have killed Mrs Chapman," Winters began bluntly. "Did you?"

For a few seconds Barbara seemed to be holding her breath. Then she spoke clearly and firmly. "No," she replied.

"You could have killed her and pretended to have found the body," Winters persisted.

"I'm a nurse," Barbara pointed out. "I would never kill anyone, and certainly not Angie."

"We've heard she'd been quite unpleasant to you," Ambrose remarked.

Flushing slightly, Barbara nodded. "I don't know why," she admitted, "except that she wasn't herself somehow. I was upset, but it had happened before and Angie always apologised. I knew she would again."

"And you put up with it?" Winters asked.

"I understood," Barbara replied, turning towards him. She sighed. "Angie gets, sorry got, depressed sometimes," she added, "but when she was happy she was good company, and I was always grateful to her."

"Why?" Ambrose prompted.

"When I moved to Chalk Heath Hospital I knew no one. Angela was a patient on my ward. She'd had some minor surgery. We got talking about singing, and she told me Calzone were auditioning." Smiling with remembered pleasure, Barbara paused. "Angie and I became good friends," she added. "We often went to concerts or the theatre together." The smile faded, to be replaced by an expression of deep and abiding loss. "I shall miss her," she added simply.

Ambrose glanced across the table. He could see the certainty leaving Sam Winters' expression. Either the woman was a very good actor or she was genuinely grieving. He tried a different approach. "Where were you between eleven this morning, and when you found Mrs Chapman's body?" he asked.

"I told you everything when you first arrived, Inspector," Barbara reminded him. "I'm not sure what more I can tell you. I took my shopping up to my room, and then had a walk in the gardens. It was cold, so I came back in."

"What time was that?"

"I couldn't say. I didn't look at my watch. After that, I sat in the library reading the newspapers. I phoned Anne, our pianist, at about eleven thirty. She'd asked me to let her know how the concert went. I forgot yesterday."

"Which phone did you use?"

"The public one in the reception. I was in the lounge by noon. I'm certain of that. Evelyn had told us off for being late for meals, and I wanted to be sure I was on time. Several of the others joined me in the lounge. When the gong sounded we all went into the dining room. Angie wasn't there, so after about ten minutes I went to find her. The rest you know."

"Can you be more specific about when you were in the garden?" Winters asked.

"It wasn't long. I heard the coach leave the hotel and go up the lane. I came inside about five minutes later. Harry might know what time he left here."

"We'll check with him," Ambrose assured her.

"Can I go now? I'm finding this very distressing."

There was no point in keeping Barbara any longer this time, Ambrose decided. Nodding, he let her go. Holding onto her chair for a few seconds as she rose, she left the library, staring ahead of her and walking very straight.

As soon as she had gone, Ambrose and Winters were both struck by the same thought. "The coach driver!" Winters exclaimed.

"Exactly," Ambrose nodded. "We need to find out where Harry's staying. And if he can account for his movements."

"As far as I can tell, he's not even set foot in the hotel, at least not officially," Winters replied. "I don't think the Tempests extended their hospitality to the choir's driver."

"That doesn't mean he didn't come in the back door when no one was looking," Ambrose pointed out. He wondered just how close Harry and Angela had been, remembering Jackie Walters' barbed comment after the accident.

He paused, thinking about who to send to interview the driver. Normally he would never have sent a WPC on her own to interview a suspect. His superiors would think it a very strange thing to do. He would probably have a hard job justifying his decision later. But Meadows was bright, and someone needed to see Harry's reaction before he had chance to learn of Angela's death from the press.

"Tell Meadows to cycle round and see if Harry's at his digs," he instructed.

"Meadows?" Winters asked in surprise.

"Yes," Ambrose replied. "Mrs Tempest will have the address. We need to know whether he has an alibi. Tell Meadows to find out everything she can about him: where he was this morning, whether he knew Mrs Chapman before, that sort of thing, and then report back to us as quickly as she can."

"With respect sir," Winters said quietly, "is that wise? You've just had to give the girl a rollicking for being too close. If 'Top Brass' find out you were interviewing her as a suspect less than half an hour ago and you're now sending her alone to meet a potential suspect…"

Winters didn't need to finish.

"I only gave some friendly advice," Ambrose pointed out, "and she could just as easily have said I was too close. I'm on the committee that invited the choir and I went to both their concerts. Even Sutton's linked through his wife, although I admit that's a bit better than being directly involved. Fortunately neither Meadows nor Kathy Sutton accepted any payment or gift from them, and I certainly didn't. If we had, you'd have had to take the case over until someone from outside stepped in. We've been down that route before. It's not pleasant."

"No," Winters agreed.

Ambrose sighed. He knew Winters was right.

"We need to show we investigated everything with the upmost speed. Ok, let's send PC Sutton to interview the driver," he sighed.

"What about the suspects?" Winters asked. "Sutton is looking after them in the dining room." He didn't need to spell out that Sutton was really on guard duty.

"Meadows will have to take over," Ambrose said. He hadn't wanted to put her in conflict with the choir, but he was running out of options.

Chapter Seventeen

Pausing at the door, WPC Meadows held her breath. She hadn't felt this scared since taking her police entry exam. Snatches of *The Messiah* kept going through her head. Usually music calmed her but this time it wasn't working.

It seemed ages since she'd sat at the front of the Town Hall, with Barbara and Evelyn, Anton turning round to joke. Now she'd be their jailor or, at least, their minder. She would have given anything to be somewhere else.

Hesitating was only going to make her feel worse. "Do your duty," she told herself firmly. Adopting a manner she hoped was calm and professional, Meadows tapped on the dining room door.

Sutton answered. "I've been sent to relieve you," Meadows explained. "DS Winters wants you." She could hear a flutter of surprise as those near the door recognised her voice.

"Certainly," Sutton replied, opening the door wider. "Do they know?" he mouthed, inclining his head towards the choir.

"No," Meadows mouthed back.

"Good luck!" Sutton whispered. For a second he hesitated. "Shall I introduce you?" he asked.

"Please," Meadows had always liked Greg Sutton. She could see why Kathy had married him. Few of her colleagues would have appreciated how difficult Meadows' position had become, much less tried to ease it for her.

"I think you've met WPC Meadows," Sutton said, turning back into the room. "You may not have known that, as well as being a fine singer, she's a policewoman. She's going to take over from me for a while." As he walked out, he could feel the tension building behind him. He was glad to be making a speedy getaway.

Sutton borrowed Meadows' bike to get to the driver's digs. The drive was slippy. He had to put his foot down to steady himself at the hotel gates. Car headlights appeared in the gloom coming down the road towards him, then passed by. Sleet stung his face as he waited. "What a day!" he thought with a sigh. He wondered whether Kathy had heard the news yet.

Pushing hard against the gravel, he set off again, around the wide curve of the lane. He knew the path to St George's estate, having used it as a short cut a few times, but only in summer. In the gathering gloom it was hard to spot, set between overgrown hedges. On either side he saw allotments, with greenhouses and sheds looming. Further ahead, a metal bollard marked the beginning of the estate.

Though everyone still referred to it as 'the new estate', most of the houses had been built in the 1930s. The streets spread right up to the edge of the allotments. It was an uninviting route from the hotel, narrow and twisty, but it was so much quicker than going through town. Sutton remembered reports of a'flasher' along the passageway. However, one of the local girls had whacked the culprit hard with her satchel, in a sensitive part of his anatomy, and he hadn't been seen since.

On such a damp afternoon, the few people he met were hurrying to get home. The whole estate felt dreary. The houses were a decent size with large gardens, but since the war the estate had begun to develop an air of neglect. The privet hedges were straggly and overgrown, the verges churned up by parked cars.

Harry the coachdriver was staying at a B&B near St George's church. To reach it, Sutton had to follow the passageways through a bewildering series of cul-de-sacs. Fortunately he knew the area well from his beat.

As he approached the original St George's area, the street suddenly widened. A few Victorian houses had survived opposite the church. Taller and larger, with terracotta decoration around the windows, they were from a bygone age. A nice looking pub, 'The Brigadier', looked very inviting. At the end of the row, a parked coach was almost blocking the street. Sutton smiled with relief; he'd clearly found the right place.

A sign swung in the front garden: "George's Place Bed & Breakfast" it announced. Underneath was painted 'Good home cooking and comfortable beds'.

"Sounds good to me," Sutton said wryly, thinking again of Kathy, as he rang the bell.

Through the door's glass panel he could see a figure coming down the stairs. The woman paused, peering through the peep hole at Sutton. Seeing the uniform, she opened the door a crack. "What is it?" the woman asked in a hoarse whisper. "Not trouble I hope." She inclined her head, as if she didn't want guests in the lounge to hear.

"Can I come in?" Sutton replied softly. He wasn't looking forward to breaking the news to Harry, or to having to question him.

Reluctantly the woman led him down the hall and into a kitchen at the back of the house. It smelt of sausage and chips. "My guests are all properly signed in," she said immediately she shut the door, "and they've all paid in advance."

"Is Mr Harry Urwin staying here?" Sutton asked.

"Yes. Don't tell me he's been speeding. That old chara couldn't get above forty."

"No. It's nothing to do with his driving," Sutton assured her. "I need to talk to him about something else."

"He's in the lounge, having a cup of tea."

The landlady led Sutton back up the hall and into the front room. "A policeman to see you," she announced as Harry looked up in surprise. "What have you been doing, you naughty man?" Her tone suggested they were on good terms.

"Nothing I know of, Gladys," Harry replied. "Is it about that accident on the way here?"

"No," Sutton assured him. He glanced towards the landlady who was hovering beside them. "I need to speak to Mr Urwin in private," he said. The murder at The Shalimar would be all over the Chalk Heath papers soon enough, without having an interfering landlady to spread the story.

With a little 'humph', Gladys turned and went out of the room, closing the door with a ill-tempered bang. She would probably listen from the hallway Sutton guessed. Walking quietly to the door, he snatched it open, nearly pulling the woman back into the room as he did so. "I asked to speak in private," Sutton reminded her.

Scarlet with embarassment, the landlady stalked back along the corridor.

Harry laughed out loud. "She is a bit of a nosy bugger," he agreed. "Looks after you well though." He indicated the tea tray in front of him. "Shall I ask her to bring an extra cup?"

Sutton shook his head. "Thanks anyway." He sat opposite the driver, lowering his voice in case the landlady had returned. "I'm afraid I have some bad news for you," he began, "and you need to keep it to yourself."

In bewilderment Harry looked up from his tea. "Is it about that young driver?" he asked. "Didn't he make it?"

"No. It's nothing to do with him. I think he's alright. I heard them talking at the 'Station. He'll be in hospital a while, but he'll make it."

"That's good news," Harry replied, and sounded genuinely relieved. "He wouldn't have done but for your inspector and Miss Barbara. Lucky we had a nurse on the scene."

Sutton nodded. He was finding it very difficult to break the news. "It's to do with Mrs Chapman," he managed to say. "I'm afraid she's died."

In disbelief Harry stared at him. "Angela's dead?" he asked.

Once again, Sutton nodded.

"Nah! She can't have died," Harry insisted. "She was fine this morning. Showed me the presents she'd bought for her nieces. Real pleased she was. They've got a lovely doll's house she said. Her brother made it for them..." Seeing Sutton's expression, Harry's voice tailed off, leaving a stricken silence.

"You were fond of her, weren't you?" Sutton asked.

"I've known her for years," Harry replied. "What happened? Did she get run over on that lane? It's a nasty bend."

There was no kind or easy way of saying it. "She was stabbed with a pair of scissors," Sutton said bluntly.

"Good God!" Harry swore. "No! Who could have done such a thing? Oh my God! Not Angie!"

"Shush!" Sutton reminded him. "Your landlady's probably listening again. It'll be better if the press don't get hold of it yet. I've been sent to ask what time you left the hotel this morning after the shopping trip. And also where you were between then and twelve fifteen."

Seeing his hororr, he added quickly, "We're asking everybody. Not just you."

It took Harry a little while to answer, but Sutton didn't think he was trying to frame a lie. The driver seemed genuinely shocked. Giving him time to regain his composure, Sutton got out his notebook and pretended to read the previous page.

"I dropped the choir off around eleven after their shopping trip and then brought the bus back here," Harry said finally. "I think I left about ten past eleven. Then I worked on the bus. The engine wasn't sounding right, so I had a cup of coffee with Gladys, I mean Mrs Locke, and went out to tinker with it. The fuel pipe was leaking a bit, so I mended that and cleaned the plugs, generally gave her a once over. After that I had me lunch here."

"What time was that?" Sutton asked, writing the details down as fast as he could. He would have to transcribe it quickly afterwards to make sure he could still read his own handwriting.

"Gladys'll know. I remember I was perishing: must have been out there working for a good hour."

"So you were eating your lunch from maybe quarter to one?" Sutton asked.

"No, later. I went upstairs to have a wash, then Gladys had to serve up. She cooked the chips fresh for me. I wouldn't have started till twenty past. I haven't long finished eating, just long enough to read the paper and have a cup of tea. I was having a real nice time till you came"

"Will people be able to confirm you were working on the coach?" Sutton asked.

"Gladys'll have seen me. And the neighbours. One of them came out to chat: an old chap who used to be a driver himself. We poked around the engine a bit together." Once again, Harry lapsed into silence.

"Driver sounds like he's in the clear," Sutton wrote quickly in his notebook. "Though we'll have to check out the neighbours." He was glad. He rather liked the man.

Looking up, he nodded encouragingly. "You said you'd known Mrs Chapman for years," he observed. "How was that?"

"We lived on the same street. She and me kid sister were pals; used to be in and out of each others' houses, giggling and clomping around in their Mam's high heels like girls do." Smiling at the memory, Harry paused. "Angie was different though," he added. "She'd only got to hear a song on the radio and she'd be singing it. If she didn't know the words, she'd sing 'la' instead. Tunes stuck with her. She learnt piano too."

"Did she have lessons then?" Sutton asked, thinking of Kathy's 'young ladies'.

"Nah. Couldn't afford it. None of us could. A lady down the road had an old upright and Angie taught herself on that, till in the end she got given it. Then she learnt the accordion and used to entertain down the pub when she wasn't even old enough to be in there. She once told me it was the only thing she ever really wanted to do: sing and make music…"

Harry's voice broke as he spoke and he paused. "Angie never had much luck," he added. "When she got the chance of a scholarship, she was ill. Then the war broke out.

"None of us managed much schooling after '39," Harry continued, "but Angie was determined. She might have made it." Once again Harry sighed. "I can't believe she's dead, let alone that someone'd kill her."

"Did she have any enemies?" Sutton asked.

"I wouldn't know nowadays. We'd pretty much lost touch. She married a chap in the navy. I didn't see her around after that. Me sister saw her occasionally, went to her shows, but you know how it is."

Sutton nodded sympathetically. He wanted to say, "You were half in love with her yourself, weren't you?" but decided that would be too intrusive. "So you got a surprise when you found she was in your coach party this week?" he asked instead.

"Actually, I knew she was one of the choir but it was a bit awkward at first. She didn't seem to want to know me; as if I was a bit beneath her. Then it wore off and she was more like her old self." Thoughtfully Harry finished his tea. "She had got a bit 'uppetty'," he admitted. "She knew she was their star and wanted things her way. But it was more than that. She seemed well….like something was on her mind."

"Oh?" Sutton asked, interested.

Staring ahead of him again, Harry nodded. "Yes. She didn't tell me what it was, but I reckon it happened while they were at their first place, Leyton Bridge. Their shows there didn't go too well, what with not having their usual pianist, and they all got snappy with each other. It was like driving a school party: yap, yap, niggle, niggle. But I reckon something personal was worrying her too."

"If you remember anything about what that might be, give us a ring at the 'Station," Sutton asked, getting up. "You've been very helpful. We'd be really grateful if you didn't say anything about what's happened until we can make a proper statement. You know what the press are like."

"Yeah, they can be you-know-what's," Harry agreed. "I suppose the tour will be cancelled and I'll have to drive them back early." He let out his breath in a long rueful sigh. "That's not going to be a fun trip is it?"

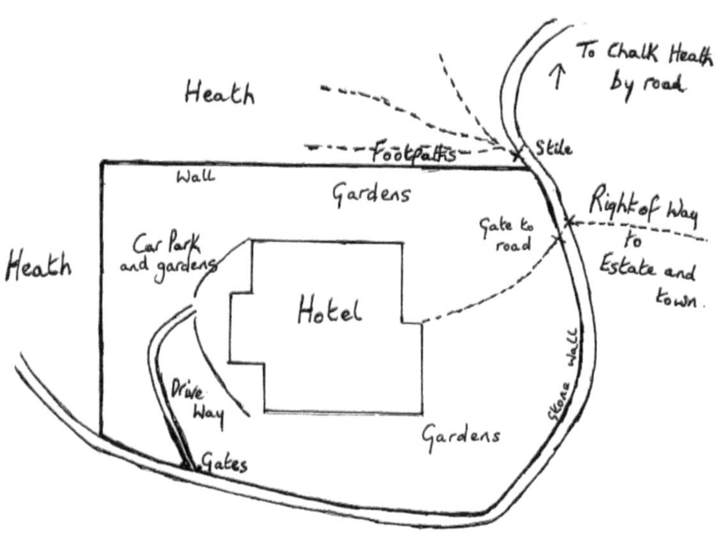

The Shalimar Hotel and grounds

Chapter Eighteen

Holding herself very erect, Meadows walked into the dining room. The hotel staff had been allowed to go about their business, but all the choir members were sitting at the tables where they'd eaten lunch. Though the plates had been cleared, the room smelt of stale food. They'd been given another cup of tea, but there was little other comfort. The fire was dying for lack of attention and a dank chill was settling in. Everyone looked tired, their faces strained by grief and shock.

Anton was the first to break the silence. "So you were bloody well snooping the whole time!" he shouted.

"Well I'll be!" Wynn began but couldn't find the right words. Turning to Meadows, he shook his head.

Anton was going red with anger. "We don't like people spying on us," he shouted, "especially the bloody police!"

"We wouldn't have invited you if we'd known," Wynn said through tight lips.

"We certainly wouldn't!" Jackie snapped. She was clearly upset. "You deceived us!" she accused. "We welcomed you as a friend and all the while you were lying to us us."

"I'm sorry you had to find out in such awful circumstances," Meadows apologised, "but I didn't lie to you. Besides, none of us could have predicted what's happened."

"Unless one of you knows more than you're letting on," she wanted to add but sighed instead. It would be better if she appeared to be on their side, as in some ways she was, she admitted. It just mustn't cloud her professional judgement.

"Sorry?" Anton spluttered. "You are as bad as the KGB." His mouth was setting into a hard line and he clenched his fist against the table. Of all the choir, he seemed to be taking the news worst. Meadows wondered whether his anger was greater because he'd thought her an easy conquest. Perhaps he was even attracted to her. She hadn't really paid attention at the time, but if he had fancied her, he must be feeling a fool now. And feeling foolish could make people very difficult.

"I wasn't spying on you," Meadows replied gently. "I joined you because Mrs Sutton said you needed a singer. That's all."

Wynn was angry too, though in a quieter, more controlled manner. "You should have told us what you did," he insisted.

"Why? How would my job make me a better, or a poorer, singer?" Meadows asked. "What mattered was whether I could hold my part and had a decent voice."

"I suppose she has a point," John admitted. "What any of us does outside the choir isn't relevant, is it?"

In surprise the others looked at him. They weren't used to him expressing an opinion.

"Well, I still think she should have told us what her job was," Jackie insisted.

"So do I," her husband agreed. "Not that any of us have anything to be afraid of," he added hastily. Meadows noticed that as he spoke, he glanced in Wynn's direction. Flushing slightly, Wynn looked away.

Dennis hurried on, turning back towards Meadows. "I'm sure none of us have ever had any trouble with the police," he continued, "but it's a matter of trust. We trusted you."

"And you don't trust the police?" Meadows asked. "Perhaps you've had some bad experiences at home. I'm sorry if that's the case. Otherwise it suggests you have something to hide." She glanced towards Anton as she spoke.

Anton let out a great snort of annoyance. "Don't you start lecturing me, girl!" he snapped. "You were very happy to flirt with me at the rehearsal."

Holding herself a little straighter, Meadows turned towards him. "I did *not* flirt with you. And don't call me, 'girl'," she ordered icily. "In England, insulting the police is an offence."

"She's right," Wynn warned Anton softly. "Go easy." Anton was about to say more, but thought better of it.

After that, everyone sat uncomfortably, talking occasionally to each other but avoiding eye contact with Meadows. It was as if they had 'sent her to Coventry', Meadows thought sadly, as the girls used to call it when she was at school. Sighing, she sat down on one of the spare chairs.

For almost ten minutes there was a painful quiet, broken only by muttered comments and the hum of the occasional car on the lane, or voices from the kitchen. Jackie began to cough and needed a glass of water from the jug on the serving table, but still no one spoke to Meadows.

Finally Meadows got up. "It's getting cold in here," she remarked. Looking round for a poker, she found a set of fire irons behind the coalscuttle and gave the fire a stir. There was a bell rope near the mantelpiece, so she tried giving it a pull. Almost at once Libby appeared, flustered but willing.

"Could you bring us some more coal?" Meadows asked her. "Please. And close the curtains too. You'll know how they work better than me."

Within minutes, the room was becoming warmer and more comfortable. "Thank you," Wynn muttered. "I suppose we are being rather silly. You're only doing your job."

"Get up and stretch a bit if you want," Meadows invited. "You must be getting cramped sitting all the time. The chairs aren't very comfortable."

Though Anton still glowered, there was a general movement as the others got up to straighten backs or rub aching necks.

"How much longer will we be kept in here?" John asked as he sat down again.

"Until the inspector has spoken to you all. It shouldn't be much longer," Meadows assured him. She tried to sound cheerful and friendly. "I know it's horrible waiting, but one of you might remember something. We need your help to find who did this dreadful thing."

"Is it possible that Angie killed herself?" Wynn suggested, almost to himself. "She often used to get depressed and she'd begun to fear she'd never make it. She wasn't so young as she was, if you see what I mean." He turned to Meadows. "Could it have been suicide?" he asked her.

"I've no idea," Meadows replied carefully. "I'm just the 'gofer'. The inspector will explore every possibility. He's very thorough."

Jackie frowned. "It could have been," she agreed thoughtfully. "I don't know…" Pausing, she tried to explain her idea. "I'm sure Angie was worried about something," she said. "She seemed distant, like she was distracted but so good she could keep going. You know what I mean? Her heart wasn't really in the music."

"I noticed a change too," Evelyn agreed. "Perhaps she'd had some bad news from home. She seemed quite happy when we left Uttley."

"Maybe she met someone at Leyton Bridge and they followed her here?" Dennis suggested. "Do you think that's a possibility?" Turning to Meadows, he frowned in appeal.

"I honestly don't know," Meadows replied. "Tell the inspector what you noticed. It might be important."

"A clue!" Jackie agreed. "Maybe someone said or did something that frightened her."

Barbara nodded. "Perhaps that was why she was being so difficult," she suggested. "I'd have said it was more like she felt bad about something though. Not that she was frightened."

Until then, Barbara had been silent and people turned towards her now with interest. Meadows noticed that Dennis glanced towards Wynn though. "Curious!" she thought. "He suspects something about Wynn."

"Well you knew her best," Evelyn acknowledged. "I wonder what on earth could have worried her? We didn't do too badly at Leyton Bridge, even if it wasn't our best."

Once again there was a pause. Much of the anger had eased, but Meadows could still feel Anton's resentment. She decided to say nothing about Barbara's visit to the Police Station in case it caused trouble for her. The others would probably think Barbara disloyal for not telling them. Unexpectedly, however, Barbara admitted it herself.

"I knew Pauline was in the Police," she said quietly.

"You knew?" Dennis demanded. "Why didn't you tell us?"

"Because I was afraid some of you would be difficult over it. And as John said, it wasn't relevant. Pauline was doing us a favour. We would have had to cancel the tour if she hadn't joined us."

"It might have been better if we had," Evelyn said wearily. "Then we would have been spared all this trouble, and Angela would still be alive."

Her reminder sobered them all. "Poor Angie!" Jackie said and blew her nose.

There was a minute or two's silence. "How did you know?" Evelyn asked Barbara finally.

"I went to the Police Station, to report my necklace stolen. Pauline was on duty. She was very kind to me. I was upset. I thought someone had been into my room to steal it."

"You should have at least told me," Evelyn complained.

"Why? What difference would it have made?" Barbara asked her. "You're all making it sound like we have something to hide."

"I agree," John said loudly. "What any of us do outside the choir is no one else's business."

His sharpness surprised everyone. Meadows made a mental note to tell DI Ambrose about the exchange. With the obvious tension between Wynn and Dennis, she was picking up quite a lot of useful information by just sitting there listening.

"Let's not turn on each other," Evelyn pleaded. "If we're to get through this awful day we've got to stick together."

There was a knock on the door. Meadows answered it. DS Winters stepped briefly into the room. "Can we have Mr Pedderson now?" he asked. He raised an eyebrow at Meadows, as if to ask "How's it going?" but said nothing more.

Looking defiant, John Pedderson got up, then followed DS Winters out of the room. As he left, Jackie lent towards her husband.

"Do you think John killed Angie?" Jackie suddenly demanded.

"What on earth makes you think that?" Dennis said in surprise.

"I don't know. I don't know what to think," Jackie's words choked in her throat. "I just think John *could* have killed Angie."

Sitting up, she found the others all looking at her in horror. "I overheard Angela teasing him. It was during the interval at the theatre. She was probably just being Angie, not thinking. But whatever it was, it upset John. He was pleading with her not to tell the rest of us. That could be a motive, couldn't it?"

"John wouldn't kill anyone," Barbara said firmly.

"He isn't as meek as he pretends," Jackie insisted. "He's really, *really* fit. None of us could have run up to that farm so quickly."

Evelyn sat up straighter, taking control. "John wouldn't hurt anyone in this choir," she said firmly. "Calzone matters too much to him. He'd been applying to join for over a year and he wanted every concert to be a success. Whatever Angie was teasing him about it was just that: teasing. Don't let the Police divide us against each other. She'll be noting everything we say."

Meaningfully she nodded in Meadows' direction.

"Bloody woman!" Anton muttered.

Beginning to cry, Jackie leant forwards on the table and put her head on her hands. "I'm so frightened," she said, her voice muffled.

Awkwardly her husband put his arm round her shoulders. "We all are," he admitted.

Chapter Nineteen

PC Higgins was in a hurry. Which obviously meant everything conspired to slow him down: delivery boys on bicycles, men on mopeds, even a small pony pulling a cart. They were all in front of him, going as slowly as they could.

The route to Uttley took Higgins through several small towns, each busier than the last. Even when he was driving through the countryside he found himself behind milk lorries or coalmen on their rounds. By now the weather was thoroughly miserable. He prayed it wouldn't actually snow.

The woman at the Planning Department had promised to stay until six, after Sutton had sweet-talked her for nearly ten minutes. Higgins watched as the clock on the dashboard ticked remorselessly. He hoped he wasn't driving a hundred miles for nothing. His visit hardly counted as an emergency so he'd been reluctant to turn on the alarm. As five o'clock approached, however, he decided it was the only way he would get to Uttley in time.

As soon as the bell sounded, the traffic opened up. Even then, there were times when drivers had difficulty getting out of the patrol car's way. Finally, at twenty past five, Higgins passed a road sign announcing '*Uttley – where the world's best boxes are made.*' It seemed an odd claim to fame, but he was very relieved to see it.

The streets became narrower and greyer, the houses packed closer. There was a faintly acrid smell on the air, like bleach. A couple of chimneys were probably the cuplrits, Higgins decided. The words 'Beejay Chemicals' painted on one confirmed that Uttley made more than just boxes. There were also engineering sheds and what looked like a clothing factory. The whole town seemed grey and industrial.

Higgins looked through the sleet at the darkening evening and was glad he didn't have to live there.

Fortunately it didn't take long to find his destination. Miss Fletcher's directions had been clear and concise. Higgins spotted the council offices immediately. Only a town hall would flaunt such elaborate porticos. Parking his car round the back as he'd been instructed, Higgins walked round to the front door. It was locked. Urgently he rapped on the glass, peering in. All he could see was a large foyer with doors opening off it. There was no sign of Miss Fletcher.

At his third attempt a figure appeared inside the building. "We're closed!" the man mouthed. Then he saw Higgins' uniform. Taking a bundle of keys from his pocket, the caretaker started down the corridor. "What time's this then?" he grumbled, his words sounding faintly through the glass doors.

He was still grumbling as he let Higgins into the building. "You're late," he complained. "I was told you'd be here for five."

"Who told you that?" Higgins asked sharply. "What did you expect me to do? Fly?" He was tired and didn't take kindly to the caretaker's manner.

"Keep your hair on," the man replied. "You're here to see Miss Fletcher aren't you? I'll give her a ring."

There was more delay while the caretaker found his way round an internal switchboard, "I don't usually do this," he explained, needlessly. "But the girls have gone home." Finally he found the right number and spoke to Miss Fletcher. "She'll see you now," he said afterwards. "I'll have to take you up."

Leading the way to an old-fashioned lift, the caretaker slid the brass doors back and let them both in. "Planning's on floor three, room 365," he explained. "Miss Fletcher's waiting there. Bit of a dragon," he added by way of a warning. "Doesn't suffer fools lightly."

The old lift shuddered alarmingly, and rose to floor three. Even there, the caretaker insisted on accompanying Higgins.

As they walked together Higgins understood why. He would have got lost on his own. They seemed to go almost the full circuit of the building, and then suddenly dive off down a corridor. Room 365 was at the far end.

"Ah, PC Higgins!" Miss Fletcher said as soon as she opened the door. "I was beginning to think you'd be too late. You can go now, Galsworthy. I'll ring for you to escort the officer back down."

Briskly, she showed Higgins into the room. "No one's allowed in after six," she explained. "Unless there's a council meeting. We can work late, I often do, but once we're out we can't come back. Rules are rules."

"Thank you for seeing me," Higgins began with what he hoped was a winning smile.

Miss Fletcher was immune to smiles. "Only doing my duty," she replied. "Your colleague said you wanted to see the paperwork for number 56, Wellington Street." She indicated a table on which were spread various plans and letters. "Bit of a saga," she added with a disapproving sniff. "Why some people can't make up their minds I don't know."

Higgins began to look at the plans on the table but found them hard to decipher. They seemed to show three different versions of a proposed extension to a pre-war detached house. On the first, the garage had been removed and replaced with a two-storey wing which included a lounge, bedroom and bathroom. This was cut back on the second proposal to a bedroom and bathroom above the garage. The third and latest plan had the garage itself turned into a bed-sitting room with a small bathroom and toilet added at the end.

"They must have spent a lot getting all these plans done," Higgins commented.

"The neighbours objected," Miss Fletcher said briefly. Her manner suggested she didn't discuss other people's business. Higgins began to see what the caretaker had meant.

Sighing inwardly, Higgins smiled again. "I see," he agreed, though he wasn't sure he did. Hoping for clarification, he began to read the letters.

"You haven't time to go through the whole lot," Miss Fletcher snapped. "I thought you were only interested in Mrs Chapman. I've already sorted her letters out." She pointed to a separate bundle.

"Thank you," Higgins said politely. He wondered whether the woman could boil water with her breath. Trying to concentrate, he examined the letters.

As the Walters' immediate next-door neighbour, Angela Chapman had objected forcibly to the first set of plans, arguing that such a large extension would lower the value of her property. She had then signed a petition organised by one of the other neighbours against the second plan. The third, much smaller extension had been more acceptable to her. She had objected, almost routinely Higgins felt, but had later withdrawn her objection so long as no windows overlooked her garden. He was about to read the next letter when Miss Fletcher looked pointedly at her watch.

"What's it all about?" she demanded. "Why would you drive all the way from Chalk Heath to see that lot?" She nodded towards the plans.

Higgins was becoming increasingly irritated. He never knew how to deal with such women: women who'd held responsible jobs during the war and weren't going to go back to being meek and feminine now. When he was young, a man knew what was expected of him: to be a breadwinner and support a wife and family at home. Now women like Miss Fletcher could buy far more bread than he ever could.

"You said we needed to see the paperwork in person," Higgins reminded her.

"I don't send confidential material by post," Miss Fletcher replied. "Not without a warrant."

Higgins had had enough. "Mrs Chapman has been murdered," he said bluntly.

For a moment Miss Fletcher stared at him. Then she sat down at her desk. "I see," she said quietly. "And arguments like these could be the reason. Why didn't you say so?"

"It wasn't a pleasant thing to have to tell you," Higgins said. "I hoped I could avoid it."

"And you think a woman can only cope with pleasant things?"

Higgins flushed. "No, of course not." He felt a fool.

"Officer, I can assure you I am no wilting violet," Miss Fletcher said firmly. "If you'd told me straight away, we'd both have saved time." Taking a letter from the top of the pile, she passed it to Higgins. "I'm casting no aspersions, but this must have annoyed the Walters a lot. Last week Mrs Chapman changed her mind. We might well have ignored her. The new plans were within our guidelines. But a late objection from a next-door neighbour would have caused a delay. And judging by their appeals, Mrs Walters is getting desperate to move her mother in with them. The old lady is very demanding, and lives the other side of town."

By now Higgins was interested. He read Angela Chapman's last letter for himself. It was well argued. She was worried about a precedent being set if her neighbours had elderly relatives living in their garages, as well as the increased number of cars that would be parked in the road.

"Could I have a photostat of this?" Higgins asked. "And of the Walters' appeal?"

"I can do better than that. We have a new Xerox machine downstairs. I have the key. I'll copy a couple of other things too, if you want. Not too many. It's expensive."

"Xerox?" Higgins asked, impressed. "I've never actually seen one."

"Your 'Station is behind the times," Miss Fletcher said, and actually smiled. "Come down with me and see how it works. I can't leave you here alone in any case. Too much confidential material around."

Higgins was beginning to revise his opinion of the woman. She might be a dragon, but she could be a helpful one. As they walked down the stairs they began to talk of Christmas and whether it would snow that night. "I don't trust that old lift," Miss Fletcher admitted. "I got stuck in it once. It took me half an hour to make anyone hear. Needless to say, the phone inside didn't work." She shuddered slightly at the memory.

"Different budgets I suppose," Higgins suggested.

"Exactly. You can buy fancy new Xerox machines, that's capital expenditure, but you can't mend them if they go wrong. Nothing's allowed for maintenance. Heaven help us if we have another war! There'll be smart new tanks with their wheels off."

Higgins laughed. They reached the copy room chatting amicably about the strange ways of Councils and Police Commissioners. The room was full of smart new equipment with instructions in bold letters pasted on the wall. "Remember to switch off!" one notice said in red, underlined three times. "It's all very well having the equipment but sometimes it's the people that need replacing," Miss Fletched joked as she Xeroxed the three sets of plans and Angela's letters. Afterwards she invited, "Why don't you have a go yourself? You'll be able to show off when your lot get round to buying one."

Hesitantly Higgins followed her instructions and when a perfect copy emerged, felt quite proud of his efforts. "I'll tell the sarge about this," he promised, "and see if he'll put in for one. We might get it by next Christmas!"

With the copies folded neatly into a large manila envelope, he followed Miss Fletcher out of the copy room. She guided him through to the foyer and the caretaker let him out.

Though he was longing to head off home, Higgins had two more tasks to do in Uttley. DI Ambrose had asked him to call at Uttley Police Station. It would be wise to let the local CID know that he was making enquiries in their town. They would understandably resent him 'muscling in' on their patch, unannounced. Ambrose had already phoned to let them know what was happening.

The sergeant at the desk was expecting Higgins but he looked at him quizzically for a moment. "Don't I know you?" he asked, frowning.

For a few moments the two men tried to recall where they'd met before. "Bill Pollark," the sergeant said, offering his hand.

Still neither could place the other. Then suddenly both burst out laughing. "Jenners Park, 1938," Higgins recalled.

"Of course! Then I joined the Met."

"And I managed to get back to Chalk Heath."

Shaking Sergeant Pollark's hand, Higgins was genuinely pleased to meet him again. Bill Pollark was a sensible bloke.

After that everything became a lot easier. Over cups of orange coloured tea, the two men swapped memories. "You've done better than me," Higgins admitted philosophically. "I never could say the right things."

"Too bloody outspoken!" Sergeant Pollark joked.

"To be honest, I'm perfectly happy as I am," Higgins admitted. "I'd rather be on the beat than doing paperwork. I never could spell." He glanced around the 'Station reception area. The walls were yellowed by decades of city smoke.

"To each his own," Pollark agreed.

Finally Higgins looked at the clock on the wall. "I'd better go," he said reluctantly. "I need to talk to the choir's pianist while I'm here.

She may know something. I'll have to break the news in any case." He took out his notebook. "Mrs Anne Jacobs, 87, All Saints Lane. Can you direct me?"

"Better still, I'll send a young rookie with you," Sergeant Pollark offered.

"Kendrick!" he called. "Drive Constable Higgins to All Saints Lane would you? You can leave your car here," he added, turning back to Higgins.

So, instead of having to hunt around a strange town in the dark, Higgins was taken straight to Anne Jacobs' home. All Saints Lane was in a better part of Uttley, the streets wider and tree lined. Mrs Jacobs should be expecting him. Sergeant Pollark had rung her before Higgins and Kendrick left. With PC Kendrick beside him, Higgins waited in the dark as footsteps sounded along the hallway.

A plump young woman opened the door. Rather than inviting them in, she held the door ajar and peered out. "Have you had the measles?" she asked.

In surprise the two police officers looked at each other. "I have," Kendrick recalled.

"I had most things when I was a nipper," Higgins replied. "Why?"

"I've got three kiddies covered in spots," Mrs Jacobs explained. She smiled ruefully. From upstairs came the sound of a child grizzling. "My husband's with them at the moment. You're welcome to come in if you don't mind."

"We'll risk it," Higgins agreed.

"What's it about?" Anne Jacobs asked, leading the way into the front room. A piano and stool almost filled the far side and there was music scattered on some of the chairs. Anne cleared it into stacks on the floor. "Sorry about the mess," she apologised. "I see my pupils in here." As neither of the policemen had answered her, she looked up in concern. "Is there something wrong?" she asked.

After his visit to Miss Fletcher, Higgins decided not to waste time trying to be tactful. "I'm afraid I have some bad news," he said. "You'd better sit down."

An expression of alarm came to Anne's face and she sat down hurriedly on the piano stool. "Do sit down too," she begged. "Don't tower over me while you give me bad news. Is it about the accident?

I was so cross when I saw that rickety old chara. I've already written asking for some money back."

Sitting down, Higgins sighed. He hated having to announce such awful news to a pleasant, likeable woman. "It's nothing to do with the accident," he said. "I'm afraid Mrs Chapman has died."

"Oh!!" Wide eyed, Anne stared at him in surprise. She had been a very pretty woman, Higgins reflected, before marriage, children and too much weight took the edge off. Even now her eyes were beautiful, filling with tears and very bright. "No! Not Angie!" she said softly.

He let her cry for a bit. Though he might not be much of a hand at paperwork, Higgins was good with people. He knew when to stay quiet. PC Kendrick wisely took his cue from him.

Finally Anne looked up, and blew her nose. "I'm sorry," she apologised. "But I was very fond of Angie, Mrs Chapman. What happened? And why have you come to tell me? Surely Kathy could have rung me? "

"You mean Mrs Sutton?" Higgins asked.

"Yes. We arranged this week together. What's happened?" Her eyes snapped open wide again. "Was she attacked?"

"I'm afraid so," Higgins replied. Her question began to seem strange to him. "Why did you think she might have been?" he asked.

"Policemen don't come when everything's normal."

Her comment was hard to deny. "An intelligent woman," Higgins said to himself. "I'm afraid Mrs Chapman was stabbed," he said aloud. "We wondered if you had any idea who might have done it, and why."

Anne swallowed hard, as if she felt sick. It took several moments for her to reply. Again, Higgins let her take her time, though he got out his notebook discreetly.

Finally Anne shook her head. "Angie could be, well, difficult," she admitted, "But no one I know would have harmed her. It must have been someone from down there. Chalk Heath I mean."

"Are you sure there were no tensions in the choir?" Higgins asked.

"There were plenty!" Anne replied and smiled briefly. "Lots of egos banging about, if you see what I mean. They're all fine singers. They can get jealous if they don't think they're getting their due, but it's never anything more than petty spats." She paused thoughtfully.

"Anton can take some handling, but he's a sweetie really." Once again she paused.

"And?" Higgins prompted.

"Well," she paused, "I have wondered lately whether he and Angie are having an affair. They're both very discreet." Anne corrected herself, gulping slightly. "I've got to learn to say 'were', haven't I?" she asked, beginning to cry again. Fumbling in her apron pocket for a handkerchief, she blew her nose.

Once again Higgins waited. The woman could be a good witness, given time. "Why did you think they were having an affair?" he asked at length.

"Glances, touching hands occasionally, you know the sort of thing. I think Anton cared more for her than she did for him. He'll be heartbroken now, even if he doesn't show it. He likes to pretend to be the tough guy."

Higgins wrote quietly. "What about the Walters?" he asked. "Hasn't there been trouble between them and Mrs Chapman?"

Sighing, Anne nodded. "That was awkward," she admitted. "It was over their plans for a big extension. They're next-door neighbours you see. For some months they hardly spoke to each other at rehearsals. I could see Angie's point. The first design would have been a monstrosity. That was all sorted though. The Walters reduced their plans and Angie withdrew her objection."

"Did you know she'd changed her mind?" Higgins asked.

In surprise Anne looked at him and shook her head. "They assured me everything was sorted," she replied. "Did they know? It must have made things very difficult this week if they did."

"That's something we need to find out," Higgins replied carefully. He changed the topic. "Tell me a bit about the choir," he invited. "Who started it?"

"Evelyn." Anne relaxed a little, clearly talking about something she cared about. "That was before my time," she added. "Evelyn had sung while she was in the services. She told me that after she was demobbed she was bored. So she decided to start a choir up herself. It was a full choir at first, about thirty strong I gather." The baby's grizzle was turning into a wail and Anne looked towards the sound in concern. "I only joined seven years ago, after I moved here and found they needed a pianist. How I ended up as their secretary I'm not sure."

"And when did it become the Calzone Singers?" Higgins prompted.

"People kept wanting 'Barber Shop', so Evelyn started a smaller group and that took over. It's quite famous." Once more Anne sighed. "This is going to make it even more famous isn't it? For all the wrong reasons."

The wailing was getting louder. Higgins was conscious he ought to let the woman go to her children soon, but he asked one last question. "Where were you this morning?"

In alarm Anne looked up, then nodded, understanding. "Here," she replied, "nursing three sick children. The doctor can confirm if you need it. He visited at about eleven o'clock."

"Anne! Can you come up?" a man's voice called from the top of the stairs. "Baby Michael needs you."

Immediately Anne got up. "I must go and help Bill," she said in concern.

"Of course," Higgins agreed. "We'll show ourselves out."

In the darkness outside the house, Higgins and Kendrick paused. "Any thoughts, lad?" Higgins asked.

The younger officer was pleased to be consulted. "She's in the clear I'd say," he suggested.

Chapter Twenty

PC Sutton arrived back at the hotel cold and wet. "It sounds like the driver's in the clear," he said to Winters, shaking his cape over the hall tiles. "Do you mind if I write up my notes before I give them to you? You'll never read my scrawl. The chap spoke so quickly I could hardly keep up."

Winters nodded. "You'd better dry off too," he suggested. "Go down to the kitchen. That's the warmest place." He paused. "Audrey Tempest and the waitress are in there talking to the chef. Ask them who has which bedroom."

"Who has which bedroom," Sutton repeated. "Yes Sir."

Winters explained. "The suspects went to their bedrooms before lunch. If they were near enough, they might have got to the victim's room without being noticed."

"Shall I do a couple of quick sketches?" Sutton asked. He bent down to remove his cycle clips. "The DI asked for one earlier."

"Why not? Nothing fancy. Just where the bedrooms are and the stairs, back door, that sort of thing. You'd better bring your notes to us first."

Turning towards the kitchen, Sutton paused. "What about Pauline Meadows?" he asked. "I left her minding the suspects."

Winters sighed. They had to let the choir leave the dining room soon. Since the coach driver wouldn't want to set off to Uttley so late, and in such weather, the choir would have to spend another night at the hotel. Nobody could be expected to spend a whole evening sitting bolt upright at a table. "Once PC Lowe is here, he can give her a break," he replied. "We'll have to let them go to their rooms before dinner. You do your sketches while the coast's clear."

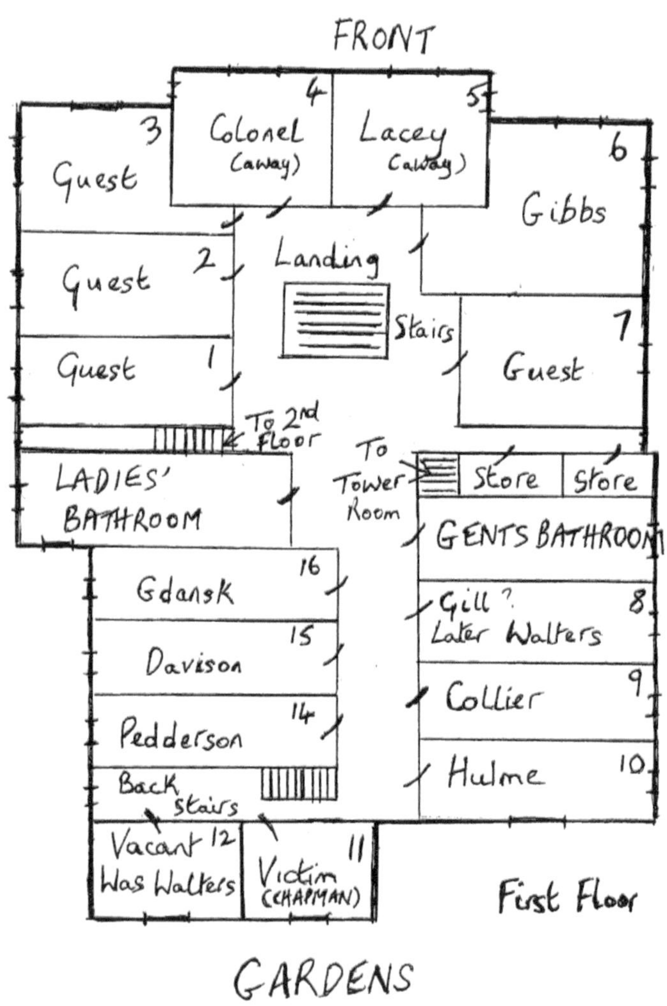

Sutton's plan of the first floor

Turning, Winters returned to the interview room. DI Ambrose was talking on the phone. "Interesting," he mouthed, indicating that he would be some time.

Nodding, Winters crossed to the bay window and looked out. He was glad to have a few minutes quiet. They had 'done a quick pass' through all the suspects. It was a technique Ambrose adopted sometimes when there was a large group. He would interview each person briefly, then let them go, giving the impression they were eliminated. Then he would call a few back in unexpectedly. Winters had seen suspects totally unnerved by being asked the same questions all over again, until they were contradicting themselves. They had solved a case that way only six months ago: 'the Limping Lothario' they had nicknamed the murderer, but the murder wasn't a joke. Nor was the astuteness of Ambrose's questioning.

The phone call showed no sign of ending. While he waited Winters began considering who the DI might want to call back in: Anton Gdansk and the Walters, possibly John Pedderson. Maybe they should call everyone back in. There was some discrepancy he was sure, something that didn't quite fit. It niggled him at the back of his mind.

Staring into the darkness, Winters thought so hard he felt as if his brain ached. Everyone's alibi seemed credible, usually supported by another choir member seeing them outside or chatting in the lounge before lunch. Perhaps this really was a case of a random attack by an outsider he admitted. He doubted it, however. Victims nearly always knew their assailants. A flurry of sleet passed the window. Winters frowned. The lane from the hotel was narrow. If it started to snow they could have trouble getting back that night.

Ambrose put down the phone and stretched his legs under the desk. "That was Higgins," he explained. "Got a lot of useful information. He's driving back now. I've told him to go straight home. He'll give us a fuller briefing tomorrow morning."

Winters nodded. "It's getting bad out there," he agreed. "Did the Planning Department come up trumps?"

"You bet. We need to question the Walters again. We may have a break-through. You'll get the gist as I talk to them. There's something amusing about John Pedderson too." Glancing down at his notes Ambrose smiled. "There's nothing so funny as folks, as my old man used to say. I'll tell you later. Let's see Jackie Walters first."

Winters stuck his head outside the door, to find PC Lowe standing near the stairs. The young constable was nervously rubbing one shoe against his trouser leg. "Not much more than a boy," Winters thought ruefully. "They get younger. Or I get older."

Whatever PC Lowe's appearance, he would prove useful. They'd been too short staffed before he arrived. With Higgins in Uttley and Sutton interviewing the coach driver, they had barely been able to see to the victim's body being taken away, let alone interview everyone. It was tough on the lad: just out of training school and having to cope with a murder case. "Still, once you've joined you can never tell what you'll be doing," Winters thought. That was why he liked the job. He'd hate being stuck in an office all day.

"Ask Mrs Walters to come in," Winters called across.

Dutifully PC Lowe went to the dining room and reappeared with Jackie Walters. She looked flustered.

Ambrose wasted no time. "I've just been talking to one of our officers," he said. "He's been in Uttley, having a chat with the Planning Department, about you and your husband."

"Oh?" Jackie responded, frowning.

"It seems you've been having a battle with your next-door neighbour, who is no other than Mrs Angela Chapman. It sounds like you had a good reason to want her out of the way."

"No!" Jackie replied hotly. "Angela was our friend as well as our neighbour. I've already told you that. We've sung in the choir together for years. Why would I want her dead?"

"Because she objected to your building plans."

"It was all sorted out," Jackie repeated. "I told you so earlier. Angie withdrew her objection. We should have the builders in by April."

Ambrose looked at her keenly. "Did you know Mrs Chapman had objected again?" he asked.

"No. That must be a mistake. Angie said she was happy with the new plans."

"Not according to the Planning Department. We have a copy of Mrs Chapman's new objection."

In surprise Jackie opened her eyes wide "She must have changed her mind," she said. "I shall have to tell Dennis. He'll be as disappointed as me." In horror she paused. "But that doesn't mean either of us would hurt her," she insisted. "Much less kill her. You'd have to be mad to even think of killing someone, wouldn't you?"

"Tell us again where you were when Mrs Chapman died," Winters asked. "Between eleven, when the coach dropped you off, and a quarter past twelve?"

For a moment Jackie held her breath. "Walking in the gardens with Dennis," she insisted, "like I said. I'm telling you the truth, honestly. We always like a little stroll before a meal. I mean, we're not as active here as at home, and the food's lovely…" Tailing off, Jackie looked at Ambrose with growing alarm. "You don't seriously think either of us killed Angie, do you?" she asked.

Ambrose had to admit that he didn't. The woman might be garrulous and foolish but he doubted if she was a killer. Her husband might be a different matter.

Dennis Walters was outwardly calmer than his wife when he re-entered the interview room, but he rubbed his face a lot and cleared his throat, often signs that someone was lying. Ambrose wasted no time. "Did you know that Mrs Chapman wrote to the Planning Department last week?" he asked.

Chewing his bottom lip, Dennis took a moment to consider his reply. "Yes," he admitted. "I asked her to."

In surprise Ambrose and Winters glanced at each other. "Why?" Winters asked.

"Because I wanted to delay the building work a bit longer. I knew I couldn't stop the plans from going through. They met all the Council's requirements. But I thought a late objection would delay things."

"Didn't you want your mother-in-law living with you?" Ambrose asked.

"Did I heck! Jackie's mother is a manipulative old woman! She makes Jackie's life a misery. If she's living with us, we'll neither of us have a moment's peace."

Winters couldn't resist smiling. "Have you told your wife how you feel?" he asked.

"Not in so many words. Jackie would fly off the handle, and when Jackie does that, life isn't worth living. Her mother is even worse."

"So you tried a little sabotage?" Winters remarked.

"You could call it that," Dennis admitted. "I've found in the past that cunning can be more effective than fighting in the open." He shrugged his shoulders. "My mother-in-law isn't in good health. I thought that if I bought a bit more time, she might die or have to go into a home before she can come to us. I'd willingly find the money for a nice residential place for her. Jackie and I even lined up several. Nowhere was good enough. She wants to ruin Jackie's life, and mine. Everything has to revolve around her!"

Coming to a sudden halt, Dennis smiled apologetically. "You touched a sore spot," he said.

"So I gather," Ambrose replied. He was beginning to feel some sympathy for the man. "Does Jackie know you asked Mrs Chapman to object?"

"Lord, no!" Uncomfortably, Dennis shifted in his chair. "And I'd be really grateful if you didn't tell her. I might as well pitch a tent on the lawn if you do."

"I can't promise," Ambrose said firmly. "But I won't say anything if it's not necessary." He tried a different approach. "Would Mrs Chapman have told her?"

"Not unless I asked her to." Shaking his head, Dennis stared at the bookcase near him. "Angie was a trooper," he said. "She always fought her corner, but she was never mean. And to be honest, the first two sets of plans were pretty awful. I couldn't blame the neighbours for objecting. The value of their property would have gone right down. But when Angie realised how much it meant to Jackie to have her mum with her, she accepted the third plan. She only objected as a favour to me."

"Were you lovers?" Winters asked directly.

"I should be so lucky!" Dennis replied. "No, Angie and I were good friends as well as neighbours. We both worked in the estimating department at Uttley Boxes, before she got a better job. And with her being a widow I used to help out with things: mend the fence, mow the lawn, that sort of thing. These past few hours have been awful! I still can't believe she's dead, or that someone could kill her."

There was a brief silence between them. The man was probably telling the truth Ambrose decided. He almost felt disappointed. He'd hoped that Higgins' news would lead to a break-through and a quick end to the case. Clearly it wasn't to be. "One last question and then you can go, for the time being at least," he replied. "Please confirm where you were between eleven and quarter past twelve."

"Walking in the gardens with Jackie. It was bloody freezing. Then lunch at noon."

Ambrose glanced at Winters to see if he had any further questions. When Winters shook his head, Ambrose got up to show Dennis to the door. Then he paused. "It sounds as though you knew Mrs Chapman well," he remarked. "Were you aware she had any enemies?"

"Not enemies exactly," Dennis replied cautiously. "A lot of people were jealous of Angie. She was talented and good looking and people often resent that. But I wouldn't have said anyone hated her enough to kill her."

Ambrose nodded. "If you think of anything that might help, tell PC Lowe and we'll have a chat again."

With an expression of relief Dennis got up. Then he paused with his hand on the doorknob. "You asked if Angie and I were, well, romantically involved," he said awkwardly. "I'll admit I was attracted to her, but I would never have been unfaithful to my wife. I think Angie was having an affair with Anton though."

"Why didn't you say so earlier?" Winters asked, looking up with interest.

"I wasn't sure. And I didn't think it had anything to do with what's happened."

"Let us be the judge of that."

Again Dennis paused uncertainly. "I saw him come out of her room on the last tour," he admitted. "I hope I wasn't jumping to conclusions, but I don't think I was. She may have ditched him for someone else this week. Anton's been grumpy ever since we left Leyton Bridge, and Angie clearly had something on her mind. Maybe she regretted doing so or he was being unpleasant about it. He has quite a temper."

Ambrose had a strong impression that Dennis knew very well who Angela had chosen, but if he did, he wasn't saying. There was something oddly guarded about the man. He appeared meek and inoffensive, but he could clearly be stubborn, even devious, if he didn't get his own way. There was a strong man hiding inside an apparently ordinary one.

After Dennis had gone Ambrose and Winters took stock of the case. "That's our two prime suspects pushed down the list," Ambrose said ruefully. "Higgins was sure it was one of them."

"I wonder who the new lover was?" Winters replied thoughtfully. "If it wasn't Dennis Walters, it must have been John Pedderson or Wynn Davison. Unless it was someone outside the choir altogether? What were you going to tell me about the Pedderson chap, by the way?"

Leaning back on his chair, Ambrose laughed. "Higgins has an old mate who's ended up in Uttley," he explained. "He reckons he saw our Mr Pedderson on a poster. Dressed as a woman. Rather a beautiful woman apparently. She, he, or whatever goes by the stage name of Lily Gardena. Performs at theatres and late-night clubs, and has quite a following. They call them 'Drag Artists' don't they?"

"'Drag Queens' I think," Winters replied, trying not to laugh.

"I wouldn't know," Ambrose retorted, though his mouth twitched with amusement. "Anyway, Sergeant..." glancing down at his notes, he tried to find the name. "Whatever he's called, Higgins' mate said his wife's quite a fan of the Calzone Singers. Goes to their concerts and drags him along. So he knows what their singers look like, and he's sure he recognised Lily Gardena as the new chap in the choir. Gone legit I suppose."

Winters rubbed his chin thoughtfully. "Didn't Kathy Sutton say something about Pedderson and the victim having an argument?" he asked.

"And Pedderson pleading with her not to tell something?" Ambrose recalled. "I don't imagine he would want the rest of the choir to know."

"I'm sure he wouldn't. Jackie Walters was pretty scathing about him being a buyer for women's clothes."

"At least he can get his stage outfits cheap," Ambrose commented, laughing. Then he was serious again. "I've known murders committed to shut people up before. Let's have Pedderson in again."

"It could be tough getting him to admit he has another life," Winters predicted.

When John Pedderson came in though, he was unexpectedly frank, disarmingly so. "I imagine Kathy told you she saw Angie and me arguing?" he volunteered almost straight away. "She's a policeman's wife isn't she? She'd be bound to tell you."

"She is," Ambrose agreed. "And yes, she did tell us. What was it about?"

Sighing, John looked towards the door, as if he longed to run through it. "I have a second career," he said. "Well, three actually if you count the choir. For several years I've performed as a review artiste, under the name of Lily Gardena. It's all good clean fun, if a bit risqué. It started as a joke while I was at Cambridge, but I do pretty well out of it; get more bookings than I can cope with. I could afford to give up the day job, as the saying is, but I'd far sooner be a classical tenor than an entertainer. Getting into the choir has meant a lot to me, and I doubt if they'd understand the other work I do."

"Quite," Ambrose agreed. It was a relief to find the young man so open, but it rather wrong-footed him. He wasn't sure how best to proceed. "Am I right in thinking Mrs Chapman found out and threatened to tell the others?" he asked.

"She saw a poster and recognised me. Normally I don't accept bookings near home, but I was made a very good offer and risked doing a spot about twenty miles away. I wish I hadn't." Pausing, John sighed again. "I don't know whether Angie was really threatening," he admitted, "or just teasing. I wasn't in a mood for teasing though. Anton had been going on at me after I got one of the pieces wrong. I dreaded him having something more to be unpleasant about."

"Did you kill Mrs Chapman to shut her up?" Winters asked.

In amazement John turned and stared at him. "Good Heavens, no!" he insisted. "Why on earth would I? It wasn't that important. I'd calmed down in a few moments, saw the funny side even. Angie said I made a beautiful woman, and she was quite jealous." Sadly John shook his head. "I didn't have chance to get to know her as well as the others. I just thought she was a bit of a prima donna. Now I wish I could take back some of the things I said. The choir will be nothing without her."

There wasn't much more they could ask him, not at that stage any way. "OK," Ambrose agreed. "That'll be all for the time being, apart from one last question: Tell us again where you were between eleven o'clock and a quarter past twelve."

"At first I was changing for lunch. I'd got very cold while we were around the town. So I put something warmer on and then went down to the lounge. When the gong went at noon I followed the others into the dining room."

"Did anyone see you?" Winters asked.

"Not when I was in my room," John replied, laughing slightly. "The others will have seen me afterwards."

Winters peered round the door and called PC Lowe. "Show Mr Pedderson back into the dining room," he instructed.

"Have you noticed how often Anton's name keeps turning up?" Winters asked when they were alone again.

"And not in a very friendly way," Ambrose agreed. Stretching his back, he stared ahead of him thoughtfully. "We should get some background info on the Uttley suspects soon. Higgins said they'll phone us. They'll do a more thorough check tomorrow. Maybe all will be revealed then," he suggested wryly.

"Our lot have started checking this end," Winters said. "The chambermaid's got form, as you know."

"I don't think it's Libby," Ambrose replied, still looking ahead of him in thought. "My mind's going in circles. We could do with a break."

"I asked Sutton to do some drawings of the bedrooms," Winters said. "He should have finished them by now. Let's have a look at them: see if we can work out who was where, and who was nearest to the victim at the crucial time. Something's not gelling."

Once again they called PC Lowe.

"Go and find Sutton," Ambrose instructed. "He's upstairs somewhere. Ask him to bring his drawings so we can study them over a cup of tea. Then relieve WPC Meadows for a bit."

"Yes sir!" PC Lowe wasn't sure whether he should salute a DI each time he appeared, then decided it would be a bit odd in a hotel foyer. "Shall I get the chef to make the tea first?" he asked.

Ambrose laughed. "Yes, that comes first," he agreed. "Tea for everyone, including the suspects."

As PC Lowe opened the door to the dining room to bring the tea in, he was surprised to be gently pushed away. "Don't interrupt for a minute," Meadows whispered. "Just stand there and listen." Then she slipped back into the room.

"You heard what I said," Wynn was saying, his voice rising in anger. "Why do you keep looking at me?"

"I don't know what you're on about," Dennis retorted.

"You keep looking at me like you know something." Wynn's accent was growing stronger as he grew angrier.

"Perhaps I do," Dennis replied.

"What?"

"Oh, do stop it!" Evelyn called across. "You sound like a couple of silly kids in the playground."

"I am not being silly," Wynn insisted, turning towards her. "Dennis is being offensive."

"How? By looking at you?" Dennis asked derisively.

The atmosphere in the room was becoming increasingly tense, some suppressed conflict between the two men surfacing.

"Shussh!" Jackie said softly, trying to calm her husband down. She only succeeded in increasing his anger.

Abruptly he pushed her hand away from his. "We might as well have this out into the open," he said.

"What exactly?" Wynn demanded. "I've had enough of your innuendos."

"If you must know, I keep wondering what Angie saw in you," Dennis replied coldly.

"What did you say?"

"You heard me. I wondered what Angie saw in you."

Anton looked up sharply. "So it was you!" he said, as if he couldn't believe what he'd heard. Then his face darkened with fury. "She preferred *you* to me?" Getting up, he appeared to be about to cross to Wynn's table and confront him physically. Then he remembered Meadows. Glancing furiously in her direction he sat down again.

"What on earth do you mean?" Jackie asked her husband in horror. "Are you saying Angie was, you know..." she couldn't bring herself to say the words. "With Wynn?"

"Are you happy now?" Wynn asked Dennis furiously. "Now you've told everybody?"

John had caught his breath in surprise. Jackie looked as though she was about to burst into tears and Evelyn was holding her hand to her mouth as if she daren't speak. Barbara was calmer. "You! A married man!" she said to Wynn in contempt. "I've never expected Anton to behave well, but I thought you were different."

Wynn held his ground. "I did nothing Angie didn't want," he said. "She came after me."

"Because she was lonely and unhappy," Barbara retorted, "and you've always seemed a nice man. She would have turned to you for understanding."

"Oh yes, it was all my fault!" Wynn mocked. "I wasn't the only one fancying her." He turned to Dennis. "You were filthy jealous. That's why you couldn't stand me and her..."

Jackie cut in furiously. "Don't you dare say such a thing about my husband!" she snapped.

It was all getting out of hand. Meadows stepped forward to calm things. "Remember where you are," she advised.

There was an angry silence. Evelyn looked around in appeal. "Fighting amongst ourselves will only make everything worse," she warned, "especially in front of the police." She nodded in Meadows' direction. "She'll report everything she's heard."

"Bloody woman!" Anton said sourly. "Spying on us."

Meadows was about to reply, but thought better of it. Instead Barbara spoke up for her. With an expression of utter disdain she turned towards Anton. "Oh do shut up!" she said. "Angie broke up with you because she couldn't stand your constant boasting and bad temper. You're not helping any of us now."

Once again there was silence.

Finally John looked across the table towards Barbara. "You knew what was going on?" he asked her quietly.

"I knew about Anton," she replied. "I was Angie's best friend. I kept her secrets."

It was time to intervene. "Evelyn's right," Meadows said. "I shall have to tell the DI what I've heard; not because I'm spying, but because it might throw some light on who killed Angela. Whatever she did, she didn't deserve to die, and not in the way she did."

Opening the door to PC Lowe, she beckoned him and the tea in.

Chapter Twenty One

WPC Meadows stood at the back door to the gardens, letting the fresh air clear her head. She was shaking slightly, though with anger not cold. A cigarette would have helped calm her nerves. There was a packet deep in her pocket, but she resisted the temptation to take it out. Even if it was unlikely anyone would see her, she had never smoked on duty and she wasn't going to start now.

Sighing, Meadows looked out into the darkness. She felt low. For the first time since her initial training she wondered whether she had made the wrong choice of job. If she couldn't stop herself being so angry with someone, was she suitable for the police force? For a moment she'd wanted to hit Anton. She was no more sensible than the couple arrested last week for brawling in the street. A good policewoman would have been able to reason with a man quietly, not become furious with him.

All in all, it had been a dreadful afternoon, Meadows thought ruefully. DI Ambrose's words still echoed in her mind. He had been polite, but she had never felt so small in her life. After two years, being on the beat around a sleepy town was getting a bit boring. Being called on by CID was far more interesting, even if she was there just to give a woman's point of view or to take care of a female suspect. Now her own stupidity had probably ended all that. DI Ambrose would never ask her again.

"Are you alright?"

Meadows swung round, to find Jane Fellowes standing beside her.

"I was just thinking," Meadows replied truthfully. "Sorry. I didn't hear you."

"I didn't mean to startle you," Jane apologised. "I came out for some fresh air. You looked, well, a bit depressed."

Uncertainly Meadows smiled, but said nothing.

“I'm not surprised,” Jane continued. “You've sung with the choir yourself. And now this dreadful thing happens.”

“It’s a shock for everyone,” Meadows commented warily

Jane peered into the gardens. “Did you find this door unlocked?” she asked. "It shouldn’t be."

“Yes,” Meadows replied, frowning. “I assumed the cook wanted some fresh air.”

“Maybe,” Jane agreed, but she stepped outside onto the terrace and looked around. “Nobody there,” she said afterwards. “Des probably forgot to pull the door to after his last smoke. I shall have to have a word with him.” She stood in the doorway, savouring the cooler air. “If Mrs Tempest let him smoke inside, there wouldn’t be a problem.”

“You must get very tired,” Meadows commented. “Working from breakfast through to dinner.”

“I’m used to it,” Jane admitted. “Are you on your break too?”

Nodding, Meadows glanced at her watch. “I have another ten minutes,” she said.

“Do you mind if I stay?” Jane asked.

“Not at all.”

They stood together in silence, leaning against opposite sides of the doorframe.

“Do you like being a police lady?” Jane asked suddenly.

“Yes.”

Meadows had answered automatically, but she paused and considered her reply more carefully. “Most of the time,” she admitted. “It can be difficult, like all jobs.”

“What do you find the hardest?”

The waitress had a way of asking a question that seemed to expect an honest answer. Yet her tone was kindly, as if she was genuinely interested in other people’s lives. It was probably why she was good at her job, Meadows reflected. She would assess what guests wanted, and do her best to provide it.

“The hardest?” Meadows repeated, looking out over the terrace thoughtfully. “Not knowing the end of stories, I think. You’re called to some incident and for a while you’re really involved with the people, yet you hardly ever hear the outcome.”

“Don’t you mind working shifts?”

"You get used to that."

"It must be hard to make friends though," Jane commented.

In surprise, Meadows turned back to the woman opposite. Her comment was unnervingly perceptive. "It is," she admitted. "I miss my friends from home. I don't get back often, and you don't meet many people when you work nights. People are suspicious of you in any case. They're afraid you'll shop them." She laughed. "Even when they haven't actually done anything."

Jane smiled. "You don't make many friends when you live in a hotel, either," she agreed. "I'd find it very difficult to share a real home with anyone now, though. I'm too used to doing things my own way. But a young woman like you... don't you ever think of getting married?"

To her annoyance, Meadows felt her face reddening. "Occasionally," she conceded "But I'd have to give up my job and be just a housewife. I'd hate that. In any case, I've never met anyone I'd like to marry."

"You will. Some day," Jane predicted.

"I can't imagine myself falling head over heels in love," Meadows said, laughing. "My feet are too close to the ground."

Jane laughed too. "Love's a funny thing," she warned. "I only knew my fellow for three months before we got engaged. Yet even after fifteen years I still miss him."

Meadows nodded in sympathy. "Was he killed in the war then?" she asked.

"He died in the bombing. He was a pilot, survived half a dozen sorties. Then he took some leave to visit his parents in Coventry."

"What rotten luck!" Meadows said softly. She was beginning to like Jane Fellowes. Then she reminded herself that the woman was a possible suspect in a murder case.

For a few moments they stood in companionable silence. "There are a couple of good looking men in your choir," Jane commented, smiling. "I suppose they're out of the question now, though" she added more seriously. "What an awful business!"

Glancing at her watch, she turned to go. "I must set out the dining room," she said, "even if everyone is still sitting there. They've got to eat, haven't they? Make sure the door's locked before you come back. A prowler could get in."

"Of course," Meadows agreed. "I just pull the door to, don't I?"

"That'll do for now. It's a Yale lock. We only use the barrel lock at night, for extra security." Hesitating, Jane looked outside again. "I can't understand why the door was open," she admitted. "We're so careful, especially since the thefts started in town."

Then she went back up the corridor, towards the dining room. Meadows heard Audrey Tempest's voice from the same direction. The two women started discussing what to do about the evening meal, then their voices faded.

For a few moments longer Meadows stood at the back door, thinking about Jane's remarks. Anton had been very rude, but people had been rude to her before. All policewomen, and men, had to get used to that. But was she a bit in love with him? Was that the real problem?

No, WPC Meadows decided honestly. She had thought the man good company, but nothing more. In fact she had been wary of him, feeling something about him didn't quite ring true.

"What was it that bothered me?" she asked herself.

The more she thought about it, the more intrigued Meadows became. "Was it his accent?" she wondered. She tried to recall how the Polish couple in the market spoke. Maybe there were local accents, just like in England. You'd never think a Geordie and a Brummie came from the same country, for instance. Perhaps it was the same in Poland.

Frowning, Meadows imagined herself back in the dining room, listening to Anton shouting at her. When he was angry, his accent seemed to slip around. It was less consistent: like hearing a piece of music played badly, the time signatures all over the place...

Suddenly Meadows understood. "It's an act!" she thought in amusement.

As soon as the idea came to her, she was sure she was right. "The man's no more Polish than my Aunt Doris!"

For a moment she savoured the idea, increasingly amused. Then suddenly she saw it wasn't a laughing matter. "If he's putting on the accent then he's acting the rest too," she realised. He could be anybody. That made him a prime suspect. She must try to speak to DI Ambrose or the DS. If they hadn't already realised, they ought to know.

Quickly she set off up the corridor. As she did so, a slight sound on the ceiling above her made her stop. Frowning, she listened intently.

Feet. That was what it was. Someone was walking above her. In a hotel that was hardly surprising. Shaking her head at her own jumpiness, Meadows was about to continue to the front of the house. Then she heard the sound again and she knew why she was concerned. Someone was on tiptoe, trying to make as little sound as possible.

Meadows listened more closely. There were two pairs of feet in fact, walking carefully along the landing towards the back stairs. A soft whisper stopped them and the feet seemed to turn aside, as if into one of the bedrooms. Then they came back and started again, even more softly.

Meadows drew in her breath. Surely there should be no one up there? All the guests were in the dining room with PC Lowe. Jane and Mrs Tempest were at the front of the house. Des had been working in the kitchen when Meadows passed earlier, and she hadn't seen him come out. Even if the chambermaid had gone back upstairs, that would only be one pair of feet. Mr and Mrs Gibbs? No, the tread was too light and why would they need to tiptoe?

There was another quiet whisper. Again the feet seemed to turn aside.

Meadows put her hand to her mouth to quieten her own breathing. Someone had entered the hotel while everyone was occupied at the front. Jane had checked the garden for intruders but not thought to look upstairs. Now someone was going from room to room, softly trying the doors and entering if they could. As they worked their way along the corridor, they headed back towards the stairs in case they needed to make a run for it.

Urgently Meadows looked around her. If she blew her whistle her colleagues would rush to assist her. But the intruders would hear it too. They could double back and escape through the front door. What on earth could she do? There, on her own?

"What a lousy day!" she thought, all her earlier anger returning with a rush. A couple of burglars were upstairs and she could do nothing about it. "They must have seen the police car at the front!" she thought furiously. "Of all the cheek!" Chalk Heath 'Station would be the butt of jokes for years to come: "Couldn't even catch a couple of thieves under their noses..."

A broom was propped against the wall near the door. Waiting until the feet seemed to have gone into one of the rooms again, Meadows returned quietly to the back door. Carefully she retrieved the broom. Taking the whistle from her pocket, she held it in her other hand. Then she crept to the bottom of the back stairs and crouched behind the bannister where she wouldn't be seen from above. With the broom held firmly, she was ready to jump up suddenly. If the intruders did come down the back stairs she might be able to trip them as they ran.

The footsteps were coming ever nearer across the landing. Meadows waited. She could hear her heart pounding in her ears. If she couldn't stop the thieves, she must at least get a good description of them. But it would all happen so fast...

There was a suppressed giggle on the stairs. It sounded unexpectedly young. Still Meadows waited.

Suddenly the feet were coming down the stairs, towards the back door. Meadows stood up urgently and shot the broom out, across the stairs and in front of the running feet. With a gasp of surprise a figure in black lunged forward over the handle and fell flat on the floor. Immediately Meadows put the whistle to her mouth and blew into it hard. In so confined a space, the noise was deafening.

There was a shriek and the second figure tripped. Still Meadows blew her whistle. Pulling the broom back she started hitting the two figures with it as they struggled to get back up.

"What the bloody hell!" a male voice gasped. "Get off!" He tried to grab the broom and pull Meadows forward with it. They struggled furiously. "Let go!" the man snarled. "Or I'll ring your neck!"

His companion rolled over, out of the way, and then started crawling towards the door and freedom. Meadows was not having either of them escape. Dropping the whistle, she lunged with the broom towards both figures.

But the man grabbed the brush and twisted it until Meadows could no longer keep her grip on the handle. Snatching the broom from her, the intruder threw it up the corridor where she couldn't reach it.

"Stay there!" Meadows shouted as the man headed towards the door. "You're under arrest!" How she thought she could arrest both of them and hold them until help came, she had no idea. She was too furious to think.

"What the hell's going on?" Des' voice shouted from the kitchen doorway.

"Help me!" Meadows shouted back, before virtually throwing herself onto the two figures. In a fury of kicking arms and legs the three of them squirmed on the floor.

Des might be heavy and slow at his work, but he could move fast if he wanted. Within seconds he was down the corridor and hauling one of the thieves up by the back of his jacket. Meadows managed to sit on the other one.

Jane and Audrey had appeared at the end of the corridor, wanting to know what the noise was about, immediately followed by DS Winters and PC Lowe. Pushing past them, they ran to Meadows' aid.

"Stop right there!" Winters shouted to the two intruders. Then he too was piling into the fray. Within minutes he was clipping handcuffs onto the one figure while Lowe and Meadows held the other. "You're both under arrest," he barked. "You do not have to say anything, but anything you do say may be given in evidence. Do you understand?"

The figure in the handcuffs merely grunted, but there was a whimper from the other intruder. Both were dressed in black jackets and trousers, with dark balaclavas pulled down over their faces.

At last there was silence, both intruders secured. "I heard them moving about upstairs," Meadows explained to DS Winters. She looked round for her whistle.

For the first time ever, Meadows saw DS Winters grin. It wasn't just a smile; it was a definite grin. "Did you now?" he asked. "Let's see what fish you caught." He pulled the balaclava off the face nearest him, to reveal a young woman with blond hair.

"Let me go! You're hurting me!" she wailed.

Meadows realised she was still sitting on the woman's legs. "So long as you don't try anything silly," she warned.

The woman shook her head, then sat up, rubbing her legs and shoulder.

"Who's your friend?" Winters asked. He pulled the other balaclava off. The boy was in his early twenties and smelt slightly of aftershave. Neither intruder looked like a typical thief. They had the appearance of bank clerks or lawyers: people you might meet at a party in a leafy suburb.

"Blimey!" Winters commented. "Where are you two from?" He turned towards Meadows. "Have you seen them before?" he asked.

"No," WPC Meadows admitted. Then she paused. "But I'll bet they were the nice young couple at the jewellers'."

"Aaah of course!" Winters agreed. "Well thought. And at the theatre when the fur coat disappeared." He shook his head. "And you look like such educated folk!" he mocked. "Turn your pockets out. Let's see what you've got."

Reluctantly the couple obeyed. A woman's purse and a watch appeared on the floor, then a silver chain that Meadows recalled Evelyn wearing. They were followed by a wallet and another watch, all probably from the choir's rooms.

"Not bad," Winters said. "Take a note of it all, Meadows. Is that the lot? Let's see inside your jackets too."

Another purse appeared and a small china ornament, probably Royal Worcester.

Audrey and Jane had stepped forward to look. "I remember this couple," Audrey said thoughtfully. "They called to see if we had any vacancies a week or so ago. We were full so I sent them to the B&B near St George's."

"And you've been coming here to help yourselves ever since?" Winters demanded.

"No!" the young woman retorted hotly. "Do you think we're mad?"

Her companion seemed more resigned to being caught, and inclined to boast. "We gathered you'd be busy," he taunted, "strutting about being great detectives! We'd have got away with it too, but for her." He nodded towards Meadows with grudging admiration. "You weren't watching the doors, were you?" the young man jeered.

DS Winters refused to be drawn but his mouth set in a hard line. "Get up!" he ordered. "We'll have you down the 'nick' in no time. Let's see if you're so cocky then."

The intruders got up reluctantly. As they did so, Winters frowned. "Are you sure you've never been here before?" he demanded. "We'll find out if you have. You might as well tell the truth now."

"Of course we haven't," the young women replied sullenly. "We never go to the same place twice. We're not daft!"

The young man shrugged. "We heard that stupid landlady talking about a murder down here," he said, "and thought the place would be worth a try. It sounded a good wheeze: nicking things from under the nose of the local plods."

Meadows glanced towards DS Winters and knew that he was thinking the same thing. If this couple hadn't been to the hotel before, there was still another thief at large.

Chapter Twenty Two

DS Winters stood on the landing, staring ahead. Something was niggling him. He had noticed something, but not enough to register it: something to do with a number. The sensation was annoying, like having an itch he couldn't scratch. For the life of him, he couldn't work out who the number belonged to, or what it meant.

Frowning, he looked down at the reception area below him. The two disconsolate thieves were sitting waiting for a police car from the 'Station. The young man was still in handcuffs but they decided the woman could be trusted. Her chances of escape were pretty remote. Besides, neither of the two officers watching her "was in the mood for any funny business", as Meadows had put it.

He hadn't always got on with WPC Meadows but as he stood watching the young thieves, Winters wished he hadn't been so hard on her. But for Pauline Meadows, Chalk Heath 'nick' would have been in a right mess. Letting a hotel be burgled right under their noses! It would have been bad enough if the hotel had been attacked by a hardened gang, but by two posh-sounding kids. Chalk Heath would be the joke of the county.

From above, the young woman looked even less like a thief than when Winters first saw her. She was well dressed and attractive, her blond hair cascading over her collar. Slender shoulders and a slight figure made her look little more than a girl. Her companion seemed just as unlikely, his hair neatly slicked back with brilliantine, the angle of his shoulders arrogant rather than cowed. Winters wondered what on earth had possessed them to turn to crime. Boredom perhaps? Maybe they were modelling themselves on the story of Bonnie and Clyde. They'd offered no explanation. Since their arrest, neither of them had said a word other than to give their names: Miranda Franklin and Josh Pendlebury, and even those could be false.

Shaking his head, Winters continued across the landing. Using Sutton's drawing as a guide, he found the stairs to the tower and went up. He wanted to know why the pocket watch had been found up here, if no one had been using the room.

The door was unlocked. Winters put on the light and stood beside the bed, looking round. With windows on all four sides the room was bitterly cold. The air smelt musty, suggesting no guests had stayed there for several months, though the two beds were made up in readiness. He glanced out into the night. The gardens seemed a long way down. When the hotel was a private house, the tower must have been a lovely feature: the sort of place where children would love to play.

Winters sighed. He would be late back tonight and miss reading a bedtime story to his own children. He'd promised to be back in time and hated disappointing them. Fran wouldn't be pleased either. They were going to pack the Christmas gifts together. He had looked forward to a night in, too.

Pulling himself up sharply, Winters moved away from the window. He checked whether there were any signs of disturbance. He couldn't tell where the watch had been found, but a faint ring on the dressing table just in front of the mirror suggested an ornament had been removed. Presumably the thieves had taken the little Worcester figurine from there. It was galling to realise they'd got so far into the hotel without being heard. "Could they have come up here before?" Winters asked himself in concern.

Perhaps, he admitted. With the choir coming and going, there would have been lots of noise to distract people. But why would tonight's thieves have targeted the hotel twice? Did they do a practice run? It was possible, yet the young couple denied coming before and they seemed to be telling the truth.

"It doesn't make sense," Winters thought crossly. The whole case was full of leads that went nowhere. "Why would a thief take something and then return it? Not just return it but leave it up here, when the room was unoccupied? It would be bound to raise suspicion."

They might do it as a joke, he mused. 'Bonnie and Clyde' seemed the sort to play silly pranks, just to prove they could. But things had gone missing in the hotel for some time, before the young couple arrived in Chalk Heath. Winters was certain of it, however much the Tempests pretended otherwise.

"Perhaps someone is trying to confuse us?" Winters wondered.

He noticed that the mirror was screwed on to the dressing table. There was no way a thief was going to take a mirror, Winters thought with amusement. Certainly not such a large one. It had three separate panels, one in the middle and one hinged on each side so you could move them back and forwards. Presumably ladies liked to look at their make-up or hair from different angles, he decided.

Winters caught a glimpse of his reflection in the mirror on the dressing table. A deep frown furrowed his brow. He found his mind drifting back to his visit to the hotel yesterday. It seemed an awful long time ago, and in a happier time. You never knew times were happy until they were gone, he reflected. It had been a pleasant afternoon even if he was investigating a theft: the beetle drive in the lounge, old Mr and Mrs Gibbs chattering away, having tea with the choir…

Winters paused. "Now that's a possibility," he said to himself softly.

Going back down the stairs, he crossed the landing to the front of the house and checked the rooms there. The Gibbs were at home. He could hear their radio, and the sound of Mr Gibbs humming along to a tune. The old man seemed happy, oddly so given what had happened that afternoon.

"I wonder," Winters thought. "If I were a retired thief, where would I hide out? How about a hotel in a sleepy little town? No one would notice you. You'd just be one of the long-term residents: a nice old guy and his friendly wife. You wouldn't be asked any questions."

At first he tried to push the idea to one side. He was there to investigate a murder, not whether an elderly man had a murky past. Turning away from the Gibbs' door, he tried the other rooms. Most were locked. Colonel and Miss Lacey were away and the guests who stayed for the concert had gone. Their rooms would have been left ready for the weekend, though whether the hotel would be able to re-open then would be up to the DI. He hoped for the Tempests' sake it would be.

But try as he would, Winters couldn't concentrate. His mind was settling more and more on Mr and Mrs Gibbs. The more he thought about the idea, the more intriguing it became. He filled in his imaginary scenario. "But supposing I got a bit confused, started nicking things again?" he asked himself. "And supposing my wife made me put them back? Or supposing my wife put them back herself, but didn't know where I'd taken them from?"

Returning to the Gibbs' door, he listened again. The old man was singing happily to himself: "My old man said follow the van…"

His idea wasn't a distraction, Winters decided. It was worth investigating. They needed to know who the earlier thief was. If the thief was a resident there was less chance of an outsider having attacked Mrs Chapman.

Crossing the first floor landing, Winters found the second flight of stairs and followed them up to the Tempests' private suite.

As he had hoped, Audrey Tempest had retreated there. She opened the door wide, expecting her husband. When she saw DS Winters her shoulders slumped though her manner was as polite as ever. "Have you lost your way, Sergeant?" she said in greeting. "You can't get to the tower room through here."

"I've come to see you," Winters replied gently. "Can we have a little chat?"

Her smile was becoming increasingly forced, but Audrey showed him in with old-fashioned courtesy. They walked together along a hallway. Several little steps suggested different levels of the original house had been joined together, but the décor was tasteful and the carpet looked new. As he passed, Winters glanced into a bedroom and then an office. Both looked comfortable, a welcome haven from the demands of guests and staff. When they reached the lounge it was warm and cosy, with red velvet curtains drawn against the cold and sprigs of berried holly arranged around the hearth. Audrey's face was pale however, and she shivered slightly.

"What is it now?" she asked wearily. "Surely there can't be any more trouble?"

"I'm not sure you've told us everything," Winters replied. He softened his words with a reassuring smile.

"I don't know what you mean," Audrey insisted, but her voice faltered. "Would you like a cup of tea?" she asked, as if out of habit. "We have a kettle up here."

"Thank you, no." Winters indicated a chair the other side of the fire. "Come and sit by me," he invited. "There's nothing to worry about. I know you'll have acted from the best motives, but you must be honest with me now. We have to eliminate every possibility or a murderer may go unpunished. Do you understand?"

Biting her lip, Audrey nodded. "What do you want to know?" she asked, her head bowed.

"How long have Mr and Mrs Gibbs been residents here?

In surprise Audrey looked up. "About eight years," she said.

"So they arrived here in '51," Winters commented. "Do you know where they came from?"

"London originally." Audrey looked puzzled. "Mrs Gibbs told me they had a nice flat," she explained, "but it was expensive. London was getting too busy for them too. So they decided to release their capital and book in with us. We offer special terms for long-term residents."

"And they pay their bills regularly?"

"Without fail," Audrey assured him. "I imagine they have private funds. We don't pry into our guests' affairs."

"Of course not," Winters agreed. "Do you know if they came straight here? From London I mean."

Audrey looked at him guardedly. "I think they tried the seaside first," she replied, "but they found it cold. They also spent a bit of time with their daughter in Australia. Why?"

"Could they have left London about ten years ago?" Winters persisted.

"Perhaps."

Winters paused, trying to recall exact dates. 'The Brown Trilby' case was before his time. He'd only just left the Military Police by then, but it was one of those cases that did the rounds every so often, to see if anyone had any new ideas. A lot of wealthy people had valuable items stolen. The Met didn't like high profile cases going unsolved. Winters smiled inwardly. He might be able to solve it for them.

"Mr Gibbs has deteriorated, hasn't he?" he continued. "He seemed quite confused earlier."

Taking the poker from the set of fire irons in the hearth, Audrey stirred the coals. Then she swept up the ash that had dropped. Patiently Winters waited. "He has his off-days," she admitted at length. "Mrs Gibbs covers for him. She's bright as a button."

"Bright enough to return something he's taken?" Winters asked suddenly.

Audrey flushed deeply but she didn't reply.

"The trouble is, she sometimes gets it wrong," Winters suggested. "Like Miss Collier's necklace. And sometimes he puts things back himself but he can't remember the room, never mind exactly where the object was. Like the watch that turned up in the tower. Am I right?"

Sighing, Audrey gave up trying to protect her guests. "I have wondered whether that's what's happening," she admitted. "But everything's always turned up. Peter and I have never felt we needed to inform the police. Telling the doctor hasn't seemed a good idea either. Mr Gibbs is much better off here. He'd hate going into a nursing home."

"So Peter agrees with you?" Winters asked.

"Of course. The Gibbs are a very nice couple. We're both very fond of them."

Winters glanced around the room. A Christmas tree was surrounded by brightly wrapped presents. Candles in metal holders decorated the ends of each branch. Beyond the curtains the wind was spattering sleet against the glass, but inside the room it was a picture of Christmas cheer. He felt very sorry for the Tempests, seeing their life's work ruined in a week. "Didn't you wonder why Mr Gibbs took other people's things?" he asked.

"We thought he was a bit of magpie, attracted to anything bright."

"You didn't ask him if he used to be a professional thief?" Winters persisted. "Or at least ask his wife?"

Once again Audrey was silent, staring into the fire. "We never ask questions about people's pasts," she said finally. "A hotel owner learns not to. Everything is in the present: how people behave now, whether they're happy with their room, enjoying their meals, that sort of thing." She paused. "A lot of people have pasts, don't they? When they go away they want to leave them behind. I don't suppose you would like to be reminded of being in the war, and I know DI Ambrose doesn't."

Winters wasn't sure he was following her now, but it was clear she knew nothing more that would help him. He tried one last question. "Does Mr Gibbs wear a trilby hat?"

In surprise Audrey smiled. "Sometimes," she said. "A battered brown trilby. Why?"

"There was a case in London, a series of cases in fact, where things disappeared from hotel rooms. A man in a brown trilby was seen in the foyer earlier."

"I see," Audrey replied, her smile fading. "But lots of men have battered old hats," she pointed out. "My father wore a panama until the brim broke. That didn't make him a thief."

"No. I'm sure it didn't." Getting up, Winters thanked her and went back downstairs.

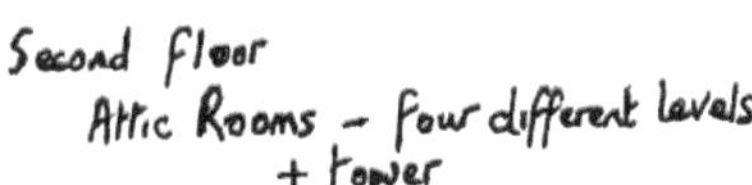

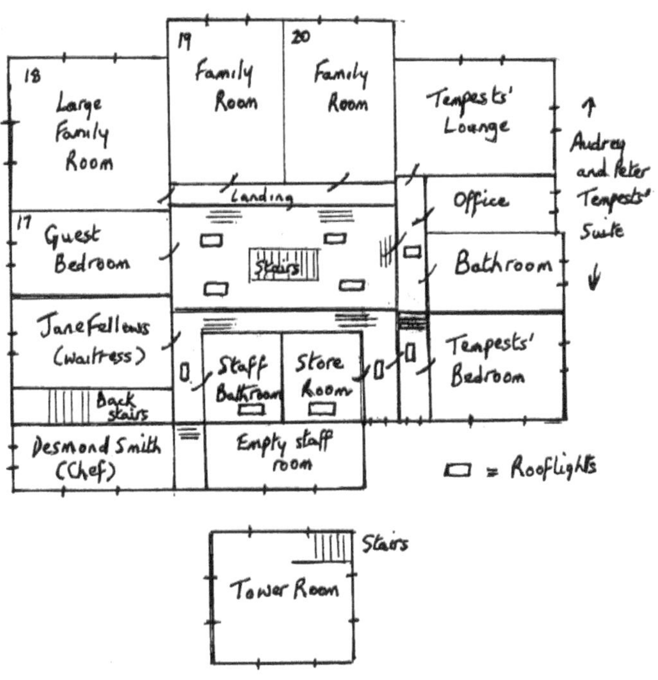

Sutton's plan of the second floor

He met DI Ambrose heading in the direction of the choir's rooms. "Ah! That's where you are," Ambrose greeted him. "I was going to have another look at the bedrooms. There must be something we've missed. I'd be grateful if you'd join me."

"I've been talking to Mrs Tempest," Winters explained. "We had a very interesting conversation. I'll tell you about it later. Has the car from the 'Station arrived?"

"Five minutes ago. Our two 'clever clogs' went off in it, still refusing to say anything. Hopefully they'll be more co-operative when they're in an interview room. If not, I'll call Jenners Park and see if they know who they are."

"You reckon they're from there?" Winters asked.

"Most likely. I suspect they moved out here when things got too hot at home. The place was crawling with police after Jack Hemmings was murdered. I bet our two decided to try another town."

"Wherever they're from they're good at their trade," Winters remarked. "They fooled a lot of people, including the Buchmanns. They nearly got away with making us look right idiots too."

Ambrose grunted. "I don't need reminding," he retorted. Then he had the grace to laugh. "Doesn't bear thinking of," he agreed.

They'd reached the victim's bedroom. Everything was still as the Forensics Team and pathologist had left it, but it smelt colder. To Winters it felt as if the victim's spirit had lingered for a while and now even that had gone. The blood stains and chalk marks on the floor seemed to be darkening as the night drew on. Despite their experience of such crimes, neither man could remain unaffected by what they saw. Both of them stood silently for a moment, in reverence to the death that had taken place.

Then they were business-like again. Ambrose re-examined the wardrobe, still smudged with finger print powder. "I can't smell anyone," he remarked. "When someone hides a while you can usually smell their sweat."

Again they stood, looking for something they'd missed before. There was nothing.

Finally they went back into the corridor. Ambrose tried the empty room next door. It was still locked. "Unless they had a key, the assailant didn't wait here," he commented. "Come to that though, who would have a key?"

"The staff," Winters replied. "Libby for sure."

They returned towards the front of the house, past one of Peter's splendid old clocks. Winters checked the time on the ornate dial against his watch. The clock might be old-fashioned but it was accurate to a minute. Like its owner, he reflected wryly.

They'd reached a small sitting area on the main landing. "There has to be something," Ambrose said in exasperation. "Let's go through it all again." He had brought Sutton's drawings. Laying them out on a small table, he sat in one of the armchairs and indicated Winters should sit opposite him. "Who was where?" he asked, leaning over the drawings.

Together, they tried to work out whether any of the choir members could have reached the victim's room within the crucial time slot, commit the murder and then get away without being seen. "John and Anton were in their bedrooms for some of the time," Ambrose pointed out, "and their rooms are quite near the victim's." He indicated both bedrooms on Sutton's drawing. "But if they did go to her room, you'd have thought they'd have been seen by Libby."

"And Barbara and Evelyn didn't come up until after the murder," Winters commented. "Libby's sure about that. Someone could be lying of course, but everyone's evidence seems to be backed up. Could Angela have killed herself?"

"Not deliberately I'd say," Ambrose replied, "though she may well have contributed to her own death, poor woman, if she pulled the scissors out." Getting up, he gathered up the drawings and went to the door. "John and Anton had the most opportunity. But I don't see how even they did it. What's your view on an outsider?"

"I don't think it was our 'Bonnie & Clyde', but it could have been someone else. Someone we've not yet identified."

They closed the victim's room again and walked down the stairs to the back door.

"Let's check outside again," Ambrose suggested. Unlocking the door, he stood in the shelter of the house, shining his torch around the terrace. The sleet had turned to rain, a hard penetrating drizzle that soaked the chairs and tables. There were no helpful footprints, no dropped cigarette cases or handkerchiefs with initials to solve the case; just wet soil, fallen leaves and a few last pansies in the borders.

"There's no point in getting soaked checking any further," Ambrose admitted. He shone his torch up the path, towards the gate in the wall. "I looked up there earlier. The gate's been forced. Quite a skilful job. The question is, did our 'Bonnie and Clyde' come here earlier, when the other thefts took place?"

"Ever heard of 'The Brown Trilby'?" Winters asked.

Puzzled, Ambrose thought for a while. Then he remembered. "Oh yes, he was in that file the Met sent round a while ago. Had a taste for diamond rings and silver cigarette cases."

"I think he's living right here."

In surprise Ambrose turned back from the door. "Is he now?" he asked. "Let's go back in the warm and you can tell me all about him."

Locking the back door behind them they returned towards the library. "By the way, Meadows rang when she got to the 'Station," Ambrose added. "She reckons Anton Gdansk isn't Polish at all. She'd intended to tell us but didn't get chance with all the commotion. I think we ought to interview him again. If he was having an affair with the victim he may have a motive. According to Meadows, so was Wynn Davison by the way. It's beginning to sound like one of those games: think of a number then..." He didn't have chance to finish.

"That's it!" Winters said suddenly. "242. That's the number I was trying to remember."

"Sorry. You've lost me there," Ambrose replied, bewildered. "What about 242?"

"Anton got the number of his squadron wrong. Squadron 242 was Douglas Bader's squadron, not one of the Polish ones. Meadows is right. The man's a fraud. Who the hell is he? And why's he pretending to be Polish?"

Chapter Twenty Three

"So why didn't you tell us?" DS Winters barked. "I've a mind to charge you with obstructing the police."

Wynn shifted uncomfortably in his chair but he held his own. "It wasn't an affair," he insisted. "It was a single night. It had nothing to do with poor Angela's death. I didn't think there was any need to tell you."

"That's for us to judge, not you," Ambrose said firmly. "When did this liaison take place?"

Looking away, Wynn flushed. "The last night we were in Leyton Bridge. We both regretted it in the morning. I'm not blaming Angie. I was an idiot. But she can be a bit of a tease." Biting his lip, Wynn changed the tense. "Could be, and I was feeling sorry for myself. We started sympathising with each other and it got out of hand."

"I've heard that story before," Winters retorted.

"In our case it's true," Wynn pointed out. "Angie was unhappy and worried about something. I was feeling sore after calling home."

"What about?" Ambrose asked.

Wynn sighed. "My wife resented me leaving her alone with the children," he replied. "She had a point. Our last choir trip was only two months ago. I can't afford to take a lot of leave this year either. Meg was angry and gave me an earful."

Ambrose looked down at the notes he'd made earlier. "You're an architect aren't you?" he remarked.

"Yes. In a small partnership."

"You must be very busy," Ambrose prompted.

"I wish we were."

Winters looked up in surprise. "I thought the building trade was booming," he commented.

"Maybe in other towns. Uttley's still arguing about what to reconstruct first. We've half a dozen projects in hand but none of them gets built." Smiling ruefully, Wynn paused. "I couldn't really afford to come on this tour," he added. "Even with free accommodation it works out expensive, but I couldn't refuse."

"I thought you were all amateurs," Ambrose said in surprise.

"Evelyn can be very persuasive." Pushing his hands though his hair in a tired gesture, Wynn sighed again. "I wanted to come," he admitted. "I'm never happier than when I'm singing. I'm a sucker for the whole business of performing; for the applause. You know…" he tailed off in embarrassment. "I suppose we all are. I did try to find a deputy. There wasn't anyone available who was good enough."

"Good enough?" Winters repeated. "You think a lot of yourself."

Wynn shook his head. "Evelyn has very high standards," he replied, "and everyone has to hold their part. It's difficult for a dep. to step in at short notice. Your police girl did very well but she only had to cover for a couple of nights. If I'd dropped out we'd have needed another bass for a whole week."

Ambrose looked down at his notes again. "You said Mrs Chapman seemed worried," he remarked. "Did she say what about?"

"No. Just that she had to make a difficult decision. I got the impression it was to do with her work. I wondered at first whether it was about her and Anton."

"She'd told you they were having an affair?" Winters asked.

"I'd guessed. I think some of the others had too."

"Did Evelyn know?"

"I doubt it. We all kept quiet about it. A group shouldn't have things going on within it, if you see what I mean. It can cause trouble. Evelyn wouldn't have approved."

"It sounds as though you're afraid of her," Ambrose remarked, smiling slightly.

Once again, Wynn shook his head. "We respect her," he said. "Calzone wasn't much more than a Glee Club when she started it. Now we're the best amateur choir around. *Were*," he added sadly. "I don't know how we'll continue after this. It's not just Angie dying. It's the ill feeling that's been let loose. I thought we were good friends, but perhaps that was only on the surface. I think we'll probably disband. My wife will be delighted."

The telephone rang. With a gesture of apology, Ambrose answered the call. He was guarded in his replies. "Yes. No. Thank you. Well done," was all he said aloud, but he was smiling as he put down the phone. "That was the 'Station," he said to Winters quietly. "Some interesting news." Then he turned back to Wynn. "Tell us again where you were between returning to the hotel at eleven and quarter past twelve," he instructed.

"In my bedroom, as I told you," Wynn repeated. "Packing some toys for the children and a necklace for my wife, as a peace offering." An expression of alarm came to his eyes. "You won't have to tell Meg about me and Angie will you?" he asked. "Please don't. I do love Meg even if things are a bit rocky between us. The children are my life. I couldn't bear to be without them."

Neither Ambrose nor Winters answered him.

Becoming concerned, Wynn looked at them in appeal. "Please say you won't!" he pleaded. "It was just one stupid night and I've hated myself ever since." He sounded increasingly distraught.

Ambrose began to feel some sympathy for the man. "If your relationship has nothing to do with Mrs Chapman's death, we won't need to," he assured him. "But what about your colleagues?"

Wynn put his hands to his eyes. "Oh Lord!" he said softly. "If one of them tells Meg…" he left the sentence unfinished. "I shall have to throw myself on their mercy."

"It might be better to tell your wife yourself," Winters advised. "Unless she's the jealous sort." For an instant he imagined himself making such a confession to Fran. It certainly wouldn't be pleasant. In fact, he probably wouldn't make it out the house in one piece.

"I'm not proud of what I did," Wynn said, his voice thick with emotion. "But I promise you I had nothing to do with Angie's death. I wasn't just taking my chance that night. I've loved Angie for a long time, even if I love my wife too. Can you understand that?"

"We deal with facts not understanding," Winters pointed out. "But I imagine we can," he added more gently.

"You can go now, but we may wish to see you again," Ambrose warned. "The dinner gong will be sounding soon. Make sure we can find you later if we need to."

As soon as Wynn had left, Ambrose got up and walked around the room. "Those chairs are as hard as boards," he remarked.

Pausing, he examined some of the leather-bound volumes on the bookshelf. Most were the sort that looked good but no guest would actually read: *The Complete Works of Tennyson*, Carlyle's *Past and Present*, Samuel Butler's *Erewhon.* The books on the next shelf looked more used, mostly biographies and wartime escape stories. "To Peter with love from Audrey" was inscribed inside a book of Rommel's campaign in the Middle East. Pencil notes and underlinings covered some of the pages. A guidebook to Syria and The Lebanon bore the imprint 'The Army Educational Corps, July 1944'. "So Peter Tempest was in the Middle East," Ambrose thought with interest.

Putting both books back, he turned to DS Winters. "What's your view of Wynn Davison?" he asked.

"A decent man who's been stupid," Winters replied. "What did the 'Station say?"

Returning to the desk, Ambrose smiled. "Jenners Park think they know our Bonnie and Clyde. A Sergeant Yates is coming over to question them. He's pretty certain they've given us false names." Ambrose's smile broadened. "And something else that'll please you," he added. "The Met has a photo of 'The Brown Trilby'. They're sending it over. It's twenty years old but we might be able to see a likeness. I gather they were very interested in your hunch. You better make sure you get credit for this."

"Thank you, sir," Winters said with pleasure. "This could be a feather in our caps. There are at least fifteen unsolved crimes linked to him."

Once again Ambrose stretched his shoulders and back. He'd allowed all the choir to return to their rooms, apart from Wynn Davison and Anton Gdansk. Anton would have been on his own for the past twenty minutes. He should be thoroughly nervous by now. "Let's get the Gdansk fellow in, or whatever he's really called," Ambrose suggested. "He's the most likely suspect. Maybe we'll crack this case as well."

"Three in one day would be good," Winters agreed.

Neither of them believed his optimism.

As soon as Anton sat down, Ambrose turned on him. "Now tell us your real name," he began coldly.

"Anton…"

Ambrose cut in before the man could complete his reply. "Your *real* name," he insisted. "You're no more Polish than I am. What is your proper name?"

For a few seconds Anton stared at him in surprise, the colour draining from his face. "John Smith," he said faintly.

Ambrose almost lost his temper. "Don't mess me about!" he snapped. "I want your real name."

"It *is* my name," Anton whispered. He seemed to have shrivelled into his chair, as if they'd pricked a balloon. "I was born Smith. For some reason my parents called me John." There was a distinct Midlands tone developing in his voice.

"So how long have you been pretending to be Polish?" Ambrose asked. He wasn't sure whether to be amused or disgusted.

"Since I moved to Uttley."

"When was that?"

"Four years ago."

Winters found the man less of a joke. "How dare you take on another man's courage?" he demanded. "The Poles were amongst the bravest and best. What did you do in the war? Were you even in the RAF?"

Looking down at his feet Anton didn't answer. His silence spoke volumes.

"I asked you a question!" Winters repeated. "How dare you pretend to be a hero? You're a nobody, you're a pack of lies!"

Still Anton didn't answer. Stripped of his pretence, he seemed to have no idea what to say.

"Why should we believe anything you told us earlier?" Ambrose demanded. "You said you didn't kill Mrs Chapman. Perhaps you did!"

"No!"

"Perhaps she rumbled you and you killed her to keep her quiet," Ambrose persisted.

Anton shook his head but he offered no explanation, lapsing into a miserable silence. Ambrose paused, glancing at Winters who shrugged his shoulders. They'd expected the man to bluster, go on lying or make up another story in excuse; not this wretched emptiness.

Ambrose tried a softer approach. "What made you pretend to be someone you're not?" he asked. Once again there was no answer. Ambrose decided to wait, indicating to Winters to remain silent too.

Finally Anton spoke. "Because I'm nobody," he replied. "Like the sergeant said."

"Few of us are what we would like to be," Ambrose responded. "But we don't assume another personality. Tell us a bit about yourself, John. Then maybe we'll understand."

"Do you mind calling me Anton? I hate the name John."

In bewilderment Ambrose tried again. "Alright, Anton," he said, "you seem to know quite a bit about flying. Except for getting the squadron number wrong."

"Ah!" Anton said softly. "That's how you found me out."

It was like getting blood out of a stone. Winters took over. "Were you in the RAF?" he repeated.

"Yes, in the Army Catering Corps. Not exactly glamorous."

Ambrose thought of Peter Tempest. He'd been 'only a back-room boy' too, as a quartermaster, but he was as proud of it as if he'd been a general at the front line. "Nothing wrong with Catering," Ambrose pointed out. "An army marches on its stomach. The same must apply to the RAF. Why be ashamed?"

"Because my parents were." Looking down at his feet again, Anton considered the past. "My father was a butcher," he said, "made a lot of money and opened a lot of branches. He expected me to be a butcher too." He shuddered visibly. "I was useless. Not like my brother. But then he was good at everything."

"Until he was shot down?" Ambrose hazarded.

"Yes," Anton replied. "Dad put his photo up in every branch." Pain still tightened his voice.

Ambrose paused, not sure what else to ask. He glanced towards DS Winters.

"So when did you decide to become someone else?" Winters asked.

"When my wife died."

"How did she die?" Winters glanced hopefully in Ambrose's direction. He wondered if it was, by any chance, a suspicious death.

Anton looked into the distance. "She was diabetic," he said. "She went into a coma while I was out at the pub. I might have saved her if I'd been there."

Winters grimaced.

"That's pretty rotten," Ambrose commented. "I imagine you would want a fresh start. But to take on a whole new personality? That would be difficult."

"I'm a good actor." Looking up, Anton smiled wanly.

Ambrose found himself picturing Joe at the school concert. He wondered whether Anton had sung or acted in plays while he was at school, and what his parents had said afterwards. "A butcher's boy going on the stage! Don't talk daft!"

"When you were younger you dreamt of going on the stage," Ambrose suggested. "Am I right?"

Anton nodded. "It's the only thing I'm good at," he agreed. At last the words were beginning to flow. "My parents thought it wasn't a proper job. So I worked in the shop in the day and paid for singing lessons in the evening. I had a few sessions at a local drama school too."

"You must have been very determined," Winters remarked. "Did your parents ever come round to the idea?"

"My mother did a bit, but not Dad. He saw everything in terms of money." There was a blotter on the desk near him. Anton picked it up and stared at it, as if he were looking at his past. A quieter, hesitant man was emerging, someone who found it hard to talk about himself; the sort of man who would sit quietly in the corner of a pub and pay for his round without question.

"Where do you come from?" Winters asked. "In real life?"

"Birmingham: not the liveliest of places, at least it wasn't then." The man was beginning to open up a bit, his voice taking on a more natural tone. "I was glad to be called up. It was better than being at home. I joined the entertainments group wherever I was posted. We did *Faust* while I was in Kenya and Shakespeare in Egypt, revues, entertained the locals, that kind of thing."

"And after you were demobbed?" Ambrose asked.

"I wanted to try and get into local theatre," he replied. "But by then I was getting married." He smiled deprecatingly. "I'm not sure how that came about, but Rosie was a sweet, kind girl who could see something in me. I needed to get a proper job but I couldn't face going back into the business, so I settled for amateur stuff and went into insurance. I hated that too…" Tailing off lamely Anton shrugged his shoulders.

"Insurance would drive me mad," Winters commented. "So where does the Polish bit come in?"

"Something sort of snapped in me after Rosie died. I was travelling through Uttley and saw an advert for a waiter. I decided to have a go, but not as me. I was fed up with being me. I'd played the part of a Polish airman just before. On an impulse I put the accent on again. Suddenly I'd got the job and all the women wanted to know me."

The explanation came to an end.

For a full minute Ambrose and Winters sat in silence, waiting for Anton to say more. Finally Ambrose asked, "Did Mrs Chapman rumble you? Was that why you quarrelled?"

"No." Anton shook his head. "Angie would never dream anyone could be a fraud. I wanted to stop the whole silly game but while she believed in me, I couldn't. I'd have looked a fool with the rest of the choir too, and at work. Once I'd started pretending I had to go on."

"Did you love her?" Ambrose asked.

To his surprise Anton shook his head again. "I don't think either of us dared risk loving someone," he replied. "But we got on well and made each other happy. We only saw each other when we were at rehearsals or on tour. It was a kind of holiday arrangement."

"So why did Angela drop you?" Winters frowned in bewilderment.

"Because I was being stupid. So many things were going wrong. We weren't up to our usual standard in Leyton Bridge and we were all edgy and cross. It was like the part I was playing was taking hold of me, making me more and more unpleasant." Looking down, Anton realised he was still holding the blotter and put it back on the desk. "I was rotten to your policewoman too," he admitted.

"She rumbled you," Winters said with a dry smile.

"I wondered if she had," Anton admitted. "It made me nervous and when you're nervous you overact. Tell her I'm sorry."

Once more there was a difficult silence. This time it was Anton who broke it. "I'm almost glad you've found me out," he said. "I'd already decided I'd have to give up and leave Uttley. Now this'll make me do it."

There was no point in continuing the interview further, Ambrose decided. Only an innocent man would tell such an implausible story, though he could be acting another part. Without further information they had little chance of knowing what was real and what wasn't.

Ambrose brought the interview back to the crucial issue. "Where were you between eleven and twelve fifteen?" he asked. "Tell us again."

"In my room checking some music and changing for lunch. I thought of going to Angie's room but decided too many people were around. Now I wish I had. I might have seen who killed her." He shook his head. "Never in the right place at the right time: that's me."

They watched as Anton slunk out of the room.

"What a peculiar fellow!" Ambrose said afterwards. "I've no idea what to make of him. He could be very clever and our killer, or an absolute idiot. Or maybe he's just an ordinary man who can't cope with life. I dunno." He stretched out wearily. "It's getting late. Let's go back to the 'Station. I'll see the choir off tomorrow. Perhaps I'll pick up something more then."

"You're letting them go home?" Winters asked.

"We've no grounds to hold any of them," Ambrose pointed out. "We'll have to hand the case over to Uttley CID," he added with a sigh.

Chapter Twenty Four

Saturday 12th December 1959

"Do you want to come in or stay in the car?" DI Ambrose asked.

"I'm not waiting around again," Joe retorted.

Ambrose sighed. "I'm sorry Joe," he apologised. "It'll only take a few moments."

"Mum could have taken me," Joe replied sullenly.

His remark stung. "I promised I'd take you and I will," Ambrose replied quietly. "We'll be there for eleven. I just need to see the choir off."

"I thought they were going tomorrow."

In surprise Ambrose paused with his hand on the car door. When he and Mary had discussed the choir's visit a month ago, Joe hadn't appeared to be listening. "They've cut their visit short," he replied vaguely.

"Why? I thought they had a concert tonight?"

"It's been cancelled." Ambrose paused, wondering how much to say. "Come in with me if you want," he invited. "I'll be interested to know what you think afterwards."

They got out of the car and went into the The Shalimar together. The foyer was full of luggage and people. Most of the choir were sitting at the small tables in the lobby finishing cups of coffee. Jackie was arguing with Peter at the Reception desk, something about the number of newspapers they'd had, but there was little conversation otherwise. Glancing quickly around, Ambrose noted that Wynn was sitting on one side of the room, Anton on the other. Both seemed to be avoiding Dennis. Barbara and John were talking softly beside the fireplace. Several people looked up and then away.

Only Evelyn got up to greet him. "Thank you for coming," she said.

"I wanted to see you safely off," Ambrose replied. He took her outstretched hand awkwardly.

"I wish things had been different," Evelyn added. "Please thank the Friends of the Theatre for their invitation." She spoke carefully, as if she were repeating a script. Then she noticed Joe who was flipping through the pages of a magazine at one of the tables. "Is that your son?" she asked.

"It's my day off," Ambrose explained, "We're on our way to Jenners Park."

Evelyn's mouth tightened. "We should have been singing there tonight," she said wistfully. "Everyone's so disppointed, it makes what's happened worse." Then she turned away, to sit beside Anton.

Peter Tempest had finished sorting out the Walters' bill. Seeing Ambrose he came across the room. "Good of you to come," he said with his usual politeness. "Your sergeant said you were off duty today; something about going to get your son's Christmas present."

"I've promised to see if Berties' has a decent guitar," Ambrose replied.

Peter nodded. "The second hand place?" he asked. "There's a new music shop just opened on Victoria Street. They've got all sorts of opening offers. You might get something better there." He glanced towards Joe. "He's grown up a lot lately hasn't he?"

Audrey appeared, carrying a large coffee percolator, followed by Jane with jugs of hot milk. "A second cup anyone?" she asked. Seeing Ambrose, she nodded in greeting.

"Would you like some coffee?" she asked. "We've just made a fresh brew. And maybe some orange juice for your son?"

"I'd rather have a coffee if you don't mind," Joe replied looking up.

Ambrose smiled inwardly. Joe didn't particularly like coffee, but he wasn't going to be fobbed off with an orange juice, like a small child. Ambrose watched in amusement as his son took a cup from Jane, then sat on his own in the far corner of the lobby.

Audrey was speaking to him again. "We're waiting for Harry to bring the coach round from St George's," she explained. "I can't help feeling sorry for them." She nodded in the direction of the choir. "They've all gone very quiet. Even the Polish gentleman just sits on his own, grieving I think. Those foreigners feel things more than us, don't they?"

Fortunately, Peter cut in before Ambrose could think of a suitable answer.

"Thank you so much for letting us re-open this weekend," Peter said. "It's our busiest time. We can't afford to lose so many bookings. Hopefully they won't all cancel when they hear what's happened."

"A lot won't," Ambrose predicted. "You'd be surprised how ghoulish people can be."

"I doubt it," Peter replied, smiling wryly.

"You will keep the victim's room locked?" Ambrose reminded him. "It's still a crime scene."

"I doubt if any of our staff will want to go into that room ever again," Peter admitted.

"Now if you'll excuse me, I need to finish some bills."

He hurried back to the Reception desk. Audrey turned away to see to the Gibbs who had come down from their room. They weren't going to miss an extra morning coffee.

As soon as Ambrose was alone, Evelyn rejoined him. "What will happen now?" she asked softly. "Will you want to question us again?"

"Your local CID may do," Ambrose explained. "And if we find any further evidence this end I'll probably come up myself. I honestly don't know."

Which he genuinely didn't, he thought grimly. Some crucial bit of information might turn up over the next few days. Otherwise it would be down to routine police work, sheer slogging investigation: the sort DS Winters was so good at. He always reminded Ambrose of a ginger haired terrier, refusing to let go. But however they cracked it, Ambrose was determined they would do so. Angela Chapman had been invited to Chalk Heath, and he owed it to her to find out why she had died on his patch.

He glanced at the far corner, hoping his son was behaving himself. To his surprise, Joe was sitting quietly on his own watching everyone in the room. "Just like I used to do," Ambrose thought in amusement. "I wonder if he does that at school?" He recalled Peter Tempest's remark. Yes, he had to agree: Joe had grown up a lot lately.

Gravel crunched outside. Heads turned in relief as the coach passed the front of the hotel. "I shall be glad to be home," Jackie said to no one in particular. "I wonder if they've heard? It's going to be awful having to tell the neighbours." She was talking too quickly, still nervous and upset.

"They'll know soon enough," Dennis assured her.

Barbara got up and joined them. "We'll have to arrange the funeral," she pointed out, her voice snagging. “When we're allowed.” She looked towards Ambrose in appeal but he couldn’t tell her when the body would be released. Sighing, she picked up her case. No one else spoke.

Harry appeared at the door. “If you're ready,” he called. “I'd like to get off as quick as we can.”

“So would we,” Dennis muttered. “Come on Jackie. Let's get out of this wretched place.” Picking up both their cases he led the way out of the hotel.

Ambrose watched as the choir gathered around while Harry loaded the luggage racks on top of the old coach. The previous night's sleet had left the gardens sodden. Breath hung on the raw morning air. It was too cold to stand around long. Deciding he could learn little more, he went back into the hotel.

“We might as well set off now,” he said to Joe. “They don't need me to wave goodbye.”

As soon as they were sitting in the car again, Joe looked at him keenly. “What's happened?” he demanded. “Whose funeral has to be arranged? And where's the woman who sang the solo? Is she the one who's dead?”

For an instant Ambrose was taken aback. He had underestimated Joe. He couldn’t discuss a case, but he didn’t want to lie to his son. “I'm afraid so,” he replied carefully. “There’s been an accident.”

“You don’t question people about accidents,” Joe pointed out.

Frowning, Ambrose started the car. “How did you know I’d been questioning them?” he asked.

“You weren't very welcome. Like you’d been asking awkward questions.”

Ambrose couldn’t help smiling at his son’s acuteness. He tried to frame a non-committal reply and knew he couldn’t fob Joe off. A statement had already been made to the local press, hopefully before the landlady at George's Place talked to too many people. The murder of a visiting choir member would be a big enough story to push others off the front page. Joe might well read what had happened in the Chalk Heath Gazette that night.

"It might not be an accident," Ambrose admitted. "But don't say anything to anyone. It's not in the papers yet."

"Jeepers!" Joe stared at him incredulously. "You mean she was murdered? That's awful. She couldn't half sing."

They headed down the lane, through a fine drizzle. The window screen wipers scraped back and forth. "I thought you didn't like that sort of music," Ambrose remarked.

"I don't usually. She was special. You could hear everyone thinking that." Frowning, Joe shook his head. "Was someone jealous of her?" he asked.

They'd reached the main road. A removal van was parked across a driveway, obscuring the junction. Ambrose concentrated on the approaching traffic before replying. "What made you ask that?" he replied. "I'm interested."

"Since when?"

Ambrose sighed. "I'm always interested in what you think," he insisted. "Even if I don't always have time to listen properly. Why did you think someone might be jealous?"

"If someone was that good at school, I would be," Joe answered.

Once again Ambrose paused before replying. He felt ill at ease, forced to reconsider his view of his own son. Joe was no longer an awkward boy but an observant young man, someone Ambrose might get to know in a new way. For several moments he drove on in silence. The main road to Jenners Park wasn't busy but visibility was poor with dirt spattering up onto the windowscreen. He needed to concentrate.

"You said I wasn't welcome," Ambrose remarked finally. "Did you notice anything else?"

Joe grimaced. "They were all sad," he replied, "for themselves if you see what I mean. Except the woman who asked you about the funeral. And the big chap sitting on his own. They really cared."

"Go on," Ambrose invited. "You have a sharp eye."

Joe shrugged his shoulders in embarassment. "Dunno about that," he replied. Then he watched the traffic thoughtfully. "The other chap on his own looked like he felt pretty awful," he added. "The whole lot weren't half different to last Wednesday." Pausing again, he frowned. "I've never really thought how it must feel to know someone's been murdered," he admitted. "No wonder you're grumpy sometimes."

"Me? I'm never grumpy!" Ambrose half-protested, laughing. Then he was serious again. "Don't repeat anything I've said to you," he warned. "I shouldn't be talking to you like this."

"I don't repeat things," Joe said. "I've heard your end of telephone calls often enough and said nothing. I'm usually told off for being too quiet, but it's safer that way. Have you any idea what it's like having a policeman as your old man?"

Ambrose smiled. "Rotten, I imagine," he agreed.

The rest of the journey was surprisingly pleasant. Ambrose managed to get Joe talking about his band and their plans. They had a couple of bookings already, he said proudly. Several people had come up to them after the concert to congratulate them and the headmaster had complimented them in front of the whole assembly. Best of all, Ambrose suspected, was the respect Joe and his friends had gained among their class mates. It suddenly didn't matter that they were no good at sport.

Ambrose was so absorbed in what Joe was saying that he almost missed the turning into Victoria Road. "I thought we were going to Bertie's!" Joe protested. "You promised!" For a moment his voice filled with the old resentment and challenge.

"Mr Tempest says there's a new music shop," Ambrose explained. "I thought we might try there first."

Looking intently at the shop signs as he drove slowly past, Ambrose found Barkers Music Ltd. It had taken over an old drapery shop and still smelt of fresh paint. Parking outside, Ambrose turned towards Joe. It was worth the drive just to see Joe's face as he saw the guitars and drum kits arranged in the shop window. His mouth shaped into a silent 'Wow!'

"Can we go in?" Joe asked.

"That's what doors are usually for," Ambrose replied, smiling.

Within seconds Joe was walking around the shop inspecting the displays like an expert. Some of the instruments were second hand but they were in better condition than those that found their way to

Bertie's pawn shop. Some were new. A couple of trumpets and a trombone reflected the light inside a tall glass case. Three flutes were clipped safely onto a display board, above a slightly battered saxophone. There was even a full sized piano on a little dais. But it was the guitars that drew Joe: propped in the window or laid across shelves, their polished wood gleaming beneath a fluorescent strip. Although most were acoustic, two flamboyant electric basses took pride of place. Both looked able to fill a dance hall on their own. "Wow!" Joe said again, this time aloud. "They've got a Fender! And a Gibson!"

"Try one if you like," the shopkeeper invited.

Joe turned towards Ambrose in wide-eyed appeal. "If you want to," Ambrose replied. "I'll see if there's some sheet music for your mum."

So while Joe tried the nearest guitar, Ambrose looked around. He chose a couple of piano pieces for Mary: arrangements of popular songs she liked. Then he wandered about the shop, looking at the instruments on show. After the past twenty four hours, he was tired and yawned as he waited. Every few minutes he glanced towards Joe to check he was still enjoying himself.

Finally Joe came over to him. "They're dearer than at Bertie's," he whispered, "but they're far better. I was thinking. If I paid you back half, would you buy me one from here?"

"How could you do that?" Ambrose asked in surprise.

"Get a job on Saturdays. Woolies are advertising. So are Benthams."

"You really want that guitar," Ambrose acknowledged. "OK. See if there's one that's good but not too expensive. You don't want to be working Saturdays for ever."

In delight Joe went back to the counter and asked the assistant if he could try another of the guitars. Shaking his head in amusement, Ambrose drifted over to a board covered in adverts and posters. Once again he yawned.

The words 'Calzone Singers' caught his attention immediately. 'CANCELLED' was written in large red letters across a poster advertising their concert that evening. "That was quick," Ambrose thought. "Evelyn must have rung the organisers last night." Interested, he read the details. 'Saturday 12th December, Jenners

Park Central Methodist Church. Grand Concert in aid of Hall refurbishment.' The Calzone Singers were given top billing with two local supporting acts in very small print below: a short organ recital by Mr Philip Crossland and songs from the shows by Miss Eileen Grant. Fortunately there was no ticket price, so no money would have to be returned, but the phrase 'Donations at the door' suggested the church had hoped to raise a lot of money for its new hall. Ambrose sighed. A murder was like a stone thrown into a river, he reflected. It sent ripples beyond its original site, affecting areas far away from the actual murder.

The shopkeeper came across to him. "Your son's very good, " he remarked, nodding towards Joe, now happily playing snatches of 'Silent Night' by ear. "I'm Tim Barker by the way. I'm a guitarist myself so I know what I'm talking about." He smiled ruefully. "There's more money in running a shop though."

"I hadn't realised how good," Ambrose admitted.

"He's got talent," Mr Barker assured him. "Most of the lads who come in can only strum a few chords. To be honest, with this modern stuff, that's all they need. Your lad has a musical ear. Given a bit of tuition he could come on a lot." He indicated a couple of cards offering lessons. Ambrose smiled, aware that he was being softened up by an astute sales man. "Joe already has lessons from a local teacher," he replied. "Thanks for your kind words any way." Changing the subject, he pointed to the poster. "Shame they had to cancel," he remarked.

"Shame? A thorough nusiance!" Mr Barker replied.

Perplexed, Ambrose turned to him. "Were you involved in the arrangements then?" he asked.

"The church did a lot of it," Mr Barker admitted. "But I want to build up a reputation as more than just a shop: as a place where musicians can meet and people can arrange concerts, that sort of thing. This was to be our first event. We tried to avoid cancelling but we couldn't find anyone to step in at such short notice. I must have spent a fortune on phone calls. The Methodists' choir offered, bless them, but people were expecting the Calzone Singers. We had to get someone as good. We couldn't."

Ambrose was suddenly very awake. "How much notice did they give?" he asked casually.

"Three days! I ask you! The wretched woman rang me on Wednesday evening. Full of apologies of course. Said she'd been trying and trying to find a deputy and couldn't, so the choir would have to cancel. You can't have close harmony with one of your sopranos missing. She did give me some other choirs to try but none of them could do it."

"It's a good job you hadn't sold tickets," Ambrose replied nonchalantly, as if only politely interested.

"Funny thing is, we got another call this morning telling us to cancel," the man continued. "I didn't take it myself. My assistant did. Said it was the choir secretary, Mrs Jakes, Jacobs, something like that. The woman I spoke to was called Chapman, their soloist I believe. They don't even know what their left and right hands are doing." Sniffing in disgust, Mr Barker returned to talk to Joe.

For a few seconds Ambrose stood staring at the poster, his mind racing. There was a telephone box just outside the shop. Calling to Joe, "Won't be a minute," he felt in his pockets to see what coins he had. "Ten pence. That should be enough," he thought urgently and pulled open the door.

Fortunately the officer on desk duty at Chalk Heath 'Station recognised his voice.

"Ring DS Winters at home," Ambrose instructed. "Don't let his wife put you off. Tell him Angela cancelled the Jenners Park concert last Wednesday."

Putting down the receiver, Ambrose almost ran back into the shop.

Joe looked at him dubiously. "Work?" he asked. "Don't tell me you're going to dash off leaving me here."

"Of course not. We'll get your guitar and go to the coffee bar like I promised," Ambrose assured him. He indicated that they should step aside out of hearing. "I've just left a message for Sergeant Winters, that's all," he said afterwards, dropping his voice.

"Why?"

"If someone cancelled one of your bookings without you knowing, how would you feel?"

"I'd kill them!" Joe whispered vehemently. Then he stopped, looking at Ambrose in horror.

Chapter Twenty Five

Sunday 13th December 1959

Ambrose slept badly. His brain kept turning ideas over, like a car engine that had been left running. He couldn't stop thinking about the Chapman case. He went through all the statements they'd taken yesterday. Each had seemed credible. Though Barbara Collier could just as easily have killed Angela as find her body, Ambrose didn't think she was guilty. Even the Walters had sounded convincing and Anton's story surely had to be true. No one would invent such a daft explanation. Yet somewhere there was a discord, a note that he could hear at the back of his mind but couldn't quite recall.

Yawning, Ambrose turned over. His mind drifted back to the music shop and going outside to the telephone box. He remembered being a young copper, calling at each of the 'points' on his beat for instructions. Everything had to be done to time, his pace measured so that he was neither too early at the telephone box nor too late.

The Chapman murder started to blur into other cases from the past. Drifting into a troubled sleep, Ambrose began to dream. He was in a large hallway with steps going upwards above him, twisting in a spiral. A very old man was cleaning on a landing five floors above him. Ambrose began to climb the stairs towards him but the old man shouted, "Go away!"

Still Ambrose climbed. "You're too early!" the man shouted. Then Ambrose saw he wasn't an old man at all, but a young woman with blood on her clothes. He had to reach her but however hard Ambrose tried, he couldn't climb the stairs. His legs were as heavy as lead. Suddenly the woman screamed and it was Mary's scream he heard. A clock chimed the hour. He had to reach her before the chimes ended. "One, two, three…" It was chiming mid-day.

As the chimes ended, moonlight glinted through a grating above him. He was in a tiny room. The air was heavy with coal dust. Mary was clinging to him as he carried her up the steps. His whole body ached. He had to get them out. Urgently he pulled at the bricks in front of him, trying to support Mary as he did so. A chunk of masonry fell, hitting his shoulder. He cried out in pain.

"Shush!" a voice said.

Ambrose snapped his eyes open, to find Mary sitting up beside him, tapping his shoulder. "It's alright," she said. "You got me out."

Letting his breath out slowly, Ambrose put his hand on hers in apology. "You must be psychic," he said wryly.

"No. I just know you pretty well by now. What's worrying you? You're usually bothered about something when you have nightmares." She leant back on the pillow beside him.

"This case is getting to me," Ambrose admitted and settled her head onto his shoulder. The moon was shining though a gap in the curtains but it gave a comforting light, not the harsh glow of his dream.

"I had a nightmare too," Mary admitted. "I was in our old Anderson shelter. Something was scuttling in the corner. I was glad when you woke me." She yawned. "There's been a plane droning around. That probably set us both off. I wonder why they're flying at night?"

"Training perhaps," Ambrose suggested. "With Krushchev strutting about, our lot will be on alert."

Mary shuddered. "I hope to God we don't have another war," she said fervently. "I want Joe to grow up in peace."

"Everyone's too scared to fight," Ambrose assured her.

"Like kids in a playground," Mary agreed scornfully. "My stick's bigger than yours." She sighed. "I hope they don't drop it by accident." She moved back to her own pillow. "We'd better go to sleep or you'll be late in the morning."

Though his wife was soon breathing regularly beside him, it was some time before Ambrose could settle. He found himself going back over the day that still troubled his dreams. Why did it haunt him so much? Other people had been bombed and lived to tell the tale, until they got thoroughly boring. He'd had to scrabble though bricks to bring Mary out to safety, but he had managed it, and she had survived. Other women in the Maternity Home hadn't. Sometimes when Joe was being cheeky to his mother, Ambrose wondered if he should tell him what she had gone through to save his life, but it wasn't fair to burden a boy with such knowledge. He was glad now that he hadn't. The boy was growing up suddenly, coming out the other side of teenage anger.

Turning over, Ambrose at last fell into a peaceful sleep.

In the morning though, his dream stayed with him. Usually he forgot the extra details, only remembering that he had dreamt about the hospital again. This time he had a niggling feeling that something else in his dream was significant; as if his subconscious had been working something out. Now he was awake whatever it was merged into the general nightmare, but it annoyed him all the while he drove to the 'Station.

A note was waiting for him on his desk. "Didn't want to bother you on your day off," DS Winters had written hurriedly. "Anne Jacobs phoned. Had odd phone call. Told her you'd speak first thing."

Puzzled, Ambrose re-read the message. Then he rang Mrs Jacobs.

Anne herself answered. She was giving baby Michael his breakfast and couldn't stay long. "He'll be throwing it on the floor if I turn my back for more than a few minutes," she apologised.

"I'll be as quick as possible," Ambrose assured her. "DS Winters left me a message but no details. Who phoned you yesterday?"

"I don't know. That's what's so strange," Anne replied. "As soon as I picked up the phone a man started shouting at me, absolutely furious. 'Where's Mrs Chapman?' he demanded. He didn't introduce himself. Just wanted to know where the 'so-and-so' Mrs Chapman was. I didn't know what to say. 'Tell the wretched woman she'll never sing with us again,' he snapped. 'And I'll see that she doesn't with anyone else.'"

"Was that all?"

"Almost. I tried to get him talking. I thought it might be important. He just repeated 'Tell her I've found a replacement.' Then he slammed the phone down."

"What time was this?" Ambrose replied, thoroughly interested.

"About four o'clock."

"Did you hear anything in the background? Anything that might suggest where he was?"

"Someone was playing a piano in the distance, unless it was a radio. It got louder for a few seconds. I thought a door might have opened and then closed."

Ambrose smiled. Anne Jacobs was a good witness. "Could he have been speaking from an office," he suggested, "in a theatre, or a concert hall?"

"Somewhere like that. When the music went louder I heard voices."

"Thank you for letting us know," Ambrose said thoughtfully. "You've been very helpful. I won't keep you from your baby."

After he'd put the phone down Ambrose sat for some time staring into space, thinking. An idea was beginning to shape in his mind. If he was right, he needed to go to Leyton Bridge immediately. Coming to a decision, he telephoned the super straight away.

Superintendent McEwan might be 'a bit of a dry stick' as his staff described him (well away from earshot) but he was respected as a fair boss, known as 'Mac' even to the rookies. His stiff military manner reminded Ambrose of Peter Tempest, though Mac had obviously been higher ranking. He was no 'Colonel Blimp' however. He could be surprisingly perceptive. Fortunately Mac didn't mind being called early on a Sunday. There was a lot going on in his patch at the moment and he liked to keep on top of things.

"It sounds like you still have several leads," Mac said as Ambrose finished his summary. "I doubt if this case is top of Uttley's list. They're unlikely to mind us carrying on, but I'd better clear it with their Brass. Don't spend a lot of time, we won't have the budget, but go over to Leyton Bridge if you think it'll help. I'll give them a ring too. Hopefully there'll be someone 'sensible' there today."

"That's what I hoped you'd say," Ambrose admitted, smiling.

"What about the thefts?" Mac asked. "They're connected with The Shalimar too, aren't they?"

"Winters is following them up," Ambrose assured him. "He's been talking to the Met. I'm not sure how far his enquiries have got."

"Tell him to keep me informed,"Mac reminded him. "Our Sam can get a bit carried away."

"Hopefully he's putting a few feathers in our caps," Ambrose promised. "But I'll see he fills you in."

As soon as he hung up, Ambrose set off to Leyton Bridge on his own. He couldn't justify taking anyone else to investigate what was, after all, a hunch. Besides, he liked a quiet drive. It gave him time to think. There was little traffic. As Ambrose headed out into the country, mist still clung to the fields. The air was cold.

Ambrose was thinking so deeply that he was surprised to find he was approaching the Netherton crossroads. It was only a few days since the accident there, but it seemed like weeks. The only sign of what had happened was a gap in the hedge. Though the junction was empty, Ambrose paused and looked very carefully before driving on. The young driver had been lucky, he thought grimly. But for Miss Collier he probably wouldn't have survived. He would be charged with dangerous driving, as soon as he was fit to plead. A young lad with a badly broken leg deserved justice.

With so little traffic, Ambrose arrived earlier in Leyton Bridge than he'd expected. An old market town, the place had a sleepy air even on weekdays. On a Sunday it seemed hardly to have got out of bed. A few of the faithful were heading towards the parish church in the centre of the town, and a small group stood on the steps of a gaunt old chapel on the other side of the square. The women at both seemed to be vying to wear the biggest and floppiest hat. Otherwise there was almost no one about. Ambrose knew the town a little. He'd visited Bob Hemmings' widow there after the jeweller was murdered. She had family in Leyton Bridge and had wanted to get away from Jenners Park.

Driving round to the market square, Ambrose parked the car and walked back to the main post office. As he'd remembered, the front window was covered with 'for sale' cards and posters. He could scarcely miss the one he wanted. In bright orange letters on a blue background it announced: 'Leyton Bridge Festival of Choirs.' In even larger letters was printed 'Special Guests: The Sequoia Singers (as heard on national radio and their recent recording). Conducted by their musical director Mr James Radcliffe, MA Cantab.' "I wonder," Ambrose said to himself thoughtfully.

The Leyton Bridge Choral Festival had featured largely in his life when he was a boy. Both his parents sang in the chapel choir and competed. The war had put paid to such events. Few had started again but Leyton Bridge was making a brave attempt to revive its festival. Judging by the number of choirs listed, the organisers had made a good start. Events had been taking place in the King's Hall throughout the week, with the final 'Grand Closing Concert' last night. Frowning, Ambrose tried to remember the King's Hall.

"Wasn't it good?" a voice asked. In surprise he turned round, to find a woman in a fur coat and matching hat also looking at the poster. She looked like an elderly brown bear. Fortunately she was friendlier.

"Sadly I missed it," Ambrose admitted. "Who won?"

"There's a notice on the King's Hall," the woman replied. "Haven't you seen it?"

"I'm afraid not," Ambrose replied. "I'm not from round here."

"Pop over and have a look," the woman suggested. "There are several winners. We thought we'd be modern and have more than one category. People don't just sing in church choirs now, do they?"

"No indeed," Ambrose replied, smiling encouragingly. The woman was clearly on the organising committee and proud of the festival.

"I mean, how do you compare 'Barber Shop' with Bach?" she enthused. "Both went down well, but they're very different."

Ambrose nodded. "I'm glad it was a success," he said. "It's good to see things getting going again. I'm from Chalk Heath. We're trying to get our theatre rebuilt. We've almost raised enough money."

"Well done you!" the woman said, almost clapping her hands. For a few moments they chatted about their respective committees and how hard it was to tear people away from their televisions. Then, glancing at the clock on the market cross the woman suddenly broke off. "Goodness! I shall be late," she said. "I'll have to sneak in at the back!" Waving as if they had been friends for years, she hurried towards the chapel.

Smiling, Ambrose watched her go. He had gained a lot of useful local knowledge, including where the Sequoia Singers were staying.

The Royal Hotel was a little way up the old High Street. "You can't miss it. Look for the big arch," his informant had assured him. The Kings Hall was before then, on the other side of the market square. Ambrose called on his way.

A badly typed notice on the door announced the results of the Festival Competitions. Ambrose glanced at the categories. The Calzone Singers were listed under 'Close Harmony Groups'. They had come third out of nine; creditable but not what they would have hoped for. After that disappointment, then an upsetting accident on the way, it was hardly surprising they were so cross when they'd arrived at Chalk Heath.

The Royal looked like the oldest and most elegant of the hotels in Leyton Bridge. An old coaching inn, it even had a large arch where carriages used to enter the courtyard. Judging by the comments he'd overheard The Calzone Singers had stayed somewhere far less comfortable. Hoping he was not too late, Ambrose went in, through a gracious hallway. A scattering of cases and a small group of elegantly dressed men and women were waiting in a lounge nearby. He noticed that there were only seven of them. If they were The Sequoia Singers they were missing a female member. All looked up at him expectantly as he entered. "Ah! Our taxi at last," one of the men said with evident relief.

"I'm afraid not," Ambrose said, managing not to laugh. "I'm looking for Mr James Radcliffe."

"Our revered Director," the man said, nodding towards a rotund middle-aged man standing beside the window. "That's him."

Thanking the speaker, Ambrose crossed the lounge towards the man. He had the air of someone who knew he was important but at that moment was decidedly irritated.

"Mr Radcliffe?" he asked.

"Yes," the man replied urbanely. "How can I be of assistance?"

Ambrose decided to keep the meeting informal if he could. "My name is Paul Ambrose," he replied. "I was hoping I would catch you before you left." He lowered his voice. "I wanted to speak to you about Mrs Angela Chapman."

"No offence meant," James Radcliffe replied sharply, "But I have no desire whatsoever to speak about that woman. If she's sent you to apologise, it's too late. Nothing would induce me to give her another chance. She nearly cost us last night's concert and our reputation."

"Mrs Chapman is dead," Ambrose said bluntly. He had intended to break the news gently but the man's manner suggested he would be unlikely to grieve.

"What? If this is some sort of joke?"

"I don't joke about such things." Taking out his warrant, Ambrose showed it to him.

"Oh Lord!" the man said. He nodded towards the sofa near the fire "I think we'd better sit down."

"Why didn't someone tell me?" he demanded as soon as they were sitting. "We would have got a deputy straight away."

"No one knew that you needed telling," Ambrose replied coldly. The callousness of the man's reaction annoyed him.

As if only just hearing what he'd said, the choir leader put his hand to his face. Under his self-important manner there was a decent man. "I'm sorry," he apologised. "That must have sounded heartless. But when Mrs Chapman didn't turn up it was panic stations; almost too late to find a replacement. I assumed she'd just let us down." He bit his lip and stared into the fire uncomfortably. "What did she die of? An accident?"

"Someone killed her."

"Oh my God!" James Radcliffe looked genuinely shaken.

Ambrose let him be quiet for a few moments. "She didn't let you down," he added quietly. "She died at about midday on Friday."

"Oh Lord!" For several moments the choir leader was silent. "What do you need to know?" he asked at length. "Everyone's going to be very shocked." He nodded in the direction of the men and women sitting waiting with their cases. "They were looking forward to her joining. She had what we needed: an excellent voice and the looks to go with it."

"Tell me how you met her," Ambrose began, taking out his notebook. "You said something about giving her a chance."

Mr Radcliffe nodded. "One of our sopranos, Harriet Nicholson, you may have heard of her? Anyway, she was offered a radio contract at very short notice," he explained. "She would have been mad to refuse, and I didn't want to stand in her way. I was judging the 'Close Harmony' category and heard Mrs Chapman sing. She was ideal. So I asked her if she would like to replace Harriet on a trial basis. It would see us though for a few weeks at least. It could also have been the break through Mrs Chapman needed: recordings, radio, maybe television. I have a reputation for spotting talent."

Though Mr Radcliffe's reply was a little smug, he was probably telling the truth, Ambrose reflected. He had spotted Angela's talent, and good as she was, she hadn't had that elusive break until he offered it. She must have been excited and nervous, afraid of losing what might be her last chance of a professional career, but not wanting to let the Calzone Singers down. Several of her colleagues had thought she seemed worried.

"Did she tell you she had a prior commitment?" Ambrose asked.

"She said her choir had bookings in Chalk Heath, but she'd get a deputy and would join us for last night's concert. She was going to come across early, for a quick rehearsal. I gave her the music. It wasn't demanding: just the usual crowd pleasers."

"Did you hear from her afterwards?"

Looking anxiously towards the window, James Radcliffe nodded. He seemed to be expecting someone to arrive: their taxis presumably. "She phoned from the hotel with a couple of queries," he replied, "and I called her later to check whether she'd found a deputy."

"Had she?"

"No. She couldn't find anyone at such short notice. Most of her contacts were taking part in the Festival. They wanted to get off home once their heat was over. She said it would be alright though. Calzone's last concert had been cancelled. She would catch the four o'clock bus over here. When she didn't arrive I tried to phone the hotel but the line was permanently engaged. So I rang Calzone's secretary. Her number was on their entry form."

A taxi was pulling up in the forecourt. "How can I contact you?" Ambrose asked quickly, "I shall need a statement."

"I'll give you my home address." Taking out his diary Mr Radcliffe wrote rapidly and then tore the page out. "This is all dreadful!" he said, passing the page to Ambrose. "Quite dreadful. Will you need statements from the others? They barely knew her and we'vee got a few days off after this. It'll be Wednesday before I'm back in London."

"They'll need to confirm what they were doing on Friday between eleven and twelve thirty," Ambrose said. "Collect their answers before you separate, please, and I'll arrange for someone to pick them up from your home."

"Will you tell everyone what's happened?" Mr Radcliffe asked urgently. Another taxi was arriving.

"I'm afraid you'll have to," Ambrose answered. "There isn't time now, or you'll miss your train."

The choir leader looked at his watch. "We're cutting it fine as it is," he agreed. "Reception asked for the taxis an hour ago. I forget how backward these small towns can be." Offering his hand in farewell, he got up. "I wish you'd brought me better news," he said. "Now we still have to find a replacement for Harriet and a fine singer has been taken from us. It's hard to make sense of life sometimes."

After the group had left in a flurry of cases and farewells, Ambrose ordered himself a cup of coffee. For half an hour he rested before driving back. Then he headed straight to the car park.

He was crossing the square when the clock on the market cross began chiming. "Of course!" he said to himself. "That's it!" In his surprise, he'd spoken aloud. A woman passing by looked at him dubiously and stepped aside.

"I've just realised something," he apologised but the woman sniffed and crossed the road.

Ambrose couldn't help laughing.

Chapter Twenty Six

As soon as Ambrose returned, PC Higgins came into his office. "Uttley have been on the phone," he said. "Their DI wants you to ring him. Hold the receiver well away. He doesn't need a phone."

Smiling, Ambrose looked at the note Higgins had passed him. "Interesting," he remarked and turned towards Winters. "DI Cavendish, Uttley, continuing Chapman investigation," he read aloud. "Has fresh evidence. Two prime suspects."

"They haven't hung around," Winters commented. "Can't have much on."

"Or Angela Chapman was very well known," Ambrose pointed out. "I hope they're not going to ignore our views. I have a few ideas myself." Frowning, he picked up the phone.

Higgins' warning was justified. "Cavendish," a voice boomed. "Thank you for ringing. We have a problem, don't we? You have the crime scene. We have the suspects. Thought we ought to put our heads together." The boom turned to a laugh. "Bit difficult with a hundred miles between us, eh? You might like to come up for a chat. We've interviewed all the choir again. Got a couple of leads you missed, not that you had a lot of time I suppose."

"No" Ambrose agreed coolly, bridling at the slight insult. "I'll be interested to hear what they are."

DI Cavendish seemed oblivious to any voice other than his own. "Pedderson looks the most likely," he boomed on. "Thoroughly odd character. Impersonates women. Calls himself Lily Gardena." Once again the boom became a loud laugh.

"I think you'll find that's in my notes," Ambrose pointed out. "Pedderson told us about his performances himself."

"Did he tell you the victim knew?"

"Yes. She recognised him from a poster."

"She may have done," DI Cavendish replied, "But she also got some dirt from one of our chaps. Sorry to have to say that. Pedderson was arrested after a brawl at a nightclub. Chapman was dating one of our PCs at the time. He told her. He's been carpeted since."

"I'll bet," Ambrose said, with feeling.

"That was a month ago," Cavendish continued. "Plenty of time for bad feeling. Usherette at the theatre's come forward. Says she saw them arguing. Couldn't hear what was said though."

DI Cavendish had a way of speaking in loud fragments that sounded like British Rail announcements. Ambrose felt wrong footed; annoyed that he hadn't known about John Pedderson's arrest. There hadn't been time to check criminal records.

"Pedderson claimed he and Chapman had sorted things out," Ambrose replied. "Is he sticking to that?"

"Swears blind he didn't kill her. Can't give an alibi for his movements though. None of the others saw him shopping. Hasn't kept any receipts. Can't remember which shops he went to. He could have returned to the hotel, done Chapman in, then gone back to catch the coach."

Despite his initial irritation, Ambrose was becoming intrigued. "The man's a good runner," he recalled. "But he'd have had to change his clothes. Someone would have noticed that."

"Unless the victim pulled the scissors out herself?" Cavendish suggested.

"And there was no blood until then," Ambrose agreed. It was a possibility he had considered. "No," he said. "Even if he didn't need to change, I don't think he could have caught the coach back. The hotel's a good way out of town."

"You know your area," Cavendish conceded. "OK. We'll scrap that. What about afterwards?"

"That's more likely," Ambrose said. "No one saw Pedderson until he came down to lunch. That's in my notes too."

"Saw that. Very clear." Despite his manner DI Cavendish clearly was no fool. "The man isn't helping himself," he continued. "Being deliberately vague I reckon. Might be trying to distract us from someone else. Miss Collier for instance."

"That's an interesting idea," Ambrose replied. "Is she your other prime suspect?"

"Has to be. At the scene straight away. Medical knowledge. Victim been unpleasant to her. Bit of a cold fish. Same problem there though. No blood spatter."

"And even less time unaccounted for," Ambrose agreed. "Anything interesting in the background checks yet?"

"Only just started. Suspects well known though. Apart from the sham Pole. Asking RAF records about him. Spotted one oddity."

"Oh?" Ambrose prompted.

"Dennis Walters. Why was he Home Guard? Not in a reserved occupation. Doesn't appear to have health problem. By '42 anyone with four limbs was going. Just curious."

"There are rumours," Ambrose said thoughtfully. "And Walters struck me as being a bit of a dark horse."

"Probably classified," Cavendish acknowledged. "Worth trying."

There was an awkward pause. "Is it OK if we follow a couple of leads this end?" Ambrose asked.

"Of course! Crime on your patch and all that. Keep us informed. We'll do the same for you."

As soon as Ambrose put the phone down, Winters looked at him quizzically. "Sounds like they've got plenty on Pedderson," he remarked and grimaced. "I could hear most of their end. Are they arresting him?"

"Not yet."

"Why not?"

"Because their bloke's canny," Ambrose replied. "He doesn't rush things."

Winters looked away, taking the comment as a criticism that wasn't meant.

"It's too circumstantial," Ambrose went on. "There's no evidence Chapman threatened to tell the others. The usherette could have heard them arguing about music. As for being vague, Pedderson could be thinking Barbara did it, and is trying to confuse things. Meadows reckoned he was sweet on her. Keep an open mind. Dennis Walters sounds equally interesting."

"What do you want me to do next?" Winters asked.

"Carry on investigating the thefts: 'Bonnie and Clyde' as well as the Gibbs. Do we have enough evidence for either case?"

"Against the two youngsters, yes," Winters assured him, relieved to be on safe ground. He'd worked very hard over the past twenty-four hours to get results. "Their proper names are Estelle Lambert and Jonathan Parsons, both from Jenners Park, as you thought. Her dad is headmaster at the local Grammar. His is chairman of the Golf Club." Relishing the idea, Winters couldn't help smiling. "Needless to say, neither respected father is amused."

"Nor would I be," Ambrose admitted. For a second he had an appalling vision of Joe being charged with something equally dreadful. He pushed the idea aside. "Did it for kicks I suppose," he suggested.

"At the start perhaps, but they got very good at it," Winters pointed out. "They may go down. It's probably not their first offence: just the first time they've been caught, although how anyone would prove that is another rmatter."

"And Mr Gibbs?"

"That's going to be harder," Winters admitted. "I'm sure I'm right, but there aren't any fingerprints to match against his. 'The Brown Trilby' was too careful. The photo might be him but it was taken a long time ago. I thought he was about to confess this morning but his wife cut in quick. Unless he does cough up it's going to be difficult to prove anything." Shaking his head with a mixture of amusement and sadness, Winters added, "I've always liked the old guy. He seemed harmless enough. You can never tell with people, can you?"

"No indeed," Ambrose agreed.

He went straight into the superintendent's office afterwards and briefed Mac.

"Thanks for coming in today, sir," Ambrose started.

"Don't flatter yourself, I have many other things to deal with!" Mac laughed. "So where are we?"

"I reckon we have two possible motives," Ambrose replied. "The victim cancelling the concert might have been the last straw for someone. Or Pedderson could have been trying to shut her up. Personally I don't think Pedderson's our killer. I'd like to send Higgins to question the waitress and the chambermaid again. I want to know how the chambermaid could have been in two places at once. "

"Higgins?" Mac asked, raising an eyebrow.

"I'd rather not ask Sam Winters," Ambrose explained. "He tends to make up his mind too early and the maid's from a bad family. Is Meadows around? There ought to be a female present."

Mac glanced at the schedules on the wall behind him. "She should be in," he said, "Are you sure Higgins won't have any trouble? A girl isn't enough back up, even if she is related to Boadicea."

Laughing, Ambrose assured him that 'Bonnie and Clyde' were safely tucked up in Jenners Park 'nick'.

Higgins found WPC Meadows warming her hands at the old pot bellied stove. "You're out in the cold again," he called. "Sorry. We're off to The Shalimar." In surprise Meadows grabbed her hat. She didn't have pleasant memories of The Shalimar Hotel and would rather not go there again, but she knew better than to argue.

A smell of soup and hot bread greeted them as they arrived. Luncheon was being served. Peter Tempest welcomed them warily. Despite the events of the past week, he still looked the exemplar of an English gentleman: spotless blazer, regimental tie, flannels perfectly creased. He just needed the panama hat, Meadows thought wryly, though the weather was hardly right for croquet on the lawn.

"How can I help you, officers?" Peter asked. "I'm afraid you've caught us at a busy time." He led them into the library and shut the door behind them. "Mercifully not everyone's cancelled and we have quite a few bookings for next week," he added. "We've left poor Mrs Chapman's room locked of course. Have there been developments?"

Meadows looked round the room. Everything was back in place, a vase of dried lavender scenting the air, the Sunday papers ironed and placed in their leather holders, ready for guests to read. It seemed incredible that a murder investigation had begun in that room. "We'd like to speak to Miss Fellowes and Libby Nunn again," Higgins replied.

"Jane is just finishing serving luncheon. I can take over if it's necessary." As he spoke, Peter examined the writing desk. Seeing that the pad of paper was almost used, he took another from the drawer, and then changed the blotter. Not a minute could be wasted his manner suggested, though very politely.

"Yes, it is necessary," Higgins insisted. He wasn't going to be put off.

With a stiff smile, Peter left the room.

Jane arrived within minutes, carrying two china cups and saucers on a matching china tray. "Mrs Tempest thought you might appreciate a cup of tea," she said, setting the tray on one of the small tables. "I gather you want to speak to me again." Like Peter, her tone was as courteous as ever, but the frown around her eyes betrayed concern.

Thanking her, Higgins indicated the chair beside him. He nodded to Meadows, who took out her notebook ready to write down the waitress' answers. "The DI would like you to go over things again," he explained, "You might remember some extra detail." He helped himself to one of the cups of tea and deliberated for a moment as he drank. Then he looked at the questions Ambrose had dictated to him. "Did you go upstairs between breakfast and lunch?" he asked.

Jane shook her head. "No. I was too busy setting out the buffet."

Once again Higgins glanced at his list. "When did the choir first realise Mrs Chapman was missing?"

Holding her breath to steady it, Jane recalled the exact order of events. "About ten past twelve," she answered. "Luncheon was booked for noon. The choir wanted to rehearse that afternoon. Mrs Chapman was late so her friend went up to fetch her. The others started eating."

"And was anyone else missing at that stage?"

"Yes, their leader, Miss Hulme." Jane allowed herself a slight smile. "Apparently she'd given them all 'what for' earlier about being on time, so they were quite amused she was late."

"Did they seem concerned about anything?" Higgins asked.

"Not that I could see."

Higgins paused to make sure Meadows had everything written down. "Question three," he read, "when did you go upstairs to find Libby?"

"Half past twelve. Mrs Tempest beckoned me from the door of her office. She said the vacuum might annoy the guests, and asked me to tell Libby to switch it off."

"Did you go straight up?"

"Of course."

"And where was Libby?" Higgins asked. Like Ambrose before him, he found Jane Fellowes' brief answers irritating.

"Vacuuming the long corridor," she replied.

"Can you recall which bedroom she was near?" Higgins had brought Sutton's sketches with him. Taking them out of an envelope, he spread the map of the first floor on the table in front of her.

For a moment Jane looked intently at the sketch. "Room seven," she replied.

"Mr Tempest has repaired the carpet there. I checked Libby hadn't snagged the join."

"Did you see anyone as you came downstairs?" Higgins continued.

Jane shook her head. "I could hear voices in the office, but no one came out. I realise now the ladies must have been waiting for the police." For the first time her voice shook.

"Thank you. You've been very helpful." Higgins got up to show her to the door. Then he paused. "You look rather pale," he remarked. "Are you alright?"

To his surprise Jane's eyes filled with tears. "I'm afraid all this is making me unwell," she admitted. "This is my home. If you close it, I shall have nowhere to go. I wouldn't fit into a modern hotel. They want pretty young girls, not someone trained in silver service..." She stopped, her usual reserve returning. "I'm sorry," she apologised. "I'm wasting your time."

"No," Higgins reassured her. "We appreciate how much this must be affecting all of you. Thank Mrs Tempest for her thoughtfulness." He glanced at the little china tray. "Ask Libby to come now, please."

After Jane had gone, Higgins finished his tea. "Have yours before it goes cold," he advised Meadows. Then he stared in silence at the sketch in front of him.

Libby was very pale as she entered; 'scared stiff' was Meadows' description afterwards. "Miss Fellowes said you wanted me," she began, and cleaned a dirty shoe against the back of her other leg. "I've told everything I remember, honest. I didn't take nothing, and I wouldn't kill anyone, not for the world."

She was becoming distressed. Higgins glanced at Meadows and passed her Ambrose's list. Then he took out his own notebook. "It's alright," Meadows assured her. "We're not accusing you of anything. We just need to sort something out with you. You said you saw Miss

Hulme come up the back stairs at a quarter past twelve. Is that right?"

"Yes, Ma'am."

"Are you sure?" Higgins intervened.

"Cross my heart and hope to die. I saw the clock in the corridor just before. It's one of them special ones so I couldn't tell exactly, but it was near quarter past. I was cleaning one of the rooms. I couldn't say which. It all goes into a bit of a blur. I just clean as fast as I can." Libby's words were tumbling out. Higgins nodded to Meadows to take over again.

"Did you see anyone besides Miss Hulme?" she asked the girl more gently. "Miss Collier perhaps?"

"No Ma'am. I didn't see no one, not until Miss Fellowes came and told me to put the vacuum off."

"And you didn't hear anything odd when you were near Mrs Chapman's room?"

"No Ma'am. The vacuum makes an awful row. I don't hear nothing when that's on."

Meadows looked down at Ambrose's list. "Did you go back along the corridor after you finished vacuuming?" she asked.

"No!" Libby replied, shaking her head emphatically. "I got on with cleaning the front bedrooms like I was told. I get paid the same, however long I take. So I get done as quick as I can. Then I go to my other jobs until I'm needed here for dinner. I clean for two old ladies between."

"You work very hard," Meadows commented.

"I've got to, haven't I? I'm saving up. Me and Stan are trying to get enough together to buy a house; one of them new places where the Grange used to be. They're only small but it's a start in't it?"

"It is indeed," Meadows agreed, smiling in encouragement.

"I don't get it!" Higgins said in exasperation after Libby had gone. "The girl's telling the truth. You can see she is. But why didn't she see Miss Collier? And why didn't Miss Collier notice her?" Higgins frowned with the effort of thought. He was by no means slow, but tricky problems gave him trouble. "Like the boss says, it doesn't make sense," he insisted. "Why did Libby go on cleaning after the murder was discovered? As if nothing had happened?"

"Even if the vacuum drowned everything out, she'd have seen something," Meadows agreed. "She ought to have seen Miss Collier running for help."

"Unless she was already at the front of the house." Higgins stared at the sketch again, then pushed it towards Meadows. "Have a butchers at this," he instructed. "How far along the corridor do you reckon you can see the back stairs?"

Meadows took out her pencil and laid it flat on the drawing to give a sight line. "Up to about here on this side," she said, indicating room eight. "You wouldn't see her *on* the stairs from the other side. But if Libby meant 'coming from the stairs', you'd see her up to about room fifteen. Maybe further if you were standing outside the bathrooms."

"Exactly. Just what the boss said," Higgins answered. "He wants us to try an experiment. Ask Mrs Tempest if she minds us opening some of the bedrooms. Tell her we'll be sure to lock them afterwards."

Five minutes later Meadows reappeared with a bundle of keys. "She wasn't happy," she whispered. "Wanted to come up and supervise. Luckily the phone rang. I'd rather not have her breathing down my neck. She's very nice and all that, but she reminds me of my old headmistress."

Together Higgins and Meadows went up the front stairs and onto the main landing. From there they turned towards the front of the house. Outside room seven they found the join in the carpet Jane had described. "Can *you* see the back stairs?" Higgins asked rhetorically.

Meadows shook her head. "Libby didn't see Miss Hulme from here," she replied.

A large old clock stood nearby and she checked it against her watch. "Pretty accurate," she commented. "Must be worth a bob or two. There's nothing odd about it though."

"There should be some sort of star and moon," Higgins said, frowning. "This isn't the clock the chambermaid saw. This one has star fish and sea horses on it. There must be another one."

They turned back along the landing towards the choir's rooms. Higgins checked Sutton's sketch. "You go down these stairs, turn round and come up them slowly," he suggested, "I'll walk forward until I can see you."

Higgins had reached room eight before he saw Meadows. "Got you," he called.

They stood together in the corridor afterwards. "You've got to hand it to the boss," Higgins said. "He can see things when he's not even here. Just from a sketch." He shook his head in admiration. "Right. Now for the next experiment. Where's the nearest clock?"

"Has to be that one," Meadows replied, indicating a second old clock on the wall opposite. "And there's the star and moon!" she added triumphantly, pointing to the dial.

"Right! That confirms the chambermaid's story," Higgins said. "OK. The boss said to open the rooms on the opposite side to the clock and see what they're like. Heaven knows why. I need a rest. You 'reccie'. I'll make notes." He leant against a door frame, notepad in hand.

Fumbling through the bunch until she found the right keys, Meadows did as directed. Mystified, she looked into the rooms. In the first two, the bed had been made up and possessions were neatly arranged on the dressing table and chest of drawers. The next room was also in use but looked untidy, as if its occupants had rushed down to lunch.

"See anything of interest?" Higgins asked.

"I don't know what I'm looking for," Meadows objected. "They all seem to be furnished the same. They must have got a job lot of identical furniture when they started the hotel." She listed everything in order. "Room eight: Left to right: small chest of drawers, bed, dressing table and stool, wardrobe taking up most of the wall on the right. Nine's the same." She peered into room ten. "This one's identical but the other way round," she called. "It looks like a larger room's been divided into two. Anything more?"

"Can you see the clock? Libby said she was cleaning a room when she saw it."

Walking in and out of each room, Meadows checked. "No," she said in surprise. "You can't even see it in room nine, and that's the nearest."

Letting out his breath in exasperation, Higgins sighed. "I'll be damned if I can make sense of it all," he said, getting up. Putting

Sutton's sketch back in the envelope he turned to leave. "Take the keys to Mrs T," he instructed. "Then we'll go back to the 'Station. The DI said to be as quick as we could."

"Do you want me to type it all up for him?" Meadows asked. She already knew the answer.

"Now there's an offer a man can't refuse!" Higgins replied.

Chapter Twenty Seven

As soon as Ambrose arrived, the superintendent called him in. "Shut the door behind you," he said softly. Intrigued, Ambrose followed him into his office and waited. Normally Mac left his door ajar. Closing it meant either a junior was about to get a rollicking, or something serious had happened.

Mac wasted no time on greetings. "Uttley CID have been on the blower," he said. "About Dennis Walters. They asked for his wartime service. Request refused."

"On what grounds?" Ambrose asked in surprise.

"National interest." Mac looked thoughtfully out the window. "Walters was in the Home Guard, but we don't know where he served. We can assume he wasn't parading around a church hall with a broom handle. He was doing something the Government still isn't admitting to."

"Well, I'll be…" Ambrose shook his head. "You'd think he was Mr Ordinary: stuck in a boring job; bit henpecked, fancied another woman but too decent to stray." He couldn't help smiling at the contrast. Then he was serious.

"My dad reckoned Churchill had a secret army," Ambrose carried on. "Chaps trained to go underground if there was an invasion. I assumed it was wishful thinking."

He let out his breath slowly. "We're never going to know, are we? He won't tell us. He'd be bound by the Official Secrets Act."

"This brings Walters back into the frame," Mac pointed out. "If there *was* a resistance movement, and he was part of it, he'd know how to kill and leave no prints."

"He had a good alibi," Ambrose replied thoughtfully, "Mainly from his wife though. She could have lied to protect him, or because she was afraid of him." He frowned. "I dunno. I got the impression he was devious rather than violent. If he was doing something special, I'd say he was a saboteur, not a fighter. Look at the way he got Angela to object to the planning proposal, just to delay his wife's mother moving in. But he could still have had special training, and if he lost his temper…" He left the sentence unfinished.

"Don't say anything about this," Mac warned, "Not even to Sam Winters. I was told not to tell you, but we have a murder to investigate. Hang it all, the war ended nearly fifteen years ago!"

"Perhaps they think we might need a secret army again?" Ambrose suggested.

"Against the Russians? It'd take more than a few chaps in a dugout to beat them." Mac grimaced. "Perish the thought! How did you get on with your other leads?"

Briefly, Ambrose recounted Higgins' and Meadows' visit to the hotel. "They confirmed my theory," he ended. "The chambermaid's either lying or mistaken. Higgins thought she was telling the truth. I want to go back there with Sam Winters. If we stand in the corridor at the right time we might see what she saw."

"No one ever sees *exactly* what another person saw," Mac warned, "but it's worth a try."

Just after noon, Ambrose and Winters escorted Libby and Audrey up the main stairs of The Shalimar. They headed along the corridor towards the back stairs. Libby was pale with fear; Audrey irritated at having the hotel's routine interrupted yet again. It didn't help that Libby couldn't recall exactly where she'd been working. "Think!" Audrey snapped.

"I don't know!" Libby wailed. "I was working. That's all." She wandered up and down the corridor trying to remember. "I think it might have been here," she said, stopping beside room nine.

Ambrose nodded. It seemed likely. She would have been able to see both the clock and the back stairs from that position. "That's all we wanted to know," he said patiently.

Winters took up position beside the door. Ambrose went into room nine. To his disappointment, the dressing table had been moved from its usual place. It had been pushed against the wall on the left hand side of the door. "Damn!" he said to himself, before moving it back to the centre of the room.

They waited for the clock to reach quarter past twelve. Rummaging in her pocket for her handkerchief, Libby began to snivel. "It's alright child," Audrey assured her more gently. "You won't be in trouble if you told the truth." Her accent on the word 'truth' did nothing to reassure the girl. She began to sob out loud. "Oh do shush!" Audrey begged. "Can't you see the policemen want to be quiet?"

The clock whirred. Then it clicked three times, the bell silenced. Ambrose looked back at the mirror on the dressing table. There was no sign of the clock, or the back stairs, just a reflection of the wall opposite and the corner of the bed. Nor could he see the clock when he turned towards the door. "I was so sure…" he said aloud. "It had to be the explanation."

Yet no matter where he stood in the room he couldn't see the clock. Going back out of the room, he turned towards Winters, "Did you see the clock strike the quarter?" he asked.

"Yes. Fine. She must have been in there." He lowered his voice. "She couldn't have mistaken anything else for twelve fifteen. The clock's perfectly clear even if it doesn't have numbers."

Libby nodded vigorously. "You can tell where the fingers are pointing," she agreed. "It's fancy but you can still tell the time. I was here at twelve fifteen, Sir, like I said."

Ambrose turned towards her in exasperation. "So how could you be at the front of the building just after quarter past?" he demanded.

"I work fast, sir."

Audrey groaned in despair.

"And why didn't you see Miss Collier?" Ambrose persisted. "Your story doesn't make sense. If you were here, you'd have seen her come out of the victim's room."

The girl clearly had no answer. They were getting nowhere; just upsetting her. Sighing, Ambrose went back into room nine. Standing in silence he considered the dressing table mirror. It was made up of three panels, not one: a wide middle stretch and two narrow side panels. A memory of a childhood game came to him. He used to play with a similar mirror at his grandparents' house, opening and closing the side panels until he saw his face reflected in a reflection, and then in another a reflection, back it seemed into infinity. He couldn't have been more than seven or eight.

"Of course!" he said suddenly. Reaching forwards, he adjusted the mirror's panels. It took a minute or two to get the angle right. Then he called to Winters. "Come and stand in the doorway," he instructed. "Can you see the clock now?"

Winters frowned in bewilderment, looking back down the corridor and then into the room. Then he too let out his breath in surprise. "Yes!" he answered triumphantly.

Ambrose turned back to Libby. "You didn't lie to us," he said. "You made a mistake, that's all. Come and stand in the doorway. Here. Beside the sergeant."

In bewilderment Libby did as she was told. At first she looked up and down the corridor or at Mrs Tempest, anywhere but where Ambrose wanted her to look. Then suddenly she stiffened. "Aw, lummy!" she said looking towards the mirror. She went very red. "Oh Lord! I'm ever so sorry. I didn't mean to get everyone mixed up. Please don't be angry with me. Please. You won't arrest me will you?"

"Of course not!" Ambrose assured her. He turned to Audrey. "Let the poor girl have a break," he advised. "She needs a cup of tea."

"I don't understand," Audrey admitted.

"Libby'll explain to you," Ambrose replied. "Won't you, Libby?"

The girl nodded mutely. Her expression still one of bewilderment, Audrey put her arm round the chambermaid's shoulders and led her downstairs.

Chapter Twenty Eight

Ambrose decided to set off for Uttley that afternoon. If they turned up unexpectedly, it might startle the murderer into doing or saying something incriminating. Leaving it until tomorrow could be too late.

"Can't you just let Uttley's chap, Cavendish, make the arrest?" Mac demanded.

But Ambrose insisted. "Uttley CID has no grounds to stop the choir leaving town," he replied. "Besides, I don't have any real proof."

"So you're just hoping that one look from you and the murderer will confess?" Mac sounded sarcastic.

"Something like that," Ambrose admitted. "If I'm right as to who it is, then I think they just might cave in."

Mac shrugged his consent. He had to admit that, given time to make plans, any of the choir could disappear. Anton wanted to avoid confessing he was a fraud. He would probably slip away soon, saying he was joining Polish friends in Birmingham or London. Pedderson was single too. In his line of work (both lines) he would be able to find a job elsewhere. The same applied to Barbara. She could apply for a transfer to another hospital without arousing suspicion. If any of the others felt guilty enough, they could just announce they were going away on holiday and never come back. Ambrose was determined not to give them the chance.

Higgins was recruited to drive Ambrose and Winters to Uttley. Having made the trip once already, he knew the way. Mac would make the necessary telephone calls while they travelled, to alert DI Cavendish to their arrival.

Ambrose didn't speak much for the first hour and Winters knew better than to start a conversation. Ambrose reminded himself he mustn't let personal feelings intrude but a sense of regret kept darkening his thoughts. If the committee hadn't invited the choir to come to Chalk Heath, a beautiful woman might still be alive. The singers would have gone straight home after the competition and he wouldn't now be travelling up to Uttley to arrest one of them.

"Oh come off it!" Ambrose told himself severely. He might as well say "If that accident hadn't happened", or "If they'd sung better at Leyton Bridge". Life and death was full of such ifs and buts. If their secretary's children hadn't caught measles, she might have stopped tensions in the choir getting out of hand. With her accompanying them, the singers might have won their competition. Then they would have been happy, instead of blaming each other for the least thing. It was pointless going over it all, but it didn't stop him doing so.

Winters was equally quiet. When he got back he would have to arrest old Mr Gibbs, and possibly his wife. Joe Gibbs was almost certainly 'The Brown Trilby' and Mrs Gibbs was probably guilty of aiding and abetting him, or at least of withholding evidence. Two hotels had kept registers from before the war, showing that a Joseph Gibbs had stayed there a few days before thefts were reported. The Met had also traced him to addresses near other burglaries.

Normally Winters had little sympathy for those he arrested. They knew the law and they broke it. That was all there was to it. But he had always liked Mr Gibbs and he couldn't help feeling sorry for him now. It must be terrible to lose your memory when you were once top of your profession, even if it was a criminal one. He rather respected Mrs Gibbs too. She'd realised her husband was deteriorating and covered for him. She'd helped him retain his dignity and even an aged thief deserved that. None of which excused either of them, of course, as Winters reminded himself severely.

Higgins had learned to keep quiet when his superiors did and was not a talkative man by nature. Besides, he needed to concentrate. The afternoon was drab and grey. With three of them in the car, the inside of the windows steamed up immediately. Mud soon spattered the outside. The windscreen wipers only cleared a small arc in the muck. Twice Higgins had to stop the car to clean a bigger area. Only when Ambrose and Winters began to relax a little, did he feel it was safe to speak. "What did we miss?" he asked, frowning into the murk ahead. "Meadows and I went over those rooms with a fine tooth comb."

"You didn't play with mirrors when you were a kid," Ambrose replied, smiling.

"Sorry Sir. I don't get you."

"Remember the dressing table mirror? It has side panels on hinges. If the one nearest the door was bent forward a bit, it reflected the clock in the corridor. It didn't when it was flat. The chambermaid must have been working just inside the room, and seen the clock in the mirror."

"Ah!" Higgins said thoughtfully.

Darkness was closing in as they approached Sunnybank old people's home. Anne Jacobs had begged them to park round the back. "Don't spoil the old folk's Christmas," she'd pleaded on the telephone. She was not playing for the choir that afternoon, having to look after her children. "One of the old gents at Sunnybank plays the piano," she explained. "And the choir sings *a capella* most of the time in any case."

So, driving carefully by the side of the building, Higgins found a spot next to a battered old mini bus. "Do you want me to come in?" he asked hopefully. He didn't fancy waiting an hour or so in a cold car.

"No. We don't want to go in mob handed," Ambrose replied. "The two of us will do for our side. We're meeting Cavendish inside."

Ambrose, Winters and Cavendish waited in the foyer until Matron came out to see them. She wasn't at all happy. "No, you can't interrupt," she said firmly. "Our residents have been looking forward to their sing-along all week. It's not just carols, you know, but some of the wartime songs they love. Bless them, they come alive again when they hear those. Wait until we're finished. The choir can't run away while they're singing, can they?"

Cavendish had to agree it was unlikely.

"I can't think what you want with them," Matron added with a disapproving sniff. "Everyone knows the Calzone Singers. You're not going to tell me they're a pack of thieves, are you?"

"We only want to speak to a few of them," Ambrose assured her. He bent down to whisper something in the Matron's ear. She looked surprised, then shrugged.

"You can use my office when they've finished singing. Second door on the left. You won't all fit in." Glancing down at the watch pinned to her apron she bustled off to check the tea was being prepared.

If the situation hadn't been so sad, Ambrose would have laughed at being bossed around like that. "We might as well sit down," he suggested.

A row of hard plastic chairs lined the foyer wall. The three officers settled down to wait. Beyond the swing doors, a roomful of voices was singing, 'Pack up your troubles in your old kit bag…' As each new verse began, the voices tailed off then joined in again at the chorus, heartily if not in tune.

"Sounds like they're enjoying themselves," Winters commented.

They began to talk about the case. To Ambrose's relief, Cavendish could turn down the volume when he wasn't on the telephone. "You're sure you know who did it?" he asked Ambrose quietly.

"No. I'm not," Ambrose admitted. "But we've broken a cast iron alibi and that's a good enough place to start."

Cavendish waited to see if Ambrose would elaborate, but he didn't. He'd been deliberately cryptic on the telephone. Despite many attempts, Cavendish had been unable to get Ambrose to name the killer.

Winters knew his boss too well to even ask. Ambrose would never explain his theories until he'd had chance to check every angle.

After a long pause, Cavendish tried a different approach.

"My money's on Dennis Walters," he said with a knowing expression. Clearly he'd been taken into his superintendent's confidence, like Ambrose. "He's a dark horse, could be a trained killer, and the victim had been a nuisance to him for some time. I reckon he snapped."

"With respect, I can't see what Walters would have gained," Winters joined in. "He'd already got what he wanted from Angela and if she died, her planning objection would have fallen away. Walters was clearly desperate to keep his mother-in-law from moving in. I'd say it has to be Pedderson. He needed to shut the victim up.

He's also the only one who could have run fast enough to get back to town in time to join the bus."

Ambrose stayed silent. Beyond the swing doors 'It's a Long Way to Tipperary' came to an end. It was followed by 'Only a Bird in a Gilded Cage'. Ambrose was aware of a growing tension. He had no idea how the choir would react. He wasn't even certain he was right. The other two were making fair points.

"Oh Gawd!" Cavendish said as "Hands, Knees and Boomps-a-Baisy" began. "Spare me ever having to sit and sing that!" Getting up, he wandered the foyer restlessly. Ambrose was glad the doors weren't made of glass. The old people couldn't see the three men waiting.

Unable to stay seated, Ambrose went to explore the Matron's office. It was tiny. He wished they weren't such a big group. He'd brought Winters with him because he'd met the choir at the hotel and might spot discrepancies. Ambrose also wanted Chalk Heath to be well represented if Uttley CID tried to poach the case. Fortunately, Cavendish didn't seem that sort.

From the lounge came the sound of 'Auld Lang Syne'. The sing-along must be finishing. Looking around, Ambrose saw a small sunroom opening off the corridor. That would be more suitable, less intimidating and not so cramped. He might persuade Cavendish to sit a little aside, where he could hear but not be too obvious. Having met Ambrose and Winters before, the suspects might talk more freely if they didn't have a stranger present.

Another pair of swing doors opposite led to the end of the main lounge, and was the nearest access to Matron's office. Beyond them, The National Anthem was being thumped out on a piano. The old people sang firmly and patriotically, back in a pre-war world. Quickly Ambrose explained his request to his colleagues. To his relief, Cavendish agreed, positioning himself beside the back window in the sunroom. Ambrose and Winters waited nearer the doors.

In preparation Winters took out his notebook and checked his pencils. With a start, he suddenly realised he had no idea who Ambrose had asked to speak to first.

An assistant appeared at the far end of the corridor, pushing a trolley laden with cups, saucers and medications. It squeaked all the way to the lounge doors. Then another followed with a tea urn and plates of mince pies. At last the doors swung open and Evelyn Hulme appeared, looking bewildered. She started to go towards Matron's office. Then she saw Ambrose and Winters. For a second she looked as if she might faint. Urgently she put her hand onto the doorframe to steady herself.

"Hello Evelyn," Ambrose began, stepping between her and the front door. "We'd like to talk to you again. Come and sit here." Taking her by the elbow, he indicated a chair in the sunroom.

To his surprise Evelyn did as she was asked, without question. She seemed to be expecting him. "Have you come to ask me about Angela?" she replied almost in a whisper.

"I'm afraid you don't have an alibi any longer," Ambrose explained, sitting beside her. "The maid has changed her evidence. She now says you came up the back stairs at quarter *to* twelve, not quarter past. That was about the time Mrs Chapman was killed."

Again Evelyn surprised him by making no attempt at denial. Instead she swallowed hard and said in a calm, controlled voice, "I've written a statement. It's at home. If you drive us back that way, I'll pick it up."

Ambrose hardly knew how to proceed. "Why would we be driving you somewhere?" he asked.

"Because we have to go to the police station. I need to confess to killing …" Her control breaking, Evelyn stopped, her mouth going slack with emotion. Then she managed to continue, speaking as if from a script. "To killing Mrs Angela Chapman. I didn't mean to. I didn't even realise I'd killed her. But I shall pay the penalty."

Cavendish was looking across in astonishment. Winters was writing furiously. "I should have confessed straight away," Evelyn ploughed on huskily, "but I couldn't believe what had happened. I think I was in a state of shock. I felt that if I waited it would all go away…" Gulping back a sob, she clutched at the arm of the chair until her knuckles went white. "And I needed to see the choir through Christmas. We had so many engagements…" she tailed off.

"Evelyn, think what you're saying," Ambrose warned. "You're confessing to murder or manslaughter at least."

"Yes," she agreed quietly.

Ambrose glanced towards his counterpart, who nodded. "This interview will now take place under caution," Cavendish said in an official tone. "You do not have to say anything, but anything you do say may be given in evidence? Do you understand?"

"Yes," Evelyn said again. "Shall we go?" She rose unsteadily. "Please don't let the old folk see. Tell them I'm not well. I don't want to ruin their Christmas. And if it's possible not to tell the choir yet." She was crying now, tears running down her face.

"Sit down again," Ambrose instructed, afraid she might collapse. "Tell us what happened. It might help you."

Evelyn dropped back into the chair, ashen-faced. Trying to regain her compose, she stared ahead, as if recalling her prepared statement. "We were on a shopping outing in Chalk Heath," she began. "I overheard a customer talking. He said our concert in Jenners Park had been cancelled and wasn't it a shame? I knew no one but Angela would cancel a concert without telling me. Besides, I'd seen her talking to one of the judges in Leyton Bridge, all flushed and happy." She spoke in a dull monotone, barely taking a breath between each sentence. "I guessed he'd made her some sort of offer. I couldn't speak to her on the coach. So I went for a walk immediately we got back, to try to calm myself. Then I went up to Angela's room. I just wanted to ask why she'd done it."

"And then?" Ambrose prompted.

"I couldn't believe it. Angie didn't even apologise. She just announced that she'd been offered a place in the Sequoia Singers. She'd intended to tell me but I was always too busy, as if it was my fault. She'd done her best to find a deputy. When she couldn't, she'd cancelled the concert, so we wouldn't be without a full line-up at the last minute. It was too good a chance for her to miss she said. She was sure I would understand. Then she started sorting out what she was going to change into for lunch." The script came to a sudden end.

"What did you do after that?" Ambrose asked.

It was some time before Evelyn could speak again. When she did, her voice shook with remembered anger as well as fear. "I begged her not to leave us, or at least to stay until we could find a replacement. We'd meant so much to each other. But she started boasting about how good her new choir was. We were only amateurs. She said she had to get a bus to Leyton Bridge to rehearse for a concert that night. She didn't have time to argue with me. Then she turned her back on me, like I was an idiot. I was so furious I didn't know what I was doing. I grabbed the nearest thing and hit her. Then I stormed out of the room."

"Did you realise you'd picked up a pair of scissors?" Ambrose asked.

Her eyes filling with tears again, Evelyn shook her head. "Not at the time," she replied. "But outside in the garden I realised what I'd done. I told myself she'd be OK. It was just a little pair of scissors. She'd be alright if I called a doctor. So I ran back upstairs to see how she was. Barbara was coming out of her room. When she said Angie was dead I couldn't believe it." With an agonised sigh, Evelyn paused. "I didn't know I'd hit an artery," she said softly. "After that, all I could think of was getting the choir home without involving them. If I pretended it wasn't me, we'd all be allowed to leave. When the maid said she'd seen me at twelve fifteen, not earlier, it seemed like I was doing the right thing."

As if her hands were offensive to her, Evelyn stared down at them. Clearly she still found it hard to believe what she'd done. "I knew I'd have to confess sometime," she said. "I couldn't live with knowing I'd killed someone, especially a friend, even if I didn't mean to."

Ambrose stood up, "We'd better go now, before the old folk or your colleagues come out," he advised.

Shakily Evelyn rose and held her wrists out towards him.

"What's that for?" Ambrose asked in surprise.

"Aren't you going to handcuff me?"

"I don't think we need to," Ambrose replied. He glanced towards DI Cavendish who nodded in agreement.

They were preparing to leave when Matron appeared at the end of the corridor, talking to one of her staff. "Can you tell the choir Miss Hulme isn't feeling well, and has gone home early?" Cavendish asked her.

In surprise she stared at him, and then at Ambrose and Winters. Finally she looked at Evelyn. "I hope you're feeling better soon, Miss Hulme," she said.

Evelyn couldn't reply. Frowning in bewilderment, Matron turned towards the lounge.

Unseen by the rest of the choir, Ambrose and Cavendish escorted Evelyn out of the foyer, and into the December evening.

Chapter Twenty Nine

January Twenty First 1960

Meadows pushed her plate aside and drank her tea. For the first time that year, the door to The Copper Kettle had been left open slightly. The sweet scent of fresh air was creeping into the usual fug of chip fat and cigarette smoke. Through the window beside her table she could see the florist shop opposite. An enamel bucket stood outside, full of daffodils. They were just beginning to open. "Imported of course," Meadows acknowledged, but the sight lifted her spirits.

The letter beside her plate lifted them too, arriving by second post that morning and addressed c/o Chalk Heath Police Station. She hadn't had time to read it until then but she'd glanced at the signature. She had no idea why Barbara Collier should have written to her but she was glad that she had. In different circumstances they might have been friends.

Unfolding the carefully written sheets Meadows read the first paragraph.

13, Newdigate Street,

Uttley.

January Nineteenth

Dear Pauline,

I hope you don't mind me writing to you. I've meant to for ages but each time I've started I've given up. I wanted to thank you for the help you gave us while we were in Chalk Heath. You were always kind and fair, even when we were shouting at you. I'm so sorry we behaved badly to you. All I can say in excuse is that it was a dreadful few days. I hope being involved with us didn't cause you trouble at work.

I also thought you might like to know what's been happening. I don't suppose you're told much after a case is finished. That must be really frustrating. We had an awful Christmas and New Year with Evelyn being arrested and the rest of us having to cancel bookings and tell people what had happened. The newspapers were horrible. Reporters hung around outside our houses and got lots of things wrong, even our names.

We're beginning to emerge now. DI Ambrose has been a tremendous help and I'm writing to thank him too. He broke the news about Evelyn to us personally and has given us lots of useful advice. He even persuaded Evelyn to get a good lawyer. Now Mr Freeman says he can get the charge reduced to manslaughter. Apparently it helps the defence if someone kills in a moment of passion rather than plans it, and Angie provoked Evelyn. Even I have to admit that.

He might be able to get Evelyn off completely he says. He'd argue the case wasn't proven beyond reasonable doubt. Angie might have committed suicide, and even if she didn't, she contributed to her own death. Evelyn says she wants to be convicted of manslaughter, though. She killed Angie and she has to take responsibilty.

At first, I was angry that she wouldn't be charged with murder. An eye for an eye and all that, and Angie was my friend. Now I'm almost sorry for Evelyn. Knowing she'll go to prison must be awful, especially for someone like her. Mind you, she'll probably start half a dozen choirs before she's released."

Pausing, Meadows looked out the window. At least Barbara could smile a bit now, as well as feel sympathy for a woman she had every reason to hate. Not many could reach that point so quickly. Barely a month had passed, though it seemed longer. The florists opposite still displayed reminders of Christmas: silvered cones and sprays of golden twigs to use as winter decoration.

"Poached egg on toast and some of your delicious fried tomatoes please," a voice ordered at the counter. "Lovely day. A real touch of spring."

"Don't be fooled," Doreen warned. "We could have a blizzard tomorrow."

"You're a right old Misery!" PC Sutton teased her.

Recognising his voice Meadows turned and nodded in greeting. Then she looked back at the letter.

"We didn't know what to do with ourselves at first. We spent Christmas at the Walters' house, not exactly jolly but better than being on our own, or trying to go to parties we couldn't face. Rather than let so many people down, especially the old folk, we formed a little quartet: Jackie, Dennis, John and I. John can sing baritone as well as tenor and Wynn said he didn't have the time. I think his wife's always disapproved of the choir and what happened confirmed her opinion. Anton left Uttley with police permission as soon as Christmas was over. He's got another job in Birmingham and is staying with Polish friends there. He wrote to me last week and asked me to enclose a note for you."

In surprise Meadows broke off and checked the envelope. A second envelope was indeed enclosed. It felt stiff, as if there was a greetings card inside. She was not sure she wanted to open it. Frowning, she put the envelope back and returned to Barbara's letter.

Anton will have to come back for the inquest, and ultimately the trial if he's needed, but DI Ambrose doesn't think we'll all have to give evidence. It'll be mainly me and the hotel staff. Anne says she'll give Evelyn a character reference - how she's devoted her life to running choirs and raising money for charity, served in the war, that sort of thing. Dennis and Jackie have asked to speak in her defence too. They'll say how hurtful Angie was being, and how Evelyn never meant to kill her, just grabbed the nearest thing. If it had been a hairbrush it wouldn't have mattered, would it?"

"No indeed," Meadows thought sadly. She paused and finished her cup of tea, now almost cold. Sutton was collecting his plate and looking round for somewhere to sit. She would have invited him to her table but he saw a space beside Higgins and joined him.

There was only one more paragraph.

Funny isn't it, how life plays tricks on you? Good as well as bad. I mentioned the quartet. The four of us have got to know each other a lot better through it. Jackie can be a bit silly but I really like Dennis. Jackie's mother had several bad falls after Christmas. She's going to have to go into a nursing home. I was surprised how relieved they both seemed, even though they'd wasted so much money on plans for the house. It's like a weight's been lifted off their shoulders. John's been a surprise too. For all he appears so quiet, when you get to know him, he's great fun. He persuaded me to go to one of his shows. I thought I'd be shocked but it was absolutely hilarious.

In surprise Meadows stopped and reread the last sentence. "Hilarious?" she queried under her breath. Then she read on.

He does a wonderful impression of Bette Davis and his Greta Garbo had the audience in stitches. He says he should be able to give up his day job soon. The trouble is he'd have to tour a lot and he says he wants to stay in Uttley. I don't know what to say, but I do like having him around. Mind you, when he told me he thought I'd killed Angie, I wasn't too thrilled.

Which brings me back to where I started. I'm sorry I've rambled on, but at least I've got the letter written. If you're ever in Uttley, please come to tea. I'll be back in Chalk Heath a bit of course for the Inquest, but I doubt if there'll be chance to talk then, so if you feel like writing a reply, I'd love to have one.

Best wishes,

Barbara (Collier)

For a long time Meadows sat looking at the letter, rereading several lines. The idea of John doing a wonderful Bette Davis made her smile. It was indeed good to hear the end of a story, and she had been personally involved in this one. Finally she summoned up the courage to open the second envelope. It contained a picture of a splendidly gothic building. 'Birmingham Town Hall' the caption announced. On the other side of the postcard Anton had written:

Please forgive me. I can't explain why I was so stupid, except I wasn't well in the head. I haven't managed to tell the others the truth yet but I will. I've gone back home to prove to myself I can be the ordinary boring bloke I really am. I've found a job as a waiter. It doesn't pay a lot but it stops my father making me work for him. I just wanted you to know so you wouldn't think so badly of me. 'Anton'

"Why should I care?" Meadows said to herself in annoyance. Shaking her head she stared at the card, turning it over in her hands several times. "The bloomin' cheek! Writing to me as if we meant something to each other!" Then she began to laugh to herself. "I suppose I should be complimented," she acknowledged. PC Sutton was coming towards her and she put the card back in the envelope quickly.

"Hope you don't mind me asking," he began, "But is that a letter from Barbara Collier?"

"Yes. How did you know?" Meadows replied in surprise.

"Kathy got one from Anne Jacobs yesterday. She said Barbara had written to you."

Nodding, Meadows indicated the chair beside her. "What did she say?" she asked.

"Not a lot. She's phoned Kathy a couple of times so there wasn't a lot of news. Mostly she keeps apologising. She's blaming herself for not coming with the choir, as if she might have stopped what happened."

"She couldn't leave her children. Not if they had measles," Meadows commented.

"That's what Kathy says, but it's going to take time for Anne to get over it. She sounded a bit happier yesterday. Calzone seems to be turning into a quartet. Anne says people like them and it's saved her cancelling so many bookings."

Reflectively Meadows nodded. "Do you think I should show the boss Barbara's letter?" she asked. "She was a suspect after all."

"I would," Sutton advised. "Then you're totally in the clear." Looking at his watch, he got up. "I need to do a bit of shopping before I go back." He flushed. "Kathy's asked me to get her some barley water. It's all she can keep down first thing in the morning."

"Ahh!" Meadows said, smiling with pleasure. "Is it public knowledge?"

"Not yet no. Just among friends."

"Then I'll keep it that way," Meadows promised. "Congratulations to you both." She too got up. "I'll go back early and see the DI."

DI Ambrose looked up at the quiet knock on his door. He'd been talking to Sam Winters about the Gibbs case but they had virtually finished. WPC Meadows was outside, looking nervous. He glanced at Winters. "Hang on a minute," he asked. "I'll just see what she wants."

"Come in," he called. "What is it?"

"I've received this letter, Sir," Meadows began, passing the envelope to him. She glanced apprehensively towards Winters, wondering if she was disturbing an important briefing. "I thought you might like to see it. It's from Barbara Collier. There's a card inside from Anton, or whatever he calls himself now."

Ambrose took the envelope and read through the contents. Winters nodded to her in greeting, then turned back to some papers he was reading.

At length Ambrose looked up, putting the letters back into Pauline's envelope. "You didn't really need to share this," he said. "It's personal and doesn't add anything new, but I'm glad you did. It shows discretion." He paused, wondering how to word his question. "How do you feel, yourself?" he asked her.

In surprise Meadows paused, not sure how to answer, especially with DS Winters in the room. She decided to be totally honest. "Still a bit upset," she admitted. "I did like them, all of them, even if they could be a bit difficult. I'd rather I'd just sung a couple of times with them, and then they'd gone home, but that wasn't how it turned out." She shrugged her shoulders. "No use crying over spilled milk as my Mum would say."

"No indeed," Ambrose agreed. "If it's any help to you, I feel much the same." He passed the letters back. "Cheer up though," he advised. "You've been put up for a Commendation."

In amazement Meadows stared at him, the colour flooding to her cheeks. "Me?" she asked foolishly. She glanced towards DS Winters who nodded in confirmation.

Laughing at her amazement, Ambrose assured her, "Yes, you. For the way you dealt with the intruders at The Shalimar. We'd have looked pretty silly if they'd got away." He turned towards Winters. "Chalk Heath's smelling of roses at present. DS Winters has just closed a file the Met have had open for decades. Nineteen cases in all."

"Mr Gibbs?" Meadows asked quietly.

"Yes. Nice old Mr Gibbs," Winters replied. "Whether he'll be fit to plead's another matter. We managed to sidetrack his wife and speak to him alone. He was happily boasting about it all when she came in. She wasn't best pleased."

"What will happen to her?" Meadows asked.

"That'll be for the courts to decide." Winters sighed slightly. "You never can tell," he added.

Epilogue

June 1960

"Cavendish here," a familiar voice boomed down the telephone. "Got the packet?"

"Arrived this morning," Ambrose replied, then realised he was slipping into his counterpart's abbreviated speech. "Thank you. They came by special delivery," he said more grammatically. "You're very prompt, as usual."

"Don't like to keep people waiting. Definitely manslaughter. Shouldn't take long."

"There'll be the extenuating circumstances too," Ambrose pointed out. "Arguments from Counsel. The usual things." Since the case he and Cavendish had developed a mutual respect.

"Seen the newspaper cutting?" Cavendish laughed broadly. "One for the books, eh?"

"Indeed," Ambrose replied vaguely, and began rummaging through the packet with his other hand. He'd noticed a cutting but assumed it was merely a report of the case in the local paper. On a busy morning it hadn't seemed a priority.

"No accounting for tastes. Reckon she must like men in women's dresses," Cavendish boomed again.

Almost dropping the packet, Ambrose found the cutting. He was thoroughly intrigued by now. "Got it," he said and read the heading quickly. Then he began to smile. "There's 'nowt' so queer as folk!" he agreed. He promised himself he would read the cutting in detail as soon as he put the phone down. It looked too good to skim. "I'll show it to Sam Winters too," he added. "He'll see the funny side."

"Thought he might. How's his 'Brown Trilby' going?"

"We're up to twentyseven thefts now," Ambrose replied. He couldn't help a hint of pride entering his voice. "The Met identified a couple more items old Gibbs had in his wardrobe. Kept them as trophies I suppose. Goodness knows what they'll do with them. Their owners are probably long gone. There's still no decision on whether he's fit to plead."

"Bit of a teaser that one," Cavendish agreed. "Rather you than me. Got an interesting one ourselves," he added. "Dog dug up a leg in the woods. Cue call-out, cordons, the lot. Then it turns out to be an artificial leg."

Ambrose laughed.

"But why would someone bury an artificial leg?" Cavendish asked. "Mightn't be so funny. We're starting to look for a real one to go with it. Must see we have enough spades."

Still smiling, Ambrose put down the phone and read the cutting he'd been sent. The photograph ought to have caught his attention earlier. Despite the make-up and costume, the face was recognisable. "Local man makes good," it announced, and in smaller letters beneath, 'Star billing at Uttley theatre."

Beside a picture of a glamorous chanteuse in fur boa and flowing blond hair, the report continued: "*Local salesman John Pedderson (34) has surprised his friends and workmates by revealing his alter ego. As Lily Gardena he has been wowing audiences in clubs around the county. Now he's been booked at the Uttley Grand Theatre to host a season of their Old Time Music Hall Shows.*

His agent, Miss Barbara Collier, commented, 'Everyone who has seen John perform will agree he'll make a wonderful host for Uttley's famous Variety Season. We are delighted that local audiences will have the chance to see his hilarious impressions.'

Both John and Barbara were members of the ill-fated Calzone Singers group. They attribute their successful partnership to the closeness of a friendship forged in tragedy.

Tickets for the Autumn season at the Grand are already on sale. Call at the Box Office now. They are selling fast."

"Well I'll be!" Ambrose said and laughed.

Other publications available from Stairwell Books

Carol's Christmas	N.E. David
Feria	N.E. David
A Day at the Races	N.E. David
Running With Butterflies	John Walford
Foul Play	P J Quinn
Poison Pen	P J Quinn
Wine Dark, Sea Blue	A.L. Michael
Skydive	Andrew Brown
When the Crow Cries	Maxine Ridge
The Geology of Desire	Clint Wastling
Homelands	Shaunna Harper
Homeless	Ed. Ross Raisin
Border 7	Pauline Kirk
Tales from a Prairie Journal	Rita Jerram
Here in the Cull Valley	John Wheatcroft
How to be a Man	Alan Smith
Know Thyself	Lance Clarke
Thinking of You Always	Lewis Hill
Rapeseed	Alwyn Marriage
A Shadow in My Life	Rita Jerram
Tyrants Rex	Clint Wastling
Abernathy	Claire Patel-Campbell
The Go-to Guy	Neal Hardin
The Martyrdoms at Clifford's Tower 1190 and 1537	John Rayne-Davis
Return of the Mantra	Susie Williamson
Poetic Justice	P J Quinn
Something I Need to Tell You	William Thirsk-Gaskill
On Suicide Bridge	Tom Dixon
Looking for Githa	Patricia Riley
Connecting North	Thelma Laycock
Virginia	Alan Smith
Rocket Boy	John Wheatcroft
Serpent Child	Pat Riley
Margaret Clitherow	John and Wendy Rayne-Davis
Sammy Blue Eyes	Frank Beill
Eboracvm the Village	Graham Clews
O Man of Clay	Eliza Mood

For further information please contact rose@stairwellbooks.com
www.stairwellbooks.co.uk

www.ingramcontent.com/pod-product-compliance
Ingram Content Group UK Ltd.
Pitfield, Milton Keynes, MK11 3LW, UK
UKHW041630190726
13854UKWH00006B/2407

9 781939 269195